I0550321

CARLIE SWEETWATER'S

SPECTACULAR SUICIDE

Inside Crazy

By Rhonda Walthall

SWORD SPEAK
— PUBLISHING —

CARLIE SWEETWATER'S SPECTACULAR

SUICIDE

Inside Crazy

By Rhonda Walthall

carliesweetwatersspectacularsuicide.com

Copyright 2019 by Rhonda Walthall
All rights reserved
This book or parts thereof may not be reproduced in any form,
stored in a retrieval system, or transmitted in any form by any
means—electronic, mechanical, photocopy, recording, or
otherwise—without prior written permission of the publisher.

Scripture quotations are from The Holy Bible, New
International Version

I

SBN 978-1-950410-02-6

Dedication

This book is dedicated to my Lord and Savior, Jesus Christ, who is my reason for living.

Acknowledgements

Though writing may appear to be a solitary game, getting a manuscript transformed into a book is more of a team sport. Lisa Creech has been a great training partner, serving as a sounding board and source of encouragement, and Miranda Creech did a wonderful job as editor by coaching me to add more clarity into the content. Then, where would I be without all my other friends and coworkers who have cheered me on?

A special thank you goes out to my husband, Ron, who helped tame my unruly computer. And last—but not least, Rachel, my daughter, thanks for taking my bio picture after painstakingly applying makeup to your ole mom.

In Memory Of

In memory of Heather Devine, whose eagerness to read my manuscripts and give constructive feedback urged me to carry on: I miss you, lovely Ms. Devine, and I wish you had lived to see the day of publication.

Table of Contents

Forewarned

In the beginning, God created the heavens and the earth, and He saw that they were good. In fact, they burst forth with spectacular, vibrance, full of color and teeming with life. Everything flourished in a picture-perfect world, living in peaceful harmony. And then He created someone designed to be akin to His own heart, someone intelligent and creative, someone with whom He could share His very soul, someone He could place in charge of all He made.

So, God made mankind, man and woman, the ones He longed to bring into the most intimate fellowship imaginable. He saw that they were good, and He loved them more than all the beautiful heavens and earth He created. He smiled at their first adventures in the garden He planted for them. He called to them throughout their day and whispered secrets of the universe into their eager ears. He told them about His eternal and glorious love as they picnicked among the trees.

But someone else lurked in the garden, someone who didn't consider mankind worthy of all the fuss that God made over them. "Just give them a choice and see what they'll do. They're not nearly as bright, loyal or loving as You make them out to be. Make it a silly, ridiculous choice—my tree over Yours—death over life. What could possibly go wrong?"

Adam and Eve felt baffled by the choice set before them. The Tree of Life was fantastic—no complaints there. The Tree of the Knowledge of Good and Evil—now that seemed mysterious! Life and goodness surrounded them daily, but what strange thing called "evil" awaited them if they chose it? And, just as puzzling, God warned that if they ate the fruit of this tree, they would do something called "dying". They struggled to understand this foreign concept, something they'd never witnessed or even heard about.

The talking serpent promised that fruit from the Tree of the Knowledge of Good and Evil would truly open their eyes, giving them access to marvelous secrets, making them gods. Thus, the stage was set; the decision made, and the earth hasn't been so good since then. In fact, mankind spent his time and energy vigorously chasing after death and finding it in many inglorious fashions.

The rest of the story is gruesome and filled with enough filth to make a prostitute blush. The Bible doesn't sanitize it, which is what makes parts of it so difficult to read. And this story, Carlie's story, is surely no Disney fare of "believe in yourself and you'll have a fairy tale ending." But through all the muck and mire, this is a tale of the only truly spectacular suicide, and it is a story born of   pain.

Bloodbath

Flashing emergency lights streamed through Carlie's bedroom window a few seconds before a police officer knocked on her door. She barely managed to lift her head and sigh. *So, they made it back from the lake after all.* She'd just gotten in and barely had time to find her razor and slit her throat before they showed up. Well, it was too late anyway. The damage had been done. This time she'd gotten it right, and she'd leave this sorry world.

Ms. Campbell's shrill voice pierced Carlie's ears even as her senses faded. The woman's frantic shrieking coupled with the officer's pounding on the door grew faint.

"Carlie, Carlie! Answer me. Come on and open up, Carlie. We've had enough tragedy for one day." Though Ms. Campbell sounded like she was sinking into some deep, bottomless well, becoming farther removed from Carlie each second, one word struck the dying girl with unexpected force.

Tragedy? What tragedy? Emily got what she wanted—how can you call that a tragedy? Through the fog of Carlie's semi shut

3

down mind, she could still see Emily's grand exit, staged for the whole boarding house to see during their annual Fourth of July picnic at Joe Pool Lake. The sun, lake and grilled burgers all faded into unimportance compared to Emily standing up on a paddle boat—Carlie hit with the sickening realization that she knew what came next—shooting herself in the head and falling into the deep, dark water.

The whole boarding house went nuts. Half of the residents screamed, a few cried, and several quick-thinkers dialed 911. Of course, the rescue attempt failed miserably just as Carlie herself planned. They couldn't find Emily's body quickly enough to save her, and Carlie found herself stuck watching and fuming from the shore until she could grab a ride with another resident who just couldn't handle the horrifying scene anymore. The events of the day flashed through Carlie's mind in quick succession.

What a fool proof suicide plan she'd come up with! It should be her body in Joe Pool Lake. The bullet was meant for her head. She should have been suspicious when Emily rushed about in such a hurry to get out on the lake. Just her luck—she only turned her back on Emily for a second, and Emily swiped her gun out of her purse. At least she didn't take her razor blade, too.

Carlie felt herself momentarily transported back to the chaos that currently came bursting through her door. Her neck was twisted, and her head—jammed between the bathroom sink and the toilet—rested in an expanding pool of blood that covered most of the black and white tiles.

Peace caressed her soul. Death. It surely was the pinnacle of life. The only thing of comfort, cooling her feverish mind, numbing the pain, extinguishing the anguish. Even Emily's thievery didn't matter at this point.

The cacophony caused by a very hysterical Ms. Campbell and the urgent police officers got drowned out by sweet silence. Carlie's world went black. Out in the world that didn't exist any longer, a handful of police and EMT's hurriedly filed into what had been Carlie's room. Emily's room. It now officially belonged to nobody. Nobody living anyway.

"She's over here in the bathroom," called out the first officer.

"Did she cut herself again?" Ms. Campbell almost sounded hopeful.

"Bilateral lacerations to the neck and bleeding out fast." The first EMT checked for a pulse. "Doesn't look good at all."

In record time, the EMT's applied pressure bandages, started an IV, and thrust Carlie's limp body into the awaiting ambulance to be hauled off to the county hospital. One gloved man kept her breathing with an ambu bag while the other rhythmically compressed her chest. They worked as one perfectly timed machine: press, press, press, press, press—breathe. Carlie's chest expanded to accommodate the influx of air.

They might as well be practicing on a mannequin for all the good they are accomplishing. She floated over the flurry of activity around her lifeless body. *Fools. So, they want to be heroes, but not this time. This is my destiny. Emily may have stolen my gun and upstaged my own spectacular suicide plan, but no one can deny me of this day...this one final day. The end of all my turmoil.*

Parkland Memorial Hospital's emergency room doors slid open. Carlie begrudgingly followed her body inside. She'd grown tired of this ER, weary of the staff, determined never to face them again, but maybe there was a bright side to dying in the hospital instead of on the bathroom floor. Here she had the same tired audience, the supporting cast of the "Let's Save Carlie Show", and here she could teach them the futility of all their medical knowledge and skill. She would be their one great failure, going out in her last victorious effort to haunt their memories forever. Carlie would be the one they just couldn't save.

You're so lame. Idiots—all of you. You never could help me. You're useless, so don't waste your time. Let me float away. Anger and pain; that's all I've known since I was what—four or five years old? That's not much to live for. Oh, why do you torture me over and over and over again? Leave me alone!

The normal, volcanic rage that erupted from her core onto all the doctors and nurses fizzled, cooled by a force even stronger than the fiery one driving her life. It posed an irresistible attraction, a magnetic field of placid surrender. This draw that sucked her deeper into its embrace contained a void full of what she wanted most: utter tranquility.

The unseen, numbing current blissfully pulled her closer to the ceiling. A bright light flooded the trauma room. Carlie turned her attention away from the doctors and nurses below as the fire that once raged within her flickered and died. The medical staff blatantly flaunted their level of ignorance and lack of understanding. Why else would they fight the best thing that ever happened to her? She turned her focus to the light. Now that caught her interest. Bright but not blinding. White, yet radiating all the colors of the rainbow. She floated higher and higher until an authoritative voice impeded her progress.

"I won't let you go—not yet." A young, deeply tanned man in a white lab coat stood back from the rest of the trauma team, leaning against the wall with his arms folded. He looked directly at her, not her battered shell on the table below. "You're not finished here. Come back." For someone who looked so laid back and calm, the power of his command caught her by surprise. And that's exactly what he issued—a command—not a hope or an observation or even the type of order given by the chief of emergency medicine. He didn't throw around words like "stat" or raise his voice to achieve the effects he wanted. This quiet man simply was a presence she couldn't deny.

And for this reason alone, she had no doubt that he could send her back into that hideous body on the gurney. Whether it was the mesmerizing strength of his voice or the glow in his eyes, she felt herself slipping from the comfortable arms of death. The body on the gurney drew her back in against her will.

NO!!!

"You must go back until you learn to do it right," the strange doctor decreed.

But why? I was home free. It's what I've always wanted. She couldn't take her eyes off him even as she protested.

"No, it isn't. It's a glimpse of what you think you long for, but how do you know for sure if you don't even know the possibilities?"

Stabbing sensations sliced through Carlie. An odd mixture of cold and warmth jolted every cell of her body. So, she'd returned after all. She kept her eyes closed and willed herself to take the journey back into that other place, but the door had closed. Her body felt like heavy concrete as she became bound once more to flesh and blood. How could this be?

Disjointed conversations collected random words to play upon her fears.

"Got a rhythm!" rang a high-pitched voice.

"Two more units of packed cells," from a tired sounding male.

"Waste," a thought whispered.

"Where's the surgical resident?" Again, the tired male, probably a sleep-deprived intern.

"Right here," another worn voice replied.

Carlie felt the pressure bandage being carefully removed, followed by a stinging sensation on her neck. Since the tender age of six, she'd been prodded, poked, sutured, had her stomach pumped, been analyzed and thoroughly instructed on improving her coping skills. She felt like Humpty Dumpty, who simply could not be put back together again. It wasn't like she just awakened one day and decided to thwart the entire medical community's best effort. After all, how could she get past her jacked up childhood and the acute loneliness and distrust that it bred? How could they expect to force her into being okay when she didn't have a clue what constituted okay?

"Severed jugular?" A new voice, female and timid.

"Good thing she didn't hit her carotid, and very fortunate that she fell the way she did. It put enough pressure to keep her from bleeding out before the EMT's could get to her."

Good for what? For keeping me imprisoned so they can torture me with more of their so-called therapy? Carlie struggled to reach the breathing tube they'd rammed down her throat, but strong, large hands quickly held her down.

"Don't fight us; we're trying to help," Ms. Timid called out.

The familiar feel of soft wrist restraints being applied quickly followed, and Carlie's racing heart exploded with frustration and fear. *No, not again. I can't stand it another moment, not another second.*

"Get the propofol going," the tired voice ordered. "Keep her sedated."

"She's not out of the woods yet," muttered an older man.

Was there still a chance the peaceful exit would open? Carlie clung to hope. After all, that interfering resident wouldn't be there every moment to keep the door closed.

"ICU. Suicide precautions. When stable, we'll transfer to psychiatry."

Ms. Timid whispered, "Hey, psych services said they'd just discharged her a day ago, and she had been admitted fifty-three times. Can you believe it? Fifty-four attempts now, and she's only twenty-one."

"Yeah, well, the word from her boarding house is that her roommate committed suicide today—shot herself in the head right in front of everyone during a picnic. That may have set her off."

Can't these people see what I am? A genetic piece of garbage, used, abused, unwanted filth. At least Emily knew what I was, because she was just as worthless, and I hate her. How could she leave me here? I hate you, Emily. Rot in hell!

The voices around her melted into oblivion as her entire soul sank into some vast chasm. Occasionally a vague awareness of bleakly humming machines surfaced...machines that breathed, that monitored, that beeped. Tattle-tale machines that would broadcast to the nurses if that wonderful doorway to the floating world opened again. She felt trapped. The freedom that loomed so close eluded her now, making her a captive to the hospital once again.

She despaired in this, the darkest pit she'd ever known—and she'd explored quite a few in her day. Even without looking, she knew that horrid, fat shell of flesh claimed her soul at least a few more days. It would be impossible to off herself under the constant scrutiny of ICU land. As consciousness ebbed and flowed with the infusion of a milky sedative, she climbed deeper into the caverns of despair.

"It's okay. I'm here with you, Carlie. I'm in this hole with you." It sounded like the same voice that forced her back into her body.

YOU! It's all your fault. Just who are you? And why are you meddling in my business? she demanded from deep within her mind. The tube they'd rammed down her throat to keep her breathing made her mute for now, but she internally launched a mental assault on the stranger. At least she could tell him off in her mind, and they wouldn't be able to chart it to hold it as evidence against her the way they did with her verbal sparring on all her fifty-three previous admissions.

"Someone who cares."

Well, go away. It's too late for me. I hate you. I hate me. I hate life.

"It's very painful to be you, isn't it, Carlie? You've been hurt so much that hope is probably beyond comprehension, but it isn't too late for you. I'm here to bring you real hope, true healing." His voice sounded so matter-of-fact that Carlie paused, unnerved by a vague foreboding. Something very odd about this doctor unhinged her, but in her medicated state she couldn't put her finger on exactly what set him apart, what made him such an aberrant in the hospital routine.

I just want to sleep. There, she didn't exactly tell him to get lost, so if he abandoned her now it wouldn't be entirely her fault. Not that it mattered anyway.

"Then sleep," he said pleasantly as if the world contained nothing other than peaceful kindness.

Carlie groaned inwardly. *Another do-gooder. I know your type.*

"Apparently not as well as you should. Good night."

Once he became silent, it dawned on Carlie that he seemed to read her thoughts. She struggled to open her eyes, squinting at the blurry man dressed in sea green scrubs and a rumpled lab coat who sat beside her bed.

Even in his silence, Carlie felt unsettled by him. She tried so valiantly to keep a watch on him, but her eyelids felt so heavy and her mind so cloudy. Her weary eyes closed once more as she succumbed   again   to   the   propofol.

Reality Bites

Day, night, day. Carlie couldn't tell how much time passed in ICU, but did it really matter? She was just passing time until she got out to do it right. This suicide attempt carried her the closest she'd ever come to ending all her misery, but next time she'd make no mistakes. There would be no Emily to steal her thunder or cutting the jugular instead of the carotid—whatever that was. She'd Google it or even buy a stupid anatomy book and find that carotid, if that's what it took, because apparently not cutting it created this entire fiasco of being held hostage as a prisoner in her own skin once again.

Scars covered every square inch of her left forearm from her wrist right up to her elbow, serving as a testament to her level of misery. Only pain could make her feel anything at all. Splendid emotions that other people claimed posed a hoax as far as Carlie could tell. When pain ceased, even briefly, she lived in fear of it returning, and when she grew weary of being fearful, she became livid. Then she lashed out at herself with anything sharp that she could find. The vicious cycle continued spinning out of control, giving way to more turmoil, anxiety and despondency.

She heard laughter in the hallway. There they went again—cackling at her discomfort. That's the way of hospitals. Her entire life was in the toilet and they—the so-called healers—always lurked in the background deriding and judging her. Then they had the nerve to tell her how defective she was as if she didn't already have a few clues on that subject. After all, just look at what her own dad did to her.   She felt the anger inside rumbling, threatening to explode.

Her eyelids fluttered open.   That creepy doctor from the emergency room quietly sat beside her bed and stared into the darkest recesses of her mind.   His tousled coal black hair and wrinkled scrubs suggested he'd been up all night.   Then he must be an intern—or maybe a medical student.   No, medical students wouldn't know how to pull off what he did.   He wasn't distracted by the frantic bustle to save her lifeless form; he'd looked directly at the real patient, the one heading out death's door, and somehow managed to slam that door shut.   Without even breaking a sweat.

Carlie swallowed and cleared her voice.   No breathing tube—must have been extubated earlier.   Well, good.   She'd give this intruder a piece of her mind.

"You!" she rasped and winced at the pain.

A perky, young nurse in royal blue scrubs hurried past the doctor, almost running into him. "So, you're awake. What's your name?"

"I'm Tinker Bell."

"Yeah, right." She shook her head, causing her brown pony tail to dance in the florescent lighting, and pecked away at the computer attached to the wall by the window. "Uncooperative as usual, huh? Well, you know the drill. You're at Parkland, and I'm Amanda, your nurse. You're on suicide precautions, and we'll be transferring you to the psych unit as soon as we get a bed. Any questions?"

"I refuse to go to psych. I want to go home." Carlie grimaced from the pain of speaking.

"Sorry. You're involuntary; you know how that works." Amanda came closer. "Come on, now. What did you expect? Every single time you try to kill yourself, we either pump your stomach or sew you back together and send you to psych. This time's no exception, except for being worse. Do you even realize how many units of blood we've had to pour into you?"

"That's why you've got to stop these half-hearted attempts," the doctor deadpanned. "You're draining our blood bank."

"Are you having any pain?" Amanda interrupted.

"Like you'd care if I did," Carlie snapped. "I'm just a piece of meat to you—someone who takes up your time and wastes your precious blood."

Amanda wrinkled her forehead. "That's not what I meant…"

"I know what you meant. Don't patronize me."

Amanda the nurse turned abruptly and retreated to a work station behind a large open window, leaving the doctor and patient alone. Carlie glared at the man in the chair.

"So, don't you have something useful to do? Why don't you go ruin someone else's life?"

He raised his eyebrows. "You can do better than that." His voice sounded as flat and void of emotion as the ventilator that had kept her breathing the last day or two.

"Leave me alone. I don't want your help—like you could really help me anyway." She muttered that last part under her breath just loud enough to make sure he heard. She knew how to push people's buttons.

"That won't work with me," he yawned.

"What? The truth?"

"Would you know the truth if it stared you in the face?" He pulled his chair closer until he filled her entire frame of vision.

She saw someone of depth, not your average pretty-boy intern. Nor did he fit into the nerd-on-a-mission category. Scars ran across his forehead, suggesting he'd met some horrendous accident earlier in his life. Maybe that's how he knew to look up for her instead of prodding and poking her limp body. His calloused hand reached for hers. A deep gash, plainly visible on his wrist, caught her attention.

"Okay, I guess you're not going to leave me alone until I ask what happened to you. Is that the deal? I'm supposed to identify with you and open up, so you can fix me? Don't you think this angle's been worked before?" Carlie sighed.

It would be nice if just one other human being on the face of this earth really understood her and cared for her, but that ship sailed years ago. She resolved to never allow herself to fall for that crap again. Besides, this man and something called a carotid were responsible for her continued suffering, so she wouldn't forgive him.

The stranger grew reflective, but Carlie thought she saw a tear in his eye. She looked away. How dare he pull out all the stops? He fought unfairly according to the rules of engagement that Carlie observed from her previous admissions. He was supposed to be all clinical and removed from emotion until she got in just the right digs, then he should beat a quick retreat. Instead, she recognized that he pushed HER buttons, and she didn't like it one little bit.

"It's time to go to psychiatry," Amanda announced cheerily.

"Yeah, aren't you glad to get rid of me? Oh, wait—without me who will you have to laugh at?"

Amanda waved a very hesitant transporter and a seasoned police officer into the room and handed the cop a large envelop with all the necessary paperwork. "This one goes straight to psychiatry—no stops. She's a high suicide risk, so keep your eye on her the whole way. Watch out for her trying to manipulate you; she's a pro at being cunning."

"A police escort? I'm so honored. Will there be lights and sirens?" Carlie smirked devilishly.

Nurse Amanda shook her head. "Sorry to disappoint you." But Amanda didn't look the least bit sorry. The tense lines in her forehead had already relaxed before Carlie got past the door.

"Try not to miss me too much," Carlie whispered hoarsely as the stretcher carried her into the hall. "I promise you'll never see me again."

Carlie strained at the wrist restraints, but the rent-a-cop employed by the hospital touched her shoulder. "Don't even try it," he ordered. "I'm here to take you to psychiatry, and that's exactly where you're going."

"Yeah, I bet you're such a big, tough man. Hide behind that badge and boss around a gal who's tied to the bed." Carlie tried to kick, but restraints held her feet. "What the hell? What did I do to you? I was minding my own business in my own bathroom when everyone came barging in ruining everything. Everything," she screamed. She struggled against the restraints. "You can't force me to live. Someday you'll have to let me out and I'll get it right. You wait and see."

The transporter stopped dead in his tracks, looking at the police officer for direction. The lawman leaned down ever so slightly and uttered a few words that had an immediate effect. "Keep it up. You know that everything you say and do will be documented, and the more you fight, the longer you give up your freedom. Is that what you really want?"

Carlie froze. He was right. She'd been down this particular path too many times with the same results. Wasn't that what they called insanity—doing the same behavior expecting different results? She shook her head.

"Now, I'm betting you don't want to go from ICU directly to seclusion, do you?"

Again, she shook her head.

"I'm not going to pretend that you like me, or I like you to get you to act nice and go quietly. But for your own selfish reasons, you might consider getting a grip and acting like a halfway sane human being at least long enough to ride in a wheelchair to the psych unit. You know why that would be a smart thing to do?"

Carlie growled, "Like you said, if I arrive tied to this bed and struggling, I get off to a very bad start. Oh, why couldn't I have just died and been done with all this?"

The officer shook his head. "I don't know all the whys and wherefores, but I do know that this is what you're left to deal with. Now if you promise to refrain from yelling and trying to escape or acting out in any other way, I'll do you a favor. I'll wait with you right here until this nice gentleman gets a wheelchair, and you'll get off to a better start. So, what do you say?"

Carlie nodded somberly. "You have a deal."

The transporter looked mortified, but he quickly pushed her back into her room and retreated to obtain a chair while the officer called Amanda back to remove the restraints. Amanda dubiously loosened the first ankle strap and held her breath as if waiting for the room to explode.

Carlie's gut churned, and every fiber of her being wanted to lash out, but she closed her eyes and tried not to pay any attention to her boiling blood.

"You're doing a good job, holding it all in," the weird guy in the sea green scrubs commented. "I know how badly you want to dish it out, but these guys didn't steal your suicide from you."

Carlie's eyes flew open. There he stood, acting so calm and cool, so out of the ordinary. He acted like he could read her mind. And he deserved her ire more than any of the other staff. After all, he totally wrecked her grand departure. Suddenly no one else in the room mattered. She had to figure how to get past him, and him alone.

"Yep, you've got that right. Just remember that I'm the one you've got to focus on. I'm your ticket to where you're wanting to go." He looked so nonplussed that Carlie wanted to scream, but that type of behavior would bring back the restraints. She bit her tongue and listened. "This hospital stay isn't going to be anything like what you encountered in the past. I guarantee that. And—by the way—when you learn to do it right, it won't be anything that you'd expect. So, word of advice here—learn to accept the unexpected. You won't believe what's awaiting you on this adventure."

Carlie stoically acted the part of the model patient while Amanda removed the last of the wrist straps and helped her into the wheelchair that the transporter brought into the room. She didn't realize how weak she'd grown until trying to pivot into the chair. It seemed to take all her strength. She glanced back at the doctor who wouldn't leave her alone. He nodded approvingly.

Captive

The heavy wooden doors under the "Psychiatry" sign opened to reveal Patty, the most annoying nurse of all psychiatry. She looked so darn serene that she almost floated on air, never ruffled by the angst of the depressed or hurried by the urgency of the manic. Carlie had her own reasons to detest Patty because of all the assignments she so freely doled out to "help" her work on her issues. Patty acted both meddlesome and detached in a way that made Carlie feel homicidal instead of suicidal.

"Oh, you again." Carlie looked away. Why couldn't she get one of the other nurses—one that would give her some slack, one that would react with more emotion to her outbursts instead of thinking up stupid therapeutic exercises for her to do?

"Welcome back," Patty deadpanned, pulling official-looking papers from the large envelop the police officer handed her. Carlie recognized the OPC papers signed by the mental illness court's judge who knew Carlie on a first name basis. That horrid judge once again made Carlie a legal hostage.

The police officer removed his gun and placed it in a locked box in the wall outside the unit.

"Put her in Room 807 down this hallway." Patty led the procession past the nurses' station and turned a sharp left onto the acute hallway, the notorious hall where cameras monitored every room—well, all except the bathrooms.

Carlie saw the two seclusion rooms from the corner of her eye. Ugh! How many of her power struggles with Patty ended there, locked into a square of four bare walls surrounding a bed bolted to the floor? No, Carlie shook her head to herself sternly. No trips to the cuckoo room this time around. Don't get into it with Patty; it will only postpone the inevitable. Besides, Patty always insisted on talking everything out, "processing the events that led up to seclusion" after the fact. Patty wouldn't get a chance this final admission.

Carlie broke into a faint, twisted grin. What would Patty think if she knew this was their last time together? She'd be trying out all her psychiatric nurse trickery—her so-called therapeutic interventions, and Carlie would have to write pages and pages of sincere-sounding psychobabble to get back out on the street.

While the transporter helped her into her new bed, Carlie could hear the police officer warning Patty about her lethal last attempt. She cleared her gravelly throat to protest, but her vocal cords responded too slowly. In the fraction of a moment that it took her to find her voice, she saw the strange doctor leaning against the wall on the window side of the sparse room, to the left of her bed.

She remembered every detail about this room. A single twin bed secured to the floor. A wooden desk, also bolted firmly in place across from the foot of the bed, served as a reminder of all the work they would expect her to do. Only the chair could be moved, and she tried throwing it through the window about a year ago, only to have it bounce off the plexiglass and break her nose.

In the corner beside the desk stood the tiniest of clothes closets filled with shelves, because apparently the rules prohibited clothes, as well as patients, from hanging on a psych unit. Even the bathroom had a locked door, so that she could only go to the toilet or shower under supervision. How lame was that?

So—bottom line—everything remained just as she remembered it except that doctor who stalked her everywhere she went. He made her realize that she didn't really care about the police officer, Patty, or her prison cell. They made up this miserable routine; he—not so much.

Why would an emergency room doctor follow her from ER to ICU to psych? Even if he worked as an intern—which she highly doubted—it made no sense. Every time she opened her eyes, he guarded her, haunting her with her ultimate failure—the failure to stay dead—a failure that he himself caused. Certainly, he had other things to do, other patients to snatch from the jaws of death—people who might actually want to live. And what weird thing had he told her back when he slammed death's oh-so-pleasant door in her face and ordered her to return to this fat, ugly body? Something about learning to do it right? Surely, he didn't mean...

"You look surprised to see me again." He rubbed his stubbly chin thoughtfully. "Not too many people have stuck with you, have they?"

She shook her head slowly, trying to size him up until that intrusive Nurse Patty pushed a computer on wheels into the room. Dragging the chair over by the bed and settling in for the task ahead, Patty immediately started asking the same million questions Carlie had answered for years.

Carlie groaned and hoarsely whispered, "Do we have to do this? I don't feel like talking. Besides, you already have all my information on file. I thought the hospital's electronic records made questions like these a thing of the past."

Patty cocked her head and scrunched up her face, tapping her finger on her rolling computer's keyboard. "Uh huh, yes. I've got your history, but I still need to know if anything's changed since your last stay. You're still at the same boarding house?"

Carlie nodded.

"Only new medical issues would be the lacerations on both sides of your neck?"

Another nod.

"Okay, but some things I have to ask now. Are you still suicidal?"

"No more than usual," Carlie whispered.

"How do you feel about being saved from your close brush with death?"

"Eternally grateful," she lied.

"Oh?" Patty leaned forward and studied Carlie's face, which of course made Carlie feel like jumping out of her skin, so she did the next best thing and closed her eyes. There, she wouldn't have to see the feigned expression of concern. More importantly, Patty wouldn't be able to see the utter darkness that consumed her. She kept her eyes tightly shut.

"That's not what the police officer just told me. Are you having any pain?" Patty typed something furiously as she spoke—no doubt something they'd lecture her about.

Carlie hesitated. Pain—yes, she hurt. But should she admit it? They—Patty and the other staff—would point out that her coping skills sucked but admitting that she had pain could be good for some narcotics. Oh, well, they always bugged her about her "ineffective coping" as they called it, so she might as well get some good pain pills out of the deal.

"Yeah, I hurt."

"Where?"

Carlie pointed to her mutilated throat.

"On a pain scale of zero to ten?"

"Twenty."

Carlie heard Patty tapping out her response on the keyboard.

"I'll call Dr. White for your orders so we can restart your meds."

Goody. Another round of Zoloft, Xanax, and Depakote. Why bother? Carlie sneaked a peek at the interfering doctor who watched intently without saying a word.

"Yeah, I'm still here." He sat on her window sill.

"What about him?" Carlie pointed toward her stalker.

Patty didn't look up from her charting. "Who? Dr. White?"

"Dr. White? His name is Dr. White, too?" Carlie frowned.

"What do you mean by that?" Patty paused as if something significant had been said at last.

Carlie's heart beat faster. Usually Patty introduced her to any new staff, but she totally ignored this goofball. What kind of twisted people played these endless mind games? They must be trying to make her think she was hallucinating so they could put her on antipsychotics. The last time she took Zyprexa she'd gained sixty pounds of unwanted extra weight onto her already well-padded five-foot, five-inch frame.

"Uh, nothing. Just wondering if the doctor seeing me this time around was another Dr. White or the same caring physician who has already brought so much healing into my life."

"He's the same Dr. White who treated you the last time you were here. By the way, what happened when you went back to the boarding house? I thought you looked forward to going to the Fourth of July picnic at the lake."

Carlie blinked back tears. What happened? Her rotten roommate stole her gun, her plan and her successful passage out of this world—that's what happened. But she couldn't say what really transpired; that would only serve their purposes. Maybe a half-truth would do. "My roommate and I had issues."

Patty clearly had no intentions of accepting ambiguous answers. "What kind of issues?"

"She was a jerk."

"What specifically did she do?"

Carlie looked back at the freaky man in the windowsill. "She stole from me," she uttered tersely.

"What did she steal?" Patty persisted.

"Does it really matter now?"

"Apparently it mattered to you."

"I don't want to talk about it now. My throat is killing me. Can you ask Dr. White for some pain pills?" Carlie rasped.

Patty sighed. "As soon as I complete your assessment. I need to know what sparked this suicide attempt."

"What makes you think I intended anything other than just relieving the pressure with some good, old-fashioned self-mutilation?" Carlie set her jaw stubbornly.

"Those cuts were too deep. You severed one of your jugular veins and nicked the other one, came dangerously close to bleeding out before they could get you to the hospital. In fact, I understand that they performed CPR on you before and during your arrival, so that's just a tad bit more than self-mutilation for someone like yourself who happens to be a pro at self-mutilation. A rookie might make this mistake, but not you."

"Okay, I'm busted. I tried to kill myself because I'm just so tired of being used by people. Is that what you want to hear?"

Patty shook her head. "All I want to hear is the truth, not what you think will get you out of here. Besides, that's pretty much out of our hands now."

"What do you mean by that?" Carlie demanded, rolling over to get a better view of her nurse.

Patty had to be as old as the hills. Her slightly rounded shoulders and her gray, wispy hair screamed senior citizen. Thick glasses perched on her nose, almost dwarfing her face. Her royal blue scrubs conformed to the standard color for all the nurses, but unlike most nurses who wore short sleeves in the one hundred plus degree Texas summers, Patty always wore a white scrub jacket. Carlie chalked it up to her overall weirdness.

"They've already decided to send you to Terrell, because the state mental hospital can keep you longer. You'll only be here until your wounds are more completely healed."

Carlie sank back into her pillow in shock. So, she truly had no hope of getting free. Tears flowed despite her best efforts.

Patty's hand touched hers. "Go ahead and cry, dear. Don't hold it in; let it out."

How could I come so close only to botch it? And you, weirdo doctor who just perches beside me like a vulture, feeding off my misery, how dare you? Who asked you to stick your big fat nose in my business? Get out of here! Leave me alone. You've done enough damage. I hate you!

"But what if I can change all that?"

My life is not some fairy tale. There's no happy ending except the ending that you took from me.

"And what makes you think that your untimely death would produce a happy ending?"

Carlie wiped the tears from her eyes and looked from the doctor to the nurse. *Why isn't Patty responding to anything you say? Why is she acting like you're not even there? What's going on?* Carlie's eyes narrowed as she searched Patty's face. She still wore the same mildly concerned expression as if someone had permanently etched it into her features, and she showed no surprise at the strange doctor's presence.

Another round of tears bitterly stung Carlie's eyes. More hopelessness, but this time mocked by a stranger who wouldn't leave her alone in her despair. Then it hit her. He couldn't possibly be real, could he?

The Suicide Specialist

After about five minutes of frantic sobbing, Patty handed Carlie a cold, wet washcloth and told her to wash her face before coming down to the dining room for lunch.

"What happened to letting it all out? I don't feel like going anywhere, and I don't want to eat. My throat is killing me; I don't want to go to Terrell; and everything's going from bad to worse, but I'm just supposed to just wash my face and go eat like nothing's wrong?" Carlie's words spilled out fast and furiously despite her sandpaper throat.

Patty gave her the famously calm, knowing look—the one that made Carlie want to scream if only her voice would work. "You've had your cry, dear, but you mustn't stay there forever. Too much crying at once is too draining for you. Now it's time to eat; you must build up your strength."

"I weigh two hundred and fifty some odd pounds. Do I look like I'm wasting away to you?" Carlie screeched.

"It's therapeutic, dear. A proper diet will help your wounds to heal, and you can't stay isolated in your room." Patty's voice was even, pleasant and monotone.

"But I don't feel like walking down there."

"Jason will bring you in a wheelchair until you regain your strength," came the automatic reply.

"I don't even feel like sitting up."

"Now, now. We've got to gently challenge your comfort zone a little here, a little there until we can build up new ways of looking at things, new ways of coping. You tend to hide out in your room, and we won't allow that this time. You'll be on suicide precautions and room restrictions from eight in the morning until nine at night, and you'll have to be out in the community for every activity and group session." Patty turned to leave. "Jason!"

"But..."

"Oh, she's good," muttered the mysterious man, still perched on the windowsill.

"What's your story?" Carlie demanded with an angry edge to her gravelly voice. She was ready to confront this smarty pants.

"Oh, me—I'm the suicide specialist."

"So, you're a consulting doctor?" Sarcasm dripped from her voice.

"Not exactly." He grinned.

"You're my sitter?" What else could be his excuse for shadowing her every move?

"No, I don't always sit."

"I've never had a male sitter; you can't be in here when I go to the bathroom or change my clothes—if I ever get my clothes from that boarding house." She still couldn't decide if he was really flesh and blood, but if he was, she had to lay some ground rules.

"Hmm. Deflecting to trivia. Effort duly noted, but if you really want to get it right next time, you'll need to get honest with me. It's going happen sooner or later—your choice." He fished a tablet out of his lab coat pocket and began to scan its contents.

"Come on, you wouldn't really help me commit suicide, would you? What's the catch?" Carlie sat up and glared at the stranger. "I think you're just toying with me...that is, if you're actually there and not a figment of my tormented imagination."

"What figment can bring you back to life from the brink of death? I know your life is too painful for you to go on, but you must be honest with me if you want my help. And, no, a figment of your imagination wouldn't know about your pain either."

"But you—yes, you're the one who screwed it all up for me just by speaking you brought me back from the brink of bliss. But how? And why would you want to do that to me? I really got it right this time. I floated over my body; I was free and light. I had no pain, so why bring me back to do it again?"

"Wrong answer," he answered crisply, almost with a twinge of impatience. "You did have pain. Go back to your thoughts as you lay dying. What were you so angry about?"

"I don't want to talk about it. What does it matter why I'm angry or why I hurt; I just want to be done with it."

"Who are you talking to, Carlie?" Jason stood in the doorway with a wheelchair, a gown, and a blanket.

"No one. No one at all." Carlie glared at the obnoxious stranger. "And I don't want to go down to the dining room. I already told Patty."

Jason laughed. "Yeah, and you know Patty. She won't take 'no' for an answer. Here." He handed the gown to Carlie. "You know the drill. Put it on backwards like a robe, and I'll cover your legs with a blanket."

Carlie slowly complied. "I hurt all over. Where are those pain pills?"

"Patty will bring them after she gets her orders from Dr. White. Sit right there. Good." Jason swiftly clicked the footrests into place under Carlie's feet and covered her legs with a tan hospital blanket.

Jason carefully pushed her into the dining room down another hall. Patients lined up to receive their trays from a familiar tech at the food cart. Liz was Carlie's favorite tech, because she'd usually manage to sneak an extra brownie to her whenever someone got discharged before lunch. It provided sort of a bribe, to behave while around Liz, but—hey—a brownie made Carlie try to act like a sane person as she inhaled its chocolatey goodness.

Liz waved to Carlie. "I've already put your food over on that table." She pointed to the one closest to the ice machine, so Jason rolled Carlie into place and locked her wheels.

An elderly woman, gray haired and hunched back, sat across the table fumbling with her sugar packet.

"Ms. Lila Mae, this is Carlie. Would you like me to sweeten your iced tea for you?" Jason reached to help Lila Mae.

"Carlie? Is this yours? I never ate breakfast." Lila Mae's voice trailed off as she searched under the plastic plate cover. "Barbecue and potato salad for breakfast? This isn't right. I know I asked for wheat toast and scrambled eggs." Her face sagged with confusion.

Jason continued setting up Lila Mae's food, stirring sugar into her tea, buttering her roll, even cutting her meat into bite-size pieces while reassuring her. "No, ma'am you had French toast, eggs, bacon, and coffee for breakfast. Remember?"

"No, I just got up. I need breakfast." Lila Mae shoved the offending food aside, splashing her drink onto her tray.

Carlie sighed and rested her face in her hands. Just the therapy she needed—to be sitting next to some looney, old bat who couldn't remember what time of day it was.

"Mind if I sit here?" inquired a thin, young lady wearing a clingy top that didn't quite meet her britches and way-too-short shorts. "I just *love* barbecue, but where are my buns? I know I ordered buns, because I always eat barbecue in a sandwich, so I can eat and run, because I've just got way too much going on to sit still and eat a whole meal. There are deadlines, reviews and appointments. Did I pencil you in? I don't remember you. What's your name and your function? I don't mean to be unkind, but I don't have time to stand on ceremony." Her words tumbled so quickly that she left Carlie speechless.

"Joylyn!" Liz exclaimed, circling around their table like a dog herding the lost lamb out the door. "Go put some clothes on. You know you can't dress like that. Get down there and change before Patty comes in."

Joylyn bolted out the door, disappearing as rapidly as she'd entered. Carlie could still hear her protesting that she had nothing else to wear and no time for the inconvenience. Then, from farther down the hall, Carlie could hear Patty's unmistakable voice offering to help solve Joylyn's wardrobe deviancy.

"Where's my breakfast?" Lila Mae looked pathetically lost, hopelessly alone.

Carlie picked at her food. "Come on, Ms. Lila Mae, this is what they serve for breakfast now." She nibbled at her chopped brisket, licking her lips in feigned delight. "Mmm. Pretty good breakfast."

The suicide specialist quietly perched on the beige counter beside the ice machine. Extracting his tablet from his backpack, he began recording his observations. The satisfied expression on his face made Carlie curious.

"What possible significance can you find in anything that's happening here?" Carlie demanded.

He just nodded at Lila Mae, who tentatively tasted her "breakfast". "What did you say, dear?" She glanced up from her barbecue.

"Nothing, Ms. Lila Mae. I just talk to myself a lot." Carlie hesitated, mulling over in her mind how she might get to the bottom of the mystery of the so-called suicide specialist.

Lila Mae pronounced her verdict on the brisket. "Not as good as biscuits and gravy for breakfast..."

"I thought you wanted wheat toast and scrambled eggs." Carlie bit her lip as soon as she'd said it.

A puzzled expression crept from the wrinkled corners of Lila Mae's eyes to her pursed lips. "Eggs..." She turned to Liz and weakly waved her napkin. "I wanted eggs for breakfast, dear."

"Ah, but they're experimenting with new breakfast menus, remember, Lila Mae?" Carlie blurted.

Liz winked and whispered, "Good save. I'll see you in the craft room after lunch."

"Come on. Have a heart. I don't think I can make it. I'm still so weak from all the blood loss." Carlie put on her most pathetic face for Liz.

"But Patty strictly told us that you're on room restriction. That means you can't return to your room until bedtime." Liz sat in the chair between Carlie and Lila Mae.

"Yeah, yeah, I know what that means. I thought Dr. White hadn't given his orders yet."

"Not all your orders. But they discussed your admission this morning when he first made rounds, and they talked about this room restriction thing." While she spoke, Liz kept her eyes on a disheveled, middle aged man on the other side of the dining room as he headed toward the trash can with his tray. "Craig, I need to take your plastic ware."

Craig paused and glared at his food tray. His knuckles turned white, and the red tray trembled. He stood frozen in one spot as if he'd been caught escaping from prison and now faced execution.

Liz moved cautiously around to face him, speaking reassuringly as she approached. "It's okay, Craig. It's just our routine here. If you'd like, I'll take care of everything for you. That way you can go wash up before occupational therapy." She reached for his tray. "Is that okay with you?"

"Uh huh." Craig surrendered his tray and stiffly shuffled toward the door.

"You remember Craig from prior admissions, don't you?" asked the suicide specialist.

"Yeah, he's like me—a frequent flier." Carlie washed down her brisket with iced tea.

"What did you say?" Lila Mae looked confused. "Did you get any eggs for breakfast? I really wanted eggs."

"No eggs for me, Ms. Lila Mae."

She paused. Lila Mae might be a bit confused about the time of day, but she did seem to at least know what she saw and heard. Carlie waved her hand in front of Lila Mae's eyes. Lila Mae blinked and looked up at her.

Carlie leaned forward and whispered, "Do you see a man sitting on the counter beside the ice machine?"

Lila Mae adjusted her glasses and searched the length of the counter. "No one's there now."

Carlie bit her lip as the suicide specialist typed down another note on his tablet. *Okay, buster, just as I thought—you're not real, and I don't have to talk with you, so leave me alone and don't you dare interfere in my life again. And stop trying to make me think I'm crazy, cause I'm not. I'm onto you, and I won't give in to whatever it is that you're scheming against me. There.*

She smiled. Her first rational decision made in the psych unit. She had maintained a good start so far. The only problem was that Nurse Patty couldn't know about this bit of progress without knowing that she'd been having conversations with some magical person who didn't exist, and that sort of thing never went well on a   unit   like   this.

Reality Testing

Joylyn returned to the dining room wearing jeans and a tee shirt, plopping down between Carlie and Lila Mae with a thud. "That nurse will be the death of me," she growled as she plowed through her green beans and brisket.

Carlie smiled at the rookie patient. "You and me, both. What are you in here for?"

"Jealousy, if you want to know the truth," she gushed with barbecue sauce oozing onto her chin. She hastily swabbed her face with her napkin, smearing her cheek in the process. "My family can't stand the fact that I'm much more brilliant than all of them combined. While they waste the night away sleeping, I'm up building a new business, one that will take the nation by storm. And you—by the way—someday you'll be able to say that you knew me when... Oh, but you won't be able to say anything because you'd be violating my confidentiality agreement seeing as how my being here is top secret and all. Isn't that the pits for you?" Joylyn barely breathed between sentences.

"So, you're here for starting a new business?" Carlie looked skeptical.

"Of course, they claimed that I had a manic episode. They don't like my creative bursts because I do more than dream; I actually do something about my ideas, and they get upset when the bills come in. But you've got to spend money to make money. Why are you so interested? They didn't send you to get information, did they? Cause I'll sue you if you breathe a word to anyone. I've got my rights to confidentiality; it's in my contract." She brushed her long auburn hair behind her ears and practically inhaled her peach cobbler.

"Your contract?"

"When I came in, I signed a contract to protect my rights even though they got a judge to sentence me here."

"You mean the Patient Bill of Rights we all get with every admission?" Carlie felt a bit miffed at this uppity, little ditz.

"Mine isn't the same as everyone else's. They had to write up a whole new contract for me because of the business I've got going."

"What kind of business is it?" Carlie nibbled on her brownie.

"Wouldn't you like to know? Then you'd try to compete, wouldn't you?" Joylyn abruptly grabbed her tray and sprang up from the table, knocking her chair over. She rushed to the opposite side of the dining room to a vacant table and sat down.

Lila Mae shook her head. "She didn't get eggs for breakfast either, I'm afraid."

The suicide specialist leaned forward. "Unfortunately, delusions of grandeur are frequently accompanied by a certain amount of paranoia. Don't take her reaction to you personally."

"I wasn't," Carlie snapped.

"Wasn't what?" Lila Mae asked.

Carlie lowered her voice to a whisper. "Did you hear that man dressed in scrubs tell me not to take Joylyn personally?"

Lila Mae shook her head slowly. "I didn't hear anyone talking to you, and there's no one in scrubs except that girl over there." She nodded toward Liz.

"Oh, boy." Carlie rubbed her weary eyes and slumped forward, holding her head in her hands. Even after convincing herself just a moment earlier that he wasn't real, she still responded to him. How could she so quickly have this lapse in judgment?

"Well, if they aren't going to serve a proper breakfast, I'm leaving," Lila Mae grumbled, pushing her chair back as she spoke.

The creep in the sea green scrubs and white lab coat slid into Lila Mae's empty chair. His curly black hair cascaded around the scars on his forehead. Carlie felt mesmerized by his coal black eyes; they looked both inviting yet intimidating. She had the distinct feeling that he could see deeper into her than any CT scan.

She glanced down at her food tray. "Lila Mae didn't see or hear you," she whispered. "I don't think you're really here, so leave me alone before you get me put back on antipsychotics."

"Oh? So, Nurse Patty has taught you something through the years." He grinned pleasantly.

"What are you talking about?"

"Reality testing. You checked with Lila Mae to see if I was real, but unfortunately Lila Mae isn't suicidal and doesn't know about the suicide specialist."

"Oh, brother!" Carlie rolled her eyes.

"What's wrong, Carlie?" Liz's voice jolted her thoughts.

"Liz, you guys are trying to make me think I'm crazy, aren't you?" Carlie's voice took a soft and resigned tone, not her usual looking-for-a-fight curtness. "Please just make him stop, and I'll be an absolute angel my whole stay here."

Liz stuffed her hands into her burgundy scrub pockets and shook her head. "I don't know what you're talking about. Make who stop what?"

Just then Patty breezed in, pushing one of those rolling computer carts again. "I've got your meds. Let me scan your bracelet." She pulled the hand-held scanner to Carlie's wrist before holding each packaged pill up and pressed the button that would allow Carlie to have some sweet relief. "There are two hydrocodone, your Depakote and Zoloft. You'll get your Xanax at bedtime, and there's an order for Ambien at night if you need help getting to sleep. I believe you're already familiar with all of these meds?"

Carlie nodded, all the while keeping an eye on the suicide specialist.

"Okay," Patty handed Carlie a pen and the clipboard. "I need you to sign med consents for each psychoactive med. As you know, Zoloft is to help your depression, and Depakote is a mood stabilizer, and—of course—Xanax is for anxiety. Oh—I almost forgot—here's the consent for Ambien, which is your usual sleeping pill. Since you've been on all of these a long time, I won't go over all the information about them unless you have questions, but here's a printout on each one that you can keep. Any questions?"

Carlie shook her head and scribbled her signature on the consents. After she slammed down her medicine, Patty ordered her to open her mouth and stick out her tongue. Carlie complied with the mouth search for hidden pills and stood on wobbly legs to leave.

"Not so fast." Liz held up her hand. "Patty, I think Carlie needs to talk with you about her suspicions that we're trying to make her think she's crazy and her request to 'make him stop'—isn't that what you said, Carlie?"

"What's going on, Carlie?"

"Thanks a lot, Liz." Carlie's stomach churned as she held onto the table for support. This could turn bad quickly.

Patty gently touched Carlie's shoulder. "Let's go to your room to talk privately. I'm here to help, you know."

That's what I'm afraid of. Carlie's shoulders sagged. It didn't matter what happened, Patty always found an excuse to talk with her.

"I thought I wasn't supposed to return to my room."

"We'll have a brief chat before you go to occupational therapy. I need to know what's going on with you. How else can I help you?"

As the other patients finished their trays, they filed out the door except Joylyn, who chowed down on the contents of a second tray like she hadn't eaten in a week. Patty reached for the empty medicine cup and plastic silverware.

"You are through with these, aren't you?" She handed the plastic fork, knife, and spoon—dangerous weapons that they were—to Liz. "How's the count?"

"All here except one set, and Joylyn should be done with hers in just a few minutes."

Patty waved Jason over to return the computer to its proper place and motioned for Carlie to sit back down in her wheelchair. A feeling of dread clamped down on Carlie's chest while Patty dutifully pushed her back to her room. *So much for staying under the radar!*

Carlie gingerly transferred from wheelchair to her bed, and Patty pulled up a chair. "Explain to me what's going on," she said softly. "Whatever it, is, I want to help."

Carlie's head drooped slightly. *And so it begins.* "It sounds silly, I know, but I thought a man was watching me in the dining room—that's all. I wanted him to stop staring at me."

Patty's wrinkled forehead caught Carlie's eye. Evidently Patty didn't buy a word of her story. She never did.

"Which man?"

"Huh?"

"Which man? We have several, you know."

The unwilling patient scowled at the window ledge where the suicide specialist made himself quite at home, leaning back against the window with his feet up on her bed. If she gave a description matching any of the patients, Patty would question him, and she'd make enemies. But still, should she tell the truth? She quickly evaluated and choose the lessor of two evils: instead of making enemies, she resigned herself to getting dosed with an antipsychotic med. She took a deep breath. *Zyprexa, here I come.*

Her raspy voice ignored the twisting in her gut and forged ahead with the truth. "Uh, he has dark, curly hair..."

"Yes?"

"And he wears scrubs and a lab coat, and he has scars on his forehead and wrists."

Patty stared into Carlie's eyes in silence before asking, "Have you seen him anywhere else?"

"Yeah, in the emergency room and again in ICU."

"Do you hear him saying anything?"

"Not much."

"But sometimes?"

"Look, I don't want to go back on Zyprexa. I look like a hippo as it is, and I know I'm not crazy. He's some intern who keeps watch over me; he says he's the suicide specialist."

"The suicide specialist?" Patty lifted her eyebrows, but her tone grew soft and almost distant.

Carlie grimaced and gingerly touched the bandages on her throat. "I really don't feel like talking. Can I go to the bathroom before I go to occupational therapy?"

"Okay. Just leave the door cracked, and I'll be right here."

Carlie weakly hobbled to the bathroom. *What do you know? That went better than expected. In fact, it went better than my attempt to walk right now.* Her legs buckled under her, and she staggered to the right. She clung to the door, swaying dangerously before Patty came to her aid.

"It's okay to ask for help, you know." Patty looked at her curiously.

"Uh, thanks." *Is the world upside down? I've basically confessed to Patty that I'm hallucinating up a storm, and she acts like nothing is out of the ordinary. And here I am thanking this annoying woman after having a session with her. Maybe I'm in some alternate reality where up is down. Or maybe I've totally lost it, and she doesn't want to rock the boat. After all, that's kind of how they treat Craig; they don't come right out and tell him he's as nutty as they come.*

The only thing worse than having to talk with Patty was doubting her own mind and looking to a nurse—of all people—for validation. This was just all kinds of crazy.

Code C

Craig somberly paced the hall in front of the occupational therapy room. Occasionally he paused to examine some ominous floor demon before beating a quick retreat, his head hanging about as low as one could hang, his blood vessels bulging in his neck and his fists rhythmically pounding the sides of his thighs. He ground his teeth fiercely, making horrible crunching sounds as if they were cracking from the force of his clenched jaw.

The so-called suicide specialist held out his arm to keep Carlie away from Craig, an act she considered totally unnecessary since anyone who'd ever been hospitalized with Craig knew better than to cross his path whenever he glared at any particular object, whether it actually existed or not. She stopped wheeling her hospital chariot, as she liked to refer to wheelchairs, and pondered turning back to her room. Her neck still throbbed in spite of the pain pills, and she honestly didn't feel like wheeling herself around, so she settled back in what she judged to be a safe distance to observe the Craigster fireworks.

Jason, the lanky tech who'd whisked her down to the dining room, strolled down the hall. "Hey, Carlie, I'm glad to see you're up to driving yourself now," he said in even tones. "Come over here." He motioned with his hand, keeping his eyes on Craig, and reaching for the phone in his pocket.

Carlie complied with Jason's instructions and wheeled herself around the corner while Craig continued to pace, grimace, crunch his teeth, and pound his thighs faster and faster. She could still hear everything when the showdown took place, and she knew it always happened rapidly.

Jason cupped his hand over the phone and whispered, "Code C now in front of OT."

Carlie rolled her eyes. "Code C? Isn't that just a little obvious?" she hissed.

The suicide specialist put his finger to her lips, which felt surprisingly hot and left her lips tingling. Carlie retreated to the water fountain next to the day room and let the cool stream soothe her lips while a small army of nursing staff and campus police assembled in the hallway.

"Stay down here," Patty ordered crisply, "until we tell you it's safe to come to OT."

Carlie nodded compliantly and parked beside the water fountain.

Even from the adjoining hallway, she knew the routine, having been on the receiving end of it many times. She heard Patty call out, "Craig, we noticed that you are pacing and punching your legs. You seem upset. Are you upset, Craig?"

The suicide specialist sat beside Carlie. "You're doing splendidly so far," he said. "I'm glad you're making progress this quickly."

"What on earth are you talking about? Progress? What progress? I've just been stuck back in the funny farm where I've been processed like a fat cow about to be slaughtered, fattened up in the dining room, and now I'm sitting out in the hall talking to someone who doesn't even exist. I'd hardly call that progress."

"But I do exist, and it doesn't do you any good denying that I'm here. How else can you account for your miraculous revival from death's door—literally death's door—you know, the one with the bright, inviting light."

Carlie scowled. "Then why doesn't anyone else seem to see or hear you? Why didn't Patty introduce you? What's your name?"

He leaned closer and shook her limp hand. "Let me introduce myself. I'm Dr. Emmanuel, and I'm here to save you—but only if you let me."

Carlie sighed and shook her head. "I didn't let you save me; you just barged right in and totally wrecked my best suicide attempt ever. I'm really quite angry at you for ruining the best day of my life."

"I know you're angry," Dr. Emmanuel said with a gentle voice, "and I'm glad you're being real with me right now by admitting that you're angry."

"Yeah, I do anger really well. I've got that one down pat, so give me a gold star for all the progress I've made—I'm mad as hell, and I can't do a damn thing about it." Carlie sounded more resigned than angry, but her glare could almost peel paint off the wall in front of her.

"Interesting that you should use such accurate terminology, even though you don't seem to grasp the full implications of what you just said." He lifted his eyebrows and scrutinized her face curiously.

That just about did it for Carlie. Where did he get off acting like she was some lab rat for him to study? "I don't know what you're yammering on about, but I'm getting sick of dealing with you all up in my face."

Dr. Emmanuel scooted in front of her laser gaze and lifted her drooping chin. "I love you."

"What?" She sputtered and gasped. "Are you coming onto me? This is so unprofessional! I'm gonna report you. I don't have to deal with sexual harassment on top of everything else. Buddy, you're gonna pay. I'll, I'll call the hospital administration, Advocacy, Texas Department of Health—you name it—the *Dallas Morning News,* Chanel Four or Eight or whatever."

"Okay. Sexual harassment is the last thing you need after everything you've been through." Dr. Emmanuel sat cross legged on the floor, pulled the little tablet from his brown backpack, and began to type. "But of course, you'll have to tell them that it came from a man no one else sees or hears, and I'm afraid you won't seem like a credible source seeing as how you're being held as an involuntary psych patient. But if you feel you must tell someone, go right ahead. Of course, you'll also have to tell them that I said nothing about sex. I simply told you that I love you."

Carlie seethed inside. How could he act like that? He couldn't just throw around the L word and pretend that it had nothing to do with sex. It always had. Period. "Don't play games with me," she growled.

"You mean like the games your father and pawpaw played?"

"I don't want to talk about them!"

"What about the youth pastor?"

Carlie sprang to her feet just as Jason came around the corner. She gulped at the trickling stream from the water fountain, so she wouldn't have to make eye contact with Jason. Too many feelings swirled mercilessly, too great a storm threatening to tear up her insides.

"Hey, Carlie," Jason greeted, "Patty sent me to bring you to OT."

Carlie took her seat and nodded, keeping her head low while Jason drove her to a large table in the OT room. Across the table slumped a young man Carlie had met the week before. He never said a word; he simply drooped in his chair like a wilted soul who had no strength to carry on. Carlie felt safe sitting with Jeffrey. She wouldn't have to make conversation or even acknowledge his presence.

She carefully scoped out the room. Joylyn loudly bossed some elderly patients at another table. "No, no! You'll never be able to work for me if you can't do better than that. Use the pretty colors I picked out and stay between the lines. No, Beatrice, you're mixing too much water in your paint, and—that's not funny, Jack—you haven't even started your project, so you're definitely not employment material. If you people can't follow simple instructions..."

Mrs. Barnes, the matronly therapist, intervened. "Joylyn, come work on your own project. I told you that this is not the place to find future employees. You've got to stay focused on your own work."

"When is breakfast?" Lila Mae asked innocently.

Carlie breathed a sigh of relief. Dr. Emmanuel had disappeared; only the regular crazies and staff carried on in front of her. She picked out a craft from the box in the middle of the table and began to string beads to make a bracelet.

As her fingers worked, she fumed about that intrusive suicide specialist that she'd hallucinated, but finally concluded that as far as hallucinations went, he came across as less frightening than some. In fact, he might be meddlesome, but he seemed to mean well. She'd known other patients with really nerve-wrecking hallucinations like snakes coming out of their food or hearing voices plotting their murder. Whatever managed to turn Craig into a powder keg must be scary as well. She shuddered. At least she didn't have to endure anything like that. However, her hallucination annoyed the living daylights out of her and intruded relentlessly into her private affairs, not to mention slipping in that creepy remark about loving her. It made her cringe.

By the end of OT, the pain in her neck subsided and she felt more relaxed, almost mellow. She wisely chalked it up to the pain pills kicking in. *Ah, mind-numbing pain pills and the tranquility they bring!*

She placed the almost finished bracelet around her wrist and did a double take. *What went wrong?* She'd made so many bracelets in this very room that she could do it in her sleep. It took exactly twelve of the larger beads and three decorative trinkets for just the right fit. She held her arm out to inspect her work. Something seemed off, different than usual, maybe looser. She counted the beads. The number was correct, so what went wrong? Holding her face in her hands while deep in bewilderment, she came to the realization that even her face felt weird.

Just stop it, Carlie Sweetwater. Get a grip and look around. The light green linoleum floor is the same as it's always been. Patient art litters the pale walls as usual. Mrs. Barnes still has a thick waist and a sweet, though slightly uneven smile, and she is visiting each table and exclaiming over the crafts as if she's taking a trip to a world-famous museum.   And that is her normal. Nothing out of whack about her.

Carlie turned her attention to the other patients.   The common, garden variety of psych patients filled the room: an assortment of elderly confused, elderly hallucinating, middle aged and younger who were depressed and suicidal, an occasional schizophrenic who seemed to be visiting from another planet filled with rampant conspiracies, and of course the newest manic depressive to join their ranks—Joylyn. Following bipolar protocol, she grew more and more obnoxious by the moment with her incessant talking and bouncing around all over the place. As far as psychiatric patients went, they all seemed to fit in perfectly.

Then it hit. *And this is where I fit in? With this goofy crowd? Oh, brother.* She completely buried her face in her hands.

"Are you okay, Carlie?" Mrs. Barnes asked quietly, zooming in on Carlie's subtle change in behavior as if she had supernatural, mind-reading radar.

Carlie felt her gentle touch on her shoulder and looked up. "I'm just not feeling well." She slumped a little more in her chair for effect, but then she noticed Jeffrey again and realized that all the slumping in the world couldn't compare to his crumpled look. If they made him come and sit through their various therapy groups, they'd prop a corpse up in the corner and count it as attending.

Maybe Craig wasn't as deranged as he seemed. Maybe he just knew how to get the good drugs, so he could nap after lunch instead of painting stupid pictures or making silly bracelets that would never leave this room. Carlie looked around the room. Just where did Mrs. Barnes keep all those bracelets? Locked cupboards filled up one whole wall, but it couldn't possibly be enough space to store years and years of bracelets and sun catchers, holiday decorations and construction paper art, could it?

Carlie studied the beads in front of her. Maybe, just maybe, Mrs. Barnes disassembled each bracelet, so it could be "made" repeatedly. And perhaps she washed away the paint on the sun catchers, so another group could paint them. Maybe nothing was really as it seemed in this room or any room.

Mrs. Barnes stared intently at Carlie with a type of motherly concern that soothed Carlie, unlike Patty's irritating manner of poking and prodding. "Do I need to call Patty for you?"

"Oh, no. It's just the medication kicking in." Carlie picked up her bracelet again and scrutinized it carefully. *Yes, I've used these same beads before. I remember this one with its little chipped area, and this one with the marbling running diagonally. And this shade of blue. No wonder psychiatric patients are paranoid.*

Seclusion

Carlie managed to endure the rest of the day shift, thanks to a medicinal cloud of tranquility that she received to keep her calm after Joylyn got in her face and screamed at her for being a corporate spy. It seemed Carlie had taken an undue interest in the beads the "employees" used, and the little, plastic spheres contained essential building blocks for all sorts of psychotic nonsense in Joylyn's world.

In Carlie's mind, her interest focused solely on finding enough evidence to prove her theory about craft recycling. Somehow figuring out just what was real in this hell hole became her primary mission, even though she didn't want to believe that sweet Mrs. Barnes could stoop to such nefarious acts of deceit. Joylyn, however, didn't give a flying fig about anyone else's needs but her own, so staff had to intervene.

Patty broke out the good drugs and gave Joylyn injections strong even to give the entire unit a break from her unceasing rambling, and Craig already lay sleeping off whatever cocktail he'd been given, so the ambiance became almost serene.

By the time the night shift hit the floor, Carlie almost didn't even care that prissy, little Candace had been assigned to her. She simply wanted to lie down and enjoy her float down the Xanax River, so she snuggled up on one of the couches in the day room and let her entire body go limp.

In the faded background, other patients debated over what to watch on TV. Carlie sighed. *Idiots. They don't have anything better to do than bicker about whether to watch America's Got Talent or the Rangers' game.*

"Yeah, you've never participated in such a trivial argument, have you, Carlie?" Dr. Emmanuel asked.

You again. Ha. I know you're just in my thoughts, so I'm not going to speak out loud to you. Carlie peered over at another couch in the general direction from which she thought she heard his voice. He wasn't there. She sat up and rubbed her weary eyes.

"It's fine with me if you don't talk out loud; you're still talking to me." The voice unmistakably belonged to Dr. Emmanuel.

She looked around the room, but she still couldn't spot him.

"Keep searching for me. You will find me when you search for me with all your heart."

Carlie froze. Those words sounded awfully familiar. She explored her memory banks. Where had she heard them before? She scanned every corner of the room while she thought about what he said. When her eyes fell upon the TV, she did a double-take. How could he be on TV?

"Do I finally have your attention?" he asked.

Uh, yeah. You're kind of hard to ignore, popping up everywhere I go, saying that you love me, telling me to search for you with all my heart, promising to teach me how to 'do it right'. I may be crazy, but I'm not stupid. I know weird when I see it, so yeah, weirdo, you have my attention. Carlie crossed her arms and glared at the idiot box.

"Good." The TV doctor looked pleased. "Let's talk about what you call 'the L word.' What makes it feel so scary?"

Carlie shoved a strand of her unruly wavy hair behind her ear and sneered. *You already seem to know. After all, you live in my head, and you already accurately listed all my abusers earlier today, so I think you've covered all the bases. Please, I don't want to recount all the sexual abuse. How many therapists have already been down that road with me?*

"But what have you learned?"

I've learned that these experiences have made me a freak. Oh, but that's not the answer you want, is it? You want to hear me say that I've learned not to trust. Well, you're right. Why should I trust anyone?

Carlie pounded the sofa's cushion defiantly and continued her internal rant. *People are only out to serve their own selfish interests. My daddy loved no one but himself.* She slammed her fist into the cushion again. *Same with Pawpaw—the dirty old man.* Another blow to the sofa punctuated her growing rage. *And that perverted youth pastor who acted so helpful and sooo interested in me.* She hurled the whole cushion at the television. *And these doctors and nurses and therapists don't spend time here out of the goodness of their hearts. They're here for the pay—and maybe a laugh or two. They don't really care. No one does.*

Carlie switched from the mental conversation she was having with her private hallucination to a loud, verbal barrage. "Now you come along, claiming you love me. Ha! Big laugh. Big freaking laugh. So, what's your angle? Want to see the crazy girl explode? You seem to get off on making me angry. Thanks a lot. You just killed a perfectly good buzz."

Carlie bolted from the couch and turned the TV off, setting off a round of grumbling from the other patients. She turned to face her peers, her face white and fierce. "How can you watch this crap? Don't you see what they're doing? They're playing with our minds just for the heck of it, and I'm not gonna take it anymore."

"Carlie, come with me now. Candace wants to see you," Calvin, one of the evening techs, announced as he ushered her into her wheelchair and pushed her away from the day room. Carlie could hear a nurse trying to calm the community.

"I don't think that girl is quite right," Lila Mae offered in the background. "She talked to the television, poor thing."

Carlie couldn't figure out if Lila Mae called her or the TV "poor thing", but she dutifully allowed Calvin to wheel her down the hall, pausing to punch the wall before launching her body into the closest armchair in the consult room. Why couldn't she keep her stupid hallucination to herself? While she fussed and fumed with all her might, Dr. Emmanuel casually leaned back, tapping his fingers on the arm of his chair.

"Do you have to do that?" Carlie snapped.

"What?" Dr. Emmanuel pulled out his trusty tablet and tapped its surface.

"Do you have to even be here?"

"You searched for me."

"No, I didn't. I mean, I heard your voice and didn't see you, so of course I tried to figure out where your voice came from. I didn't go looking for you. If anything, I searched for just a tiny bit of peace in this hell hole."

"Uh huh. Peace. So, you were searching for me."

Carlie shook her head. "Peace is what I'll get when I'm dead."

A hand touched her shoulder. "Carlie, what's going on?" Candace looked puzzled in a professionally concerned way.

All nurses must practice that look in nursing school, Carlie mused.

"Oh, brother! I'm just having a bad day, but what's new? I seem to be having a horrible life, so why do you want to talk with me? You think you can fix me in ten, twenty, maybe thirty minutes? Could you fix me if you had all day? What about all week?" Her voice raised a few decibels.

Candace twirled her strawberry blond hair and considered her words carefully. "I'm not here to fix you; I'm here to help you make progress toward healing."

"Then give me some more Xanax. I can't deal with all this anxiety." Carlie grimaced. "You know how poorly I deal with anxiety, don't you?" Maybe having a track record for violent outbursts could be helpful in getting back to that gentle Xanax River. She fidgeted convincingly in her chair, bouncing her legs with raw, nervous energy and rocked back and forth.

"Yes, well, it's not time for Xanax yet. Tell me about why you yelled and threw something at the TV, and I'll call the doctor to see what we can do."

Dr. Emmanuel leaned forward. "Here's your chance to tell her about me being an unprofessional hallucination and using the L word."

Carlie stopped rocking and lunged forward, trying to grab her tormentor by the neck. She landed in his empty chair, banging her head on the wall in the process. "Stop it! Stop trying to make me think I'm losing my mind."

She peered suspiciously at Candace. "You saw him, didn't you? Do you know what he's been doing to me ever since I came in through the emergency room?"

Candace's voice registered barely above a whisper. "Who, Carlie? Who's bothering you?"

Carlie held her head with trembling hands. "He won't leave me alone. He's coming onto me, saying he, he..."

"Yes, what did I say? I said I love you. I'm not coming onto you. I'm offering what you crave so desperately but fear so greatly."

Dr. Emmanuel stood behind Candace, looking totally calm and collected, so darn clinical in his scrubs and lab coat, but Carlie didn't think he acted clinical at all. None of the other doctors in any of her previous fifty-three admissions told her they loved her. His behavior was strictly unwarranted and definitely reportable.

"Who is he, Carlie?" Candace asked again, still wearing her artificially compassionate nurse face perkily framed by a stylish hairstyle that perfectly suited her cheerleader physique. Carlie wanted to spit at her for being so obviously fake.

"Are you for real? You don't see Dr. Emmanuel or whatever his name is standing right there?" Carlie pointed toward the figure now standing in the doorway.

Candace glanced around and shook her head. "I don't see him or hear him, but he seems to upset you significantly."

That was psych nurse talk for, "You're a raving lunatic, and I think I'd better draw up the Haldol", so Carlie knew what came next.

"Let's wheel you down to the quiet room where you can relax while I call the doctor and get something ordered for you."

Carlie hung her head. The quiet room—just a euphemism for the seclusion room—presented more unhappy memories. If she went voluntarily, she'd get some time alone with the door open, but if she balked and ramped up her anger to the point of throwing things or threatening anyone, she'd get carried down there, twisting and screaming, and locked in. If she put up a seriously good fight, maybe throw a few punches or kicks, or if she could manage to bite one of the staff, she'd get restraints. And of course, Dr. Nosey would still be hounding her while she struggled to free her arms and legs. Besides, she found herself at a tremendous disadvantage, still being as weak as a newborn lamb and unable to put up a proper fight.

Considering the options and the throbbing in her neck, she chose the path of least resistance and stood to make the familiar trek down the hall. "Please tell Dr. White not to give me Zyprexa; I'm already the size of a pregnant hippo, and I'm borderline diabetic as it is." She swerved on unsteady legs, but Calvin steadied her and got her seated in the wheelchair.

"Okay, I'll tell him." Candace looked relieved. "I appreciate you being honest with me and helping me to help you."

After Carlie stretched out on the seclusion room bed and Candace fled to the safety of the nurses' station to make her call, it dawned on Carlie that the seclusion room might just be a sweet deal after all. It got her out of the day room before bed time, and she'd get pumped full of chemical bliss.

If her regular room appeared sparse, seclusion took the prize for being the ultimate in the minimalist contest. A large plexiglass window covered with a heavy, locked metal screen lurked like a prison window behind the bed. The metal bed frame held an old mattress. That was it. That and the spy camera in the ceiling. The bathroom consisted of a toilet and a sink within the anteroom, and the thick wooden doors on each side of the bathroom had small unbreakable windows for snoopy staff who wanted to get up close to their prisoner. Dr. Emmanuel made himself comfortable on the floor without saying a word.

"You again. Why don't you just give up? I think I've made it clear that I'm not interested in whatever you're trying to push onto me."

"But how can you know that you're not interested if you don't even know what I have for you? It's not like you've got everything handled on your own, so from my viewpoint, it looks like you could use my help."

"Okay. Maybe I owe you some thanks. This bed is better than that musty old sofa in the day room. I guess being crazy has its advantages." She mustered a slight smile.

The strange doctor just shook his head. "You're not crazy."

Out in the hall Calvin warned Candace that Carlie still appeared to be actively hallucinating. Carlie glared at Dr. Emmanuel. "So, I'm not crazy, huh? Well, here I am in the quiet room hearing and seeing a guy that no one else does, so explain that if you can."

"Maybe I'm a spiritual being." He faded from her sight as if to prove his point.

"A spirit? Like a ghost or something? Look, I don't believe in ghosts, and this isn't a haunted house; this is the funny farm, and I've never been this bad off before. You're making me sick. I can't even tell what's real anymore, and it's all your fault. You hear me?" she rasped. "Just because I can't see you now doesn't mean you're not hiding around the corner somewhere. You're always there, following me, hounding me, giving me the creeps."

"Carlie?" Calvin stood in the entryway.

"What do you want?" Carlie spat.

"You seem very upset. What can I do for you while Candace gets your medicine? Would you like something to eat or drink? Would that help get your mind off..."

57

"You think I could eat anything with all this stupid mental torment going on? What's really happening? Are y'all trying to make me snap? Well, it isn't cute, and it's not funny, and it's not therapeutic in the least. I'm reporting all of you."

Dr. Emmanuel appeared beside Calvin this time. "Again, with the reporting, huh? And what do you think that will accomplish?"

"It's your right to report us," Calvin replied, "but help me understand what exactly you plan to report."

"Here's your shot," Candace called out as she burst into the seclusion room. "This is Geodon, and it should help get rid of whatever you are seeing and hearing that is disturbing you, so you should feel better. It may sedate you a little, but I think you will like it. Here's the consent." She held out a clip board.

Carlie hastily scribbled her name. *Here I am, not knowing up from down and carrying on like a lunatic, but I must give written consent to get the medication that will restore my sanity. Sometimes I don't know which is crazier—me or the mental health care system.* She handed over the clip board and willingly offered her   arm.   "Just   make   him   go   away."

Confession

Morning came all too soon with Liz escorting Carlie back to her room to get ready for breakfast. Carlie felt so groggy that she zigzagged right past the suicide specialist without speaking. She had no words for him this early in the morning after being medicated into oblivion. She squinted and swayed into the wall. The whole doggone building kept moving, and her legs felt like Jell-O.

"Are you dizzy?" Liz asked while steadying her.

"Uh, I, uh." Carlie blinked her eyes.

There came Nurse Patty, walking like a woman on a mission straight for her, beady eyes peering through her over-sized glasses. Not now. Not this early.

Before Carlie could form a single word, Patty whisked her into a wheelchair and rolled the very dizzy Miss Sweetwater into one of those extra wide showers with a handicap seat and a rail to hold onto. Before she could protest, the staff stripped her down and proceeded to hose her off with wonderfully warm water.

Then they soaped up her entire body with baby shampoo that smelled so darn soothing and comforting that she could only relax, succumb to their agenda and enjoy her shower.

Patty and Liz made an efficient team, and before Carlie knew it, she found herself dressed in her own jeans and tee shirt. Her dazed mind contemplated how her clothes curiously seemed to have stretched a size or two larger than the last time she'd worn them. Liz rolled her wheelchair down to breakfast with Carlie listing to one side and wearing her baggy clothes, wondering what other oddities would surface next.

Strange doctor shadowing my every move. Crazy OT room where I find beads that I've encountered before. Either my own clothes have grown a couple of sizes, or I shrunk when they showered me. Maybe the medication is making me lose my marbles. Or I'm in some sci-fi time warp. Or...I don't think...

Before she could formulate a cohesive theory, Lila Mae greeted her enthusiastically. "Biscuits and gravy. Scrambled eggs and sausage. Coffee and orange juice. Now this is a great breakfast. Come join me over here, dear. I know you won't be disappointed with breakfast today." The old lady positively lit up. Apparently, breakfast was all it took to make her day.

"Mmm," she continued. "Now this is good sausage. Young lady, what brand of sausage is this?"

Liz didn't know but promised to call nutrition services to find out. Not that it mattered; Lila Mae went on to something else before Liz finished her sentence. Carlie leaned back and watched everyone in slow motion.

Joylyn stared at her food through medicated eyes and moved about as slowly as Carlie. Across the dining room, Craig drooped onto his table. So, all three of the trouble makers got shot up with the good stuff last night. An experienced psych patient like Carlie knew the score.

She picked at her food. Lila Mae was right about the biscuits; they tasted moist and buttery. And the sausage had a slight hint of maple syrup. The eggs were fluffy and warm. She closed her eyes and savored the flavor just for a second, well, maybe a minute or two. Anyway, she apparently dozed off with eggs still in her mouth and her hand resting on top of her biscuit and gravy.

Patty swooped down from nowhere. "Wake up, Carlie, and swallow," she commanded, dabbing Carlie's gravy-laden hand with a wet paper towel.

"Uh, oh, uh." Carlie swallowed.

"I guess that shower didn't awaken you sufficiently. Maybe you need a nap before we have our chat. Mrs. Campbell brought all your stuff from the boarding house since you won't be returning. We'll go through it later, so you can pick out what you want to keep in your room. As you may have noticed, I took the liberty of picking out your attire for today."

All of Patty's words tumbled and jumbled around in Carlie's private fog, leaving Carlie with a vague impression that something had just taken place, but, for the life of her, she couldn't make out what. Only the last words stuck in her mind, so she sat pondering who in the world besides Nurse Patty even used the word "attire".

Before she'd reached any conclusions, she found herself lying on a cot in the day room, dreaming up a storm about hot, buttered biscuits and golden scrambled eggs, dead to the world of activity around her. Around noon she finally stirred and sat up wondering how she managed to get her own clothes.

"Hello, sleepy head," the suicide specialist grinned. "I hope you're ready to work on your issues now that you've had a good nap."

As if on cue, Patty came charging over and almost sat on the quirky doctor. "We've got to talk now that you're awake. Mrs. Campbell from the boarding house filled me in on what happened, so let's get straight down to business. I want to hear your perspective of what happened at the Fourth of July picnic and what led up to it. Now we can go to your room or the consult room, but we're going to talk."

Carlie groaned. "Y'all are teaming up on me. It's not fair; I just woke up and can't think straight."

"Good," Patty grunted. "Don't try to put any spin on it; just tell me what happened."

"I've gotta pee," Carlie grumbled. Despite her gruff, barely awake look, complete with a severe case of bed head, Carlie's heart pumped faster, and her palms began to sweat. *Oh, crap! Not the dreaded talk. Just kill me now and be done with it.*

The chariot ride to the bathroom seemed to take forever with Patty carrying on about traumatic events needing to be addressed, and how you just can't bottle these things up, and you must deal with your feelings and learn healthy ways of coping, and on and on. It made Carlie want to vomit.

"Keep the bathroom door cracked," ordered Nurse Patty. "I'll be waiting for you right here."

"Oh, goody." Carlie couldn't keep the sarcasm from her voice.

"I'm glad you're pleased, because I'll be here, too." Dr. Emmanuel's calm, pleasant voice irritated her to no end.

What happened? How do I feel about it? Oh, great! Here's what I feel—trapped.

"Trapped and angry?" asked the good doctor.

Yes, angry, and... Carlie spotted a couple of towels from this morning's shower. Impulsively she grabbed them and tried to tie them around her neck, but before she could make it work Patty barged in and took the towels from her.

"You have so much pain, but hurting yourself won't make it go away," Patty said softly.

"Yeah, there's only one way to get rid of Nurse Patty, and that's to tell her the truth." Dr. Emmanuel peered over Patty's stooped shoulder.

Carlie flushed the toilet and made her way over to her bed with Patty in close pursuit. Carlie plopped down despondently and sighed. "What the hell?"

Patty pulled a chair close to the bed and sat. "What went on between you and Emily?"

"We were roommates the last six months, and it turned out that we both had similar backgrounds. She'd been molested at an early age, and she had a thing for cutting, too. When she wasn't cutting, she was using."

"Using what?"

"I don't know; anything she could get her hands on. She stole my Xanax until I caught her and started keeping my meds in a locked box. Then she got all hysterical like I owed her something because of all the crap she'd been through. What a laugh! She didn't go through a fraction of what I did, but, for some reason, I was supposed to give her whatever she thought she needed because she was so 'fragile'. Fragile my eye; she was just a drama queen and a manipulator."

Patty's lips pursed together tightly, but she didn't say anything.

Carlie paused to glare at Patty. *So that's how she sees me; that's how they all see me. They think I'm like Emily.*

"Nah, not like Emily. Emily was an amateur compared to you!" As usual, the suicide specialist didn't seem impressed.

"She acted like the whole world revolved around her, like her pain was sooo much worse than anyone else's..."

"When really the world revolves around you, because you are the most injured, the most special of all God's creation." Dr. Emmanuel yawned. He had the nerve to yawn after putting her down.

Carlie's voice became more heated. "She monopolized everything, practically took over the entire room. I couldn't have any privacy. She even read my journal."

"And saw your suicide plan." Dr. Emmanuel sat on the foot of the bed.

"Apparently she saw my suicide plan. It was a foolproof plan, because I couldn't take it anymore and didn't want to go through any of...this. I felt so tired of the endless cycle of being the laughingstock of the hospital, of not getting any respect, of always hurting and never having any hope. I managed to get a gun that I stashed under my bed, so I could use it at the picnic."

"The Fourth of July picnic that the boarding house held at the lake?" Patty asked.

"Yeah. My strategy was to get a paddle boat and paddle out to deep water. I figured that I'd fall into the lake and drown even if I somehow screwed up shooting myself in the head like that guy a couple of months ago who blew away his jaw. You remember?"

Patty nodded solemnly. "I remember you and Roger talking quite a bit while he recovered from his injuries here."

"Well, even though his jaw was wired shut, he told me how horrible it was. I didn't want to follow in his footsteps, so the lake plan provided drowning as a fail-proof back up."

Patty leaned back, looking especially thoughtful. "You developed quite a plan, something that required quite a bit of work to set up properly."

Carlie squinted in disbelief. Could Patty possibly be impressed with her suicide plan?

"It really was remarkably well thought out," Dr. Emmanuel droned in the background.

"What happened?" Patty asked.

Carlie looked from Dr. Emmanuel to Patty. This had to be a trick, didn't it? They acted like she was brilliant because of a suicide plan she didn't even get a chance to implement. She rubbed her tired eyes and sighed. Her voice grew weak and quivered just a tad.

"Emily happened. She read my journal...uh, I guess she found my gun in my purse, 'cause I hid it there that morning while she took her shower. Then she probably ripped me off while I applied my makeup in the bathroom. I, uh, think you know the rest."

"So, she basically stole your suicide plan!" Patty stared straight ahead as the significance sank in.

Tears silently welled up until they seeped from the corners of Carlie's eyes. She sniffled and nodded.

"Yeah, Patty, I finally came up with something smart, and I still failed."

"You see this as a failure on your part?"

"Well, I, uh, I mean...it worked for Emily." She shook her head. "I couldn't stand it. Hatred consumed me. I detested her for succeeding at the plan I so carefully set up, and I loathed her for taking it from me, leaving me with nothing but an old razor blade.

"Do you have any idea how sick and tired I feel, always trying and failing? Always in and out of the hospital, nothing ever changing? I just wanted it all to be over. Cutting was a spur-of-the-moment easy reaction; I didn't even have to plan anything—just do it." She snickered. "Like the old Nike commercial, huh?"

Patty touched Carlie's arm. "There's a lot to be angry about. And disappointed."

Carlie nodded. "Yeah. I'd done the cutting right this time. I was on my way out, and it was so...so comforting. A door with a wonderfully warm light invited me deeper in, and I experienced floating above the emergency room. It felt so peaceful. I basked in the most tranquil place I've ever been."

"Then what happened?"

"Dr. Emmanuel. He closed the door, turned off the light, and made me go back into my body. He said I hadn't learned how to do it right."

Carlie sneaked a glance at Patty to see what kind of reaction that would get. Surprisingly, Patty's eyebrows lifted ever-so-slightly, and she had a far-away expression in her eyes. "And he's been with you since then?"

Dr. Emmanuel smiled. "Go on."

"Sometimes I don't see him for a few minutes, and I think he's gone, but then I'll hear his voice. Last night, he, uh, he appeared on TV."

"You seemed pretty angry at him last night according to Candace."

Carlie blinked away the last teardrop. "Yeah, I'm mad. And I know he's just a hallucination, but he seems so real."

Patty looked directly at the spot where Dr. Emmanuel placidly perched with his trusty tablet. "I see."

In the Closet

The rest of the morning sped by with a blur of therapeutic activity. Carlie shuffled off to her morning group and went through the motions of making goals for the day—her main one being pain relief—and thinking longingly about the sweet bliss of death. Next stop, she attended medication class and totally tuned out since she'd heard this lecture a million times.

She ate lunch with Lila Mae and Joylyn, that is, whenever the perpetual motion machine decided to sit a spell before darting off to steal food from other patients' plates. Carlie rolled her eyes impatiently. *Why don't they use more of that wonderful medicine that they bragged about for the entire past hour on the human tornado?*

As if to prove her level of mania, Joylyn abruptly jumped up for some inexplicable reason ranting about her usual nonsense and spilled her tea all over Carlie.

It took all the self-restraint she had to keep from smacking her nemesis upside her head. "Why don't you sit down, shut up and act like a halfway decent person for a change?" she yelled.

Joylyn, not to be outdone, screamed obscenities and called Carlie several choice names, none of which eased the tensions mounting between the two.

Jason and Liz separated them while nurses fetched syringes filled with knock out juice. Thus, the two misfits found themselves in time out rooms, and serenity returned to the unit.

Carlie closed her heavy eyes and succumbed to the welcomed sedation. There would be no coping skill assignments today! Tomorrow, yes, but not today, and in her book, today was all that mattered.

Dreams, disjointed images of rabbits and kittens, sounds of war and hip hop music filed through Carlie's mind. Nothing significant—just gobbledygook. Nothing until the nightmare began.

Oppressive darkness—the kind that felt so thick with humidity and heat that it made five-year-old Carlie pant for breath—squeezed her throat and made her eyes fly open. She could see nothing at all. Sweat trickled down her forehead and threatened to drip into her eyes. She wiped her forehead and listened closely for Mommy's signal. Despite the heat, she crouched under a heavy winter jacket that had fallen off its hanger when she ran into the closet.

The front door creaked and slammed. Slippered footsteps shuffled past the closet. Mommy's voice, sounding eager to please, accompanied the sound of her house shoes.

"Good morning, Kyle. Are you hungry for breakfast?" she asked in syrupy tones.

"Yeah, starved," Daddy snarled.

Oh, no. He's angry again. He's always angry.

"I've got biscuits in the oven, and bacon in the microwave. Would you like your eggs scrambled or fried?" Mommy asked ever-so-sweetly.

"Fried." His answer sounded abrupt and gruff.

"How was work?"

"How da hell do ya think it was? I work night shift in a freakin' county jail. Whaddoya wanna interrogate me ever' day? Gimme a break." Daddy's voice sounded increasingly hostile and his words slurred, so Carlie knew what came next.

Mommy worked extra hard to talk nicely to Daddy. "I'm so sorry, dear. I didn't mean to set you off. Just making a little conversation 'cause I love you, babe."

Cowboy boots clacked across the linoleum and a chair scraped the wall before Daddy thudded into his place at the table. Every slight noise became amplified by the deepest terror Carlie ever knew. It was happening. Again. The clanking of Daddy's fork on his plate. The slurping of hot coffee. Water running and dishes being washed. And then it came. The boots started taking one slow step after another toward the hall closet.

Her hair dripped, sopping wet with sweat by now. Her chest ached and squeezed tightly, and the closet walls threatened to close in. She tried to sit perfectly still. *Don't make a sound.* Her own heart defied her by beating more and more fiercely until she could hear the pounding reverberating off the wall. *No, he'll hear me.* She took small sips of air through her open mouth and fought the urge to scream.

She valiantly fought back the tears that stung her eyes and clenched her lips tightly. That thick coat suffocated her, and her legs screamed to be stretched, but she couldn't move. Between the walls of the closet and the vacuum cleaner, the coats, and who knew what else that was crammed in the darkness, she could barely blink without her eyelashes hitting something. Each breath consumed every bit of strength that she could muster.

The heavy trudging turned away, but Carlie knew they'd come back. They always came back, and then the fighting began.

"Where the hell ish Carlie?"

"She's sleeping over at Janna's, remember? You look tired. Why don't you get some sleep? She'll, uh, she'll be back by the time you wake up."

"Don'tchya lie ta me, woman. Wheresh the lil ho?"

"Kyle, she's...Kyle, please don't. You're hurting me."

Three slaps in rapid succession jolted Carlie and rattled her spine. Then one thud after another and screams, horrible screams from Mommy. Salty little rivers silently trickled down Carlie's cheeks. Daddy cursed vociferously, and Mommy cried, sobbing uncontrollably and moaning. But today her moans only fueled Daddy's rage.

Carlie quaked with every yell and punch that punctured her ears with terror. *Make it stop, God. Make Daddy stop.* But it kept going, escalating in sound and intensity until she thought her heart would explode from panic.

"You think that's bad, bish? I've got a lot more 'an that lil bit o slapping ta give ya. Hush up an git o're here."

Another thud and Carlie could hear Mommy hitting the floor. Then she heard another loud cry, higher pitched, and sounding like infantile shrieking. Carlie stuffed her fist in her mouth, but it was too late.

"She'sh gone, huh? I'll teach ya ta lie ta me."

Shots rang out. The first made Carlie jump; the second made her pee.

Adult Carlie woke up in a wet bed, but she trembled too violently to even try to get up to the toilet. Instead, she covered her head with her blanket and whimpered like little Carlie back in the dark closet. "Make it stop! Please make it stop!" she cried.

"The nightmare again?" Dr. Emmanuel's voice sounded genuinely concerned, and Carlie felt so overwhelmingly desperate.

"Please help me! I can't take it anymore. Please!" She reached out from her covers and grabbed Dr. Emmanuel's hand, sobbing until her pillow became as wet as her sheets.

"Go on, my dear child, go on and let it out. Let me take it from you." His voice, filled with kindness, reassured her. "That's it. Give it to me."

"I don't know how. It hurts so badly. You tell me to give it to you like I can just put it in a box and hand it over. This is part of who I am; I can't just...just..."

"Carlie, are you alright?" LaShondra, a middle-aged tech who had worked nights for years, stood in Carlie's doorway. "Who are you talking to?"

Carlie wiped her puffy eyes. "I, I just had that nightmare again. I can't take it anymore. Isn't there something they can give me to make the dreams go away?"

LaShondra's spoke softly. She'd become all too familiar with Carlie's nightmare—the one that woke her up with incontinence at least once or twice with each admission. "I'm sorry, Carlie, but I don't know of anything. How 'bout me taking you back to your own room and helping you get a nice, warm shower. That'll freshen you up a bit. Then you can have a snack since you slept through supper. I can ask Candace about any meds that might help."

Without waiting for a reply, LaShondra turned on the light and started helping Carlie into a wheelchair. Carlie had to admit that she preferred her own bed to the one in seclusion, so she went along for the ride.

In a New York minute, LaShondra had water running in the shower, towels and a fresh gown stationed next to the sink and ever-popular baby shampoo in her pocket.

Carlie felt frazzled and still a bit disoriented, but she made a valiant effort to stand. Unfortunately, the floor and the walls swayed, which seemed an all-too-common occurrence for her. She reached to steady herself, but her legs started to give way.

A petite Filipino nurse magically appeared on her left and grabbed hold with a vise grip while LaShondra hoisted her from the right. She got quickly deposited back into the wheelchair until someone procured a white, plastic, shower chair.

Once she safely sat in the shower chair the clean-up crew to begin their work. Warm water cascaded down her already wet body. She willingly tilted her head and let the flow revive her. The clean scent of baby shampoo washed away the remaining horror from the dream, and her churning stomach settled gradually.

So, this is what I've become: a full-grown adult who has to be held up by one person while someone else lathers me up with baby shampoo. Baby shampoo—how fitting. I'm still the same child in that closet, even if I am twenty-one.

Soon she propped herself up in her clean bed and nibbled on smoked turkey and cheese topped with lettuce and tomato, sandwiched between two slices of delicious multi-grain whole wheat bread. She popped a few baked potato chips into her mouth after sipping her chocolate milk. Serenity started kicking in, but Carlie knew it was largely due to the injections she'd received during her sparring match with Joylyn. She meekly thanked her caretakers and munched on another chip.

"There you go, gal! Two big steps in one night; I'm so proud of you," Dr. Emmanuel beamed.

Chewing slowly and methodically, Carlie frowned. "What steps?"

"You asked for help, and you actually thanked someone for helping you. How does it feel?" He pulled the chair up close and studied her eyes.

"I feel maybe lighter; I don't know. I feel like I can breathe. Does that make sense? I couldn't breathe in my dream; my chest seemed like it was being crushed. I needed someone, something...I couldn't go on. But you—I don't understand you. I don't know how I can trust you or who you really are."

His large brown eyes seemed to captivate her spirit—not in a spooky way this time, not intimidating, but with a new hope. The scars on his forehead and wrists somehow reassured her that maybe, just maybe, he told the truth about being the one person who could really understand her trauma.

"That's alright. Try me for yourself. See with your own eyes that you can lean on me. I'll never be exactly predictable or do things the way you think they should be done, but trust me even more during those times. I promise I won't let you down. Not ever."

"And you're really going to teach me how to commit suicide and do it right?"

Without blinking, he silently nodded.

"Then teach me now. Why wait another moment? Can't you see that I live in torture every day, every night? You got what you wanted; I asked for help, so help me. Show me how to 'do it right'. Get me out of here and help me put an end to all this once and for all. You're the reason I'm still here, so you kind of owe it to me, you know."

"You're not even close to ready yet." He shook his head.

"So, what do I have to do to be ready? Just tell me what it is, and I'll do it," Carlie insisted.

"But that's the point," Dr. Emmanuel explained. "You can't. You are unable to do what it takes—at least at this point. If I told you what it takes, you'd muddle everything up trying to hurry the process, and it can't be rushed. Everything at its proper time, and it's something that only I can do to get you ready and only if you let me."

"But that makes no sense."

"And you're talking with someone that no one else can see or hear. Does anything really make perfect sense to you? Does it make sense that you had such a jacked-up childhood? That everyone who should have protected you hurt you instead? That the help they offered you only hurt you more deeply? That pain this deeply ingrained can't be cured by any pill or shot or talk therapy? Yet, they expect you to get better. Sixteen years of therapy—over a decade and a half—and what healing do you have to show for it? Their best wisdom hasn't touched the surface, and you don't even understand the extent of the darkness you face. You think you do, but you still only have the child's understanding...the frightened child who couldn't even see right in front of her nose in that dark closet."

Carlie sat silenced by his reply. He knew something, but how? He didn't appear much older than her. He may have read the police and therapy reports, but he wasn't there. She held her head in her hands and tried to figure it out. How could her hallucination know some deep dark secret about her past? How could he be her only chance of relief? None of it made sense, but it also didn't make sense that her imaginary friend knew about her day of horror before she even told him her story. Could he just guess that there was more than what she'd told everyone for years, or did he have actual information?

She searched her memory. No, all her nightmares confirmed her story. There couldn't be any more horrible, forgotten abuse. After all, how could it get any worse than what had been burned into   her   memory   so   clearly?

An Old, New Friend

Carlie awakened the next morning with the nightmare still playing on her emotions. No matter how hard she tried to forget, sounds from the closet played repeatedly in her frazzled brain. Trudging through the morning with Dr. Emmanuel at her side, she noticed a certain degree of comfort that he brought. At least she didn't have to face those horrible memories alone.

By noon, she felt downright worn out from dealing with ghosts from the past and almost welcomed the lunchtime drama provided by her least favorite bipolar.

A new patient close to her own age barely sat down to eat at a nearby table when Joylyn started yelling at her for being "another corporate spy sent by my enemies, my family, and the American military-industrial complex organization overseeing the destruction of true genius wherever they find it so they can stuff everyone into their tiny, pre-conceived box of old-fashioned notions of conformity"...and many more hostile rants in her most grating, shrill, and annoying voice ever.

Craig shouted, "Shut up! Don't you know they're listening?" as he pointed meaningfully at the fire detector on the ceiling.

Lila Mae stopped eating and dropped her fork on the floor.

The new girl flinched. She already had two black, swollen eyes, bruises and cuts on every part of her visible body, and a cast on her left arm. She didn't look like she could stand any more battering—even the verbal kind.

The whole nursing team swooped in to remove Joylyn from the dining room, calm Craig, and offer emotional support to the wounded girl.

Lila Mae fished around on her tray for her spoon and resumed eating. Conversations that halted started to hum once more. Carlie mused privately that normalcy on the psych unit had returned, if indeed anything on a psych unit could be considered normal. She glanced at Dr. Emmanuel, who showed no reaction at all to Joylyn's tirade. What a quirky hallucination!

What? No advice about Joylyn's manic behavior? No delightful words of insight about my own anger? Maybe you're getting bored with me. Carlie silently railed, forgetting the comfort he so recently brought her.

"I would never be bored with you, my love."

Okay. Stop with the...

"L word? Let's move past that for the moment, because something else is about to push your buttons. Let's just call it a learning opportunity." The crazy doctor turned his head toward the new patient. "She has something you need."

Carlie's stomach twisted into at least three knots as she followed his gaze. Each time she looked at the battered flesh still quaking in fear her internal alarms blasted and jolted every fiber of her being. As much as she wanted to run the other direction, she felt compelled to pick up her tray and move over to her table.

Visions of her mother getting smacked around flooded her memory banks. How many times had she gotten broken bones set? How many ER visits with traumatic injuries? Carlie fought her instincts to run. After all, if someone—just one person—had stood by her mother, maybe she'd still be alive. Maybe they would have been a family: Mommy, Bubba and her. They could have gotten away from Daddy together. If only...

"Sorry, Miss Lila Mae, I've got to meet an old friend for the first time."

The old lady waved her blessings, so Carlie slid into an empty chair opposite the bruised girl. "Hi, uh, I'm Carlie. Mind if I eat with you? I promise not to press charges against you for spying on my ultra-secret, sure-to-make-me-rich-quick, corporate structure that I don't even have except in my own mind. What's your name?"

"Taylor Whitehouse. I just got here about an hour ago." Taylor looked relieved to see a friendly face.

"So, how's it going so far, besides being accused of all sort of nefarious acts by our resident maniac?"

Taylor smiled weakly. "I like you. You're funny."

"Yeah, I'm just here for comic relief. In fact, I'm so wildly popular at the nut hut that I hang out here a lot. They call me the queen of good times." Carlie laughed. *If anything, I'm the queen of sarcasm, but if I'm making up a new persona for myself, I might as well be clever about it. Besides, I can't bear what I know this girl's been through—she's just like my mother.*

Apparently, Taylor either bought Carlie's story or felt a desperate need of a friend inside the looney bin. Of course, the population at hand didn't offer many viable options. Whatever the case, she became Carlie's shadow over the next several days. She joined Carlie and Lila Mae for every meal, tagged along to each group session, and sat with Carlie in front of the day room TV while the other patients visited with friends and family. Neither of them had visitors. Somehow Carlie knew it would be that way.

Taylor settled into the couch beside Carlie one evening. "Looks like it's you and me, kid. What do you want to watch on TV?"

"It doesn't matter. Hey, if you don't mind—well, I'm just curious. See, my dad beat my mom, and eventually he killed her..."

"I'm so sorry!" Taylor exclaimed, looking appalled.

"Oh, uh, thanks. Maybe you can help me understand. I've often wondered why she didn't leave him. I never knew her parents, so I guess I just figured they must be really messed up if she considered staying with Daddy a better option. So, I guess what I want to know is—and let me know if I'm prying—what kind of childhood did you endure? And how did it prepare you for your abusive relationship?"

Taylor shifted uncomfortably. "Wow! You get to the point, don't you? I don't mean that in a bad way. It's much worse when people beat around the bush, but you get the feeling that they're judging you for taking the beatings."

"Oh, no, please don't take it that way. I just wish I could have my mother back, and she didn't seem to have anyone—no friends or family except Daddy and us kids. So, uh, I wondered if things were so bad between her and her folks that running off with Daddy seemed like a better option."

"I can understand how you would wonder about that. Of course, I can't speak for your mother. All I can tell you is that I have wonderful parents—not perfect, but they are warm and caring. I always knew they loved me.

"Then I met this charming guy in college. He was smart, witty and good-looking. While other guys seemed more interested in acting like over-grown boys fueled by hormones, he seemed more mature. He wanted to get serious, and I felt tickled pink. He went on and on about family and the sanctity of marriage, and I thought we shared the same values. Brad filled up my days and evenings, and soon I had little time for anyone else, but I thought I had this fairy tale romance that would never end.

"We got married just six months after our first date, the day after graduation. The first sign of trouble came on the honeymoon when he discovered that I squeezed the toothpaste tube from the middle. He let me know in no uncertain terms that only a moron would do something that unthinking and disorganized. He later apologized for his harsh words and bought me a gorgeous bouquet of flowers, but that turned into the beginning of a downward trend."

Taylor sighed, and she gingerly rubbed her cast. "I chalked it up to the stress of taking finals, graduating and all the hoopla of the wedding. Way too much to pack into a short period of time." Her eyes fell to the carpet. "Unfortunately, there was always stress, and I was always wrong. He'd apologize while subtly letting me know that he loved me in spite of me being beneath his lofty standards. Oh, and he took it upon himself to change me into the perfect wife. That meant **everything** had to be done his way, or there were consequences."

"Oh, thanks. Well, at least you wiped out one theory I had about my mom. Hey, why don't your parents come to visit?"

Taylor looked ashamed. "I, uh, I mean Bradley pretty much cut me off from everyone little by little until I stopped communicating with my parents. They have no idea about the abuse or the fact that I'm in the hospital. I know they'd come, but that would mean having to explain—you know—everything. I don't want to upset them, so..."

Carlie put her arm around Taylor. "So, you go it alone. Well, no one came through for my mom, either. But in case you haven't noticed, you're not exactly alone in here. I promise to be here   for   you."

The Terrible Tale

Just as she promised, Carlie stuck close to Taylor, holding her hand as she sobbed her way through her tale of domestic abuse during one of the mid-afternoon group therapy sessions. She closed her eyes and stifled her own tears. *My mom didn't deserve this either.*

As if on cue, Patty piped up. "I see you and Carlie share a special bond. Has she told you her story?"

Carlie violently shook her head at Patty. *How can she do this to me? She knows I hate talking about it. I've told the story like a million times already to every shrink, every nurse, every therapy group. How long does my life have to be defined by what happened when I was five years old?*

"That's exactly right," Dr. Emmanuel chimed in. "I'm so glad to hear you reach this conclusion; however, this poor girl needs to know why you understand her pain."

Taylor wiped her eyes and blew her nose before searching Carlie's face for answers. Carlie gritted her teeth. *Here goes.*

"Well, I already told you part of the story about how, uh, my father used to beat my mother—you know real regularly. Then he started molesting me for grins, 'cause putting Mommy in the hospital on a semi-regular basis only went so far in screwing up our entire family.

"He came home from working the night shift one morning, and I hid in a closet because I knew what he'd do to me. I hated mornings, 'cause he'd come to my room and mess with me, and I'd have to start every day feeling dirty and angry and miserable. So, anyway, when I heard his pickup truck, I ran to the hallway closet and hid behind the vacuum cleaner.

"He took out his frustration on my Mom—I could hear him knocking her around—and went on a shooting spree. Then it got real quiet until the cops came. They found my mother and my baby brother dead and arrested my dear old dad. So that's my life story with all the sordid details."

There, she made it through her life history without having a meltdown. In fact, she pretty much felt numb through the retelling. Her face remained stony, like her heart.

"ALL the details?" The suicide specialist raised his eyebrows suspiciously.

Shut up. I'm not talking to you—not now.

"But you WILL talk with me," he decreed.

Not now. I'm a little busy here.

"Then listen and listen well." He pushed his black curls away from the scars on his forehead. "Just as you understand Taylor's pain from your experience, I understand your pain even more."

Suddenly Taylor threw her arms around Carlie—cast and all— taking her by such surprise that she froze in her chair. "After all you've been through, and you're so brave! You're such an inspiration!"

A few of the more seasoned patients who still inhabited reality groaned.

Carlie extricated herself from what seemed like a tangle of arms and glared at the rest of the group. "No! Ask them. Go on and ask them. I was freaking trying to kill myself. I'm not brave—not even close. How do you think I got these Frankenstein gashes on my neck?"

The room fell suddenly silent, all eyes on Carlie. Even Jeffrey looked up from his normal, near-lifeless slump and met her gaze with a questioning expression. Taylor's lower lip trembled, and Craig clutched his chair as if preparing for blast off. Joylyn grinned devilishly and wagged her finger at Carlie, which turned out to be the last straw.

Carlie stormed out of the room, only to be followed by perfect Patty. "Is it really so bad that someone likes you, that someone thinks highly of you? I've known you for three years now and have never seen you allow anyone to get this close to you. I see this as progress—not a setback—though I'm sure it makes you feel vulnerable."

She couldn't take it anymore. What made Patty think she knew anything about the storm brewing inside? She slammed her fist into the wall and screamed. Her stony heart shattered into a million pieces. The strange lack of emotions she'd experienced just seconds ago gave way to the violent storm brewing underneath her surface.

Whirling around to face her intrusive adversary, Carlie snarled fiercely. "You don't know anything about me. You certainly can't tell me how I feel about anything—not anything. Do you hear me?" She literally screamed in Patty's face.

When Patty took a few steps back, time went into a warp. Everything happened in slow motion, yet as a blur of fast-forwarded events, each taking place step by step as they always did.

First came the therapeutic jargon: "I hear you yelling and see you punching the wall. You look very upset, but you're right. I can't tell you what you're feeling. I need you to tell me what's going on. Would you rather go to your room...?"?

"Or go to the seclusion room, right? Isn't that where this dance always ends? I'm violent; I'm crazy. What's new? Go get the drugs and put me out of my misery." Carlie's volume now grew even louder and more belligerent than before, and her rage rivaled Craig's intensity.

The troops started to rally. They came from different directions, donning gloves as they approached, and one of the nurses had a couple of syringes in her hand.

Carlie flailed her arms. "Get away from me, you perverts." She ran down the hall to her room and slammed the door. Grabbing her chair from her desk, she propped it up against the door. Looking around, she saw nothing else to use. After all, the desk and bed were bolted to the floor, leaving her with nothing— except Dr. Emmanuel. A hostage! She lunged at him but thudded into the wall and landed on the floor at the same time the door flew open and the staff poured in. They had her trapped like a rat!

"NOOOOOO!"

Unflappable Patty calmly pointed to the bed. "You can either get on the bed, or we can give you the shots with you lying on the floor—your choice."

"Go to hell!" Carlie kicked at the closest set of legs.

Jason nimbly jumped out of the way, allowing her right leg to swing forward before grabbing it and pinning both legs down. She let out a blood-curdling scream while several of Patty's minions restrained her. Something cool and wet quickly dabbed her upper arm before she felt the first needle pierce her flesh.

"I hate you all!" she hissed. "This isn't therapeutic, Patty. You're a sadist—all of you—you brood of vipers!"

Dr. Emmanuel's finger touched her lips. "You'll feel better soon, but it's only temporary. You and I have some serious talking to do."

Strong arms lifted Carlie from the floor and laid her on the bed. Patty's gray hair stuck out all over and her glasses were missing. She huffed silently, trying to catch her breath until she regained her ability to talk in her normal nurse-robot tones.

"Carlie, you can rest here or in the quiet room. If you cooperate and don't yell, hit, kick, or do anything violent and you are able to follow directions, it ends here. We had to medicate you because you harmed yourself by punching the wall and were quickly escalating towards more violence. Do you understand?"

The more subdued Carlie nodded.

"We'll talk about it after you rest." Patty looked around. "Liz, will you sit with her for a few minutes? It usually doesn't take long before she's asleep."

Liz sat in the chair previously used as a flimsy barricade and watched as Carlie's eyelids grew heavy.

"It won't always be this painful if you give it to me. I'll teach you how to die to the pain." Once again, she heard the good doctor's voice, the one that refused to go away. She had to admit that he helped her through her nightmare last night, but--

Really? How can I trust you?

"How is not trusting me working for you?"

Carlie's world became progressively blurred and distant as she succumbed to the Haldol-Ativan-Benadryl cocktail. Punching the wall and hollering at Patty had its perks, after all. The float down

Xanax River was mild by comparison. This felt more like plunging over Niagara Falls. Carlie willingly took the dive into medicated bliss, void of nasty emotions and voices urging her to trust, open up and learn how to cope.

Somewhere in the distance, Patty's voice asked Dr. Emmanuel to help Carlie.

Carlie's eyes fluttered one last time. Did she really hear Patty talking with her hallucination? In all her fifty-three prior admissions to this same psychiatric unit, not to mention the untold number of visits to Children's Hospital for the same reasons in her youth, and a handful to the nearest state facility in Terrell she'd never had any hallucinations.

Dreams tormented her. The past haunted her, but she could always recognize reality. Until now. She'd officially sunk to new lows.

Then, again, this new doctor could be quite comforting in the strangest way. She almost half believed he did know the missing answer, just the right antidote for what ailed her. Maybe she needed to simply go with her hallucination and see what he had to offer.

"I'll help you find what's real. I promise." Dr. Emmanuel's words echoed in her groggy brain before Carlie was overcome by deep sleep—and her usual nightmare.

For the remainder of that day and the next, Carlie feverishly choked back screams in that pitch-black closet. She drifted in and out of consciousness, trembling and wet after each episode, crying out for help and clinging to Dr. Emmanuel's hand. Then she returned to the closet with a sense of urgency to find out what truth lurked in the darkness. The answer continued to elude her until she finally awakened the next day.

Mental Vacation

An Indian nurse with long silky hair pulled back into a pony tail brought Carlie her meds after breakfast. Carlie came as close to liking Anna as any nurse she'd ever had. She projected true kindness in a gentle, soft spoken manner even though Carlie couldn't always understand her thick accent. She didn't meddle like Patty, and that alone made her a better pick among the day nurses. Sure, she asked the basic questions, but she didn't pry to the same degree, and she more quickly medicated instead of making her write a ton of therapeutic nonsense.

With one gulp, Carlie downed all the pills in the little paper medication cup and opened her mouth to prove she had indeed swallowed each and every one of them.

"Dr. White phoned and wants to meet you in the consult room. He should be here in a couple of minutes, so I'll let you in." Anna pulled her keys from her scrub pocket. "Do you need anything else before you see him?"

"Uh, no, I'm fine for now." The seasoned psych patient dutifully followed her nurse down the hall while considering what she might ask Dr. White to order for her today. *Oh, yes, something to get rid of the nightmares.* She made herself comfortable in the armchair closest to the door as Anna disappeared down the hall and thanked her lucky stars that she didn't have to deal with Patty.

"Don't worry. You still have me. I—unlike Patty—never take a day off." The suicide specialist smiled warmly as he sat in the chair beside hers. "We have much to talk about today."

Sure. I want to stop this not-so-merry-go-round and get off. I'm at the end of my rope, so yeah, I'll give you a shot. What do I have to lose?

"Your fear, and of course your anger, and even your guilt." Dr. Emmanuel tapped his finger on his knee with each point that he made.

Carlie bristled internally. *I've been therapized since early childhood. If there's one thing I've learned, it's that I have nothing to feel guilty about. None of what happened was my fault. That's what every doctor, every therapist, nurse—even the janitor...*

The odd doctor held up his hand to stop her before rubbing his eyes. He sighed and shook his head. "You woke up before seeing everything that happened on your last trip to the closet."

Yeah, I didn't see the bodies in my dream, but I don't want to see them—not ever, Carlie fumed mentally, biting her lower lip to keep from talking out loud and being accused of hearing voices. *Look, I know I asked you for help in a moment of sheer terror and maybe again under the influence of medication, but—let's be clear from the start—I just want to learn how to commit the perfect suicide and end the pain. That's what you said you'd do for me. That's all I want from you. Get it?*

Dr. Emmanuel lifted his eyebrows, his gentle brown eyes searching Carlie's face. "I understand what you want, and I understand what you need. The two are not the same. I will give you everything you need."

She grimaced and clenched the padded arms of her chair. *Oh, I see. So, the double talk begins. Just who are you that you know what I need? That sounds a lot like going back on your word to me.*

He shook his head. "I always keep my word. Always."

Footsteps approaching from the hall caught Carlie's attention. Taylor waved as she hurried closer. "Hey, I overslept and missed having breakfast with you. How are you feeling?"

"As good as ever." That wasn't a lie. Deep depression dominated her baseline mood, and hopelessness designed her lifestyle. Her outburst during therapy may have been quite a show for someone who didn't know her very well, but it was simply another dip into the pool of despair for Carlie. And yesterday was a medicated blur, except for those nasty trips to the closet.

"Aren't you coming to group?"

"Yeah, in a few minutes. Dr. White's gonna chat me up first."

Taylor smiled. "I'll save ya a seat then."

Carlie grinned appreciatively. "See ya." *Well, she doesn't seem too freaked out about my meltdown; she must be adjusting to life in the nut hut pretty quickly.* She felt her cheeks flushing at the memory.

Just then Dr. White breezed in carrying what looked suspiciously like the latest in electronic gizmos. He was a meticulous man, thin and austere, dressed in a crisply starched long sleeved shirt and expensive-looking trousers and sporting a conservative, charcoal tie. He grunted a nonchalant greeting and swiped the screen with his index finger, frowning at whatever the screen told him.

Of course, Carlie had a pretty good idea of what he read about her, seeing as how she kept acting out and getting sedated that week, so she decided to beat him to the punch line. "It certainly seems I haven't learned much about controlling my emotions over the years, doesn't it? I mean, you'd think I'd be immune to telling my story to anyone and everyone and wouldn't blow a gasket like I did. So—and I guess you already know about the nightmares I've had the last two nights—they aren't getting any better. Is there any medicine that could take them away without making me weigh like a thousand pounds?"

Dr. White cocked his head to one side, looking incredulously at his problem patient. "Do you understand how serious this is? You are chronically in the self-destruct mode, and your impulse control is almost non-existent. I know you've been dealt a rotten past, but you don't appear to be invested in improving your present or your future. Instead of trying more medicine, how about you tell me what YOU are willing to do to become healthier?"

Carlie sighed. It sounded like he took a page out of Nurse Patty's manual. She fidgeted in her chair and looked defiantly at the carpet. "I do try. I journal and identify my feelings and develop all sorts of plans for dealing with them (*only because Patty makes me*), but the feelings come on so strong…"

She sighed again, and her face clouded with anger. "So now I guess it's my fault I'm so screwed up. Forget what my daddy did to me. Forget that I had to listen to him shooting my mom and brother. Forget…"

"But your dad didn't shoot your brother," Dr. Emmanuel butted in.

Carlie's face suddenly drained all its color, and she slumped back into her chair.

Dr. White cleared his throat, his pale blue eyes glued to his i-Pad. "I take it that you're not having any side effects from your current meds?" Clearly, he didn't want to go through Carlie's life history again, not that he really cared anyway.

She shook her head and scowled. Another great start to the emotional roller coaster she was doomed to ride on a daily basis. Why did it even bother her that this jerk and his i-Pad saw her as an insignificant piece of trash?

"You're not trash." Dr. Emmanuel reached over and took her hand. His flesh felt strangely soothing as if he had some magic flowing through his mere touch.

Carlie was struck with the sharp contrast in physicians. Her savior of sorts with his rumpled lap coat and tousled hair wouldn't win any fashion awards, but his big, puppy-dog eyes conveyed both compassion and power. And his consistent shadowing of her spoke volumes, especially compared with her usual two-minute, hit-and-run meeting with Dr. White, who wouldn't even look at her.

"I care for you very deeply." His voice seemed to cast a spell on her.

Instantly Dr. White faded into insignificance. His voice faded into the background when he announced his decision to keep her medication regimen the same at this time. Like that, their session ended.

A smile crept over Carlie's face as she stood to leave. Dr. Emmanuel still held her hand, walking her to group therapy like a kind father would walk a child to school. She heard him telling her that she'd be fine, that he would see to it. She didn't know why, but she believed him, at least for the moment. Maybe she had run out of strength to keep on fighting. Maybe she just didn't have anything else in which to believe. Whatever the reason, she felt strangely peaceful—and without being shot up with Haldol.

I guess you're not so bad. Of course, it wouldn't take much to be an improvement over Dr. White. I just don't get why you had to bring me back when I was dying, just for me to learn how to do it right. I mean, who decided the correct way to commit suicide?

Dr. Emmanuel's eyes narrowed. "You think it's just about committing suicide correctly? No, no. I'm not here about some shame-on-you-for-not-getting-it-right mission. I'm here to show you a more excellent way, a truly spectacular suicide."

Carlie paused before opening the door to the therapy room. *It's about my form? You did seem impressed by the suicide plan that Emily stole from me.*

"No, let's stop that train of thought right now. Don't try to figure out what I'm going to show you, because it's something you've never seen before, never heard about, never concocted in your wildest dreams."

But the results are the same, right? I mean dead is dead, and I'll be free of pain, and...

"No, not all death is the same, and in some cases, pain is intensified. What you experienced during your cardiac arrest was a sample of what will be, not what actually laid in store for you in your current condition."

What will be—not was? Where do you get this stuff?

Before Dr. Emmanuel could explain, Jason came out of the nurses' station and made a beeline for Carlie. "Anna wanted me to make sure you came to group therapy after your session with Dr. White. Everything okay?"

Carlie nodded. "Yeah, I'm headed to group now, so tell Anna she can breathe easy." She cracked the door open and scoped out the room. Sure enough, an empty chair next to Taylor sat waiting just for her. Might as well get this over.

Amazingly enough, Paul, the therapist, didn't even bring up her last catastrophe. Instead, he looked preoccupied leading the group in guided imagery and other stress-reducing techniques. Soon Carlie found herself kicking back on an imaginary sandy beach listening to pretend waves rolling in and feeling the sun in her head caress her cheeks with warmth. Since she plunged into the official nut hut mental vacation wholeheartedly, she decided to do it up right and sip a cool, nonexistent pina colada. As she bit into a sweet slice of pineapple and savored its tropical goodness, a gorgeous hunk of a shirtless waiter bent over and gently wiped her mouth with a white linen napkin. Her beached whale of a body instantly transformed itself into slim curves of movie star proportions. Oh, this little exercise could be quite pleasurable— much better than the session they had a couple of days ago.

"Having fun?" a familiar voice beside her drew her attention away from Mr. Gorgeous. She turned to find Dr. Emmanuel sprawled comfortably on his own beach chaise lounge. His scrubs and lab coat had been replaced with electric blue board shorts and a striped tank top. His curly locks brushed from his brown face by the playful breeze, exposed the scars on his forehead more than usual.

Carlie's eyes traveled down his bare arms and legs. Gashes from long ago had left sizable craters in both wrists and feet. Curiously she reached out and touched his right arm, tracing the scars with her finger. *How did this happen?*

"I died, and now I'm here for you."

Did you kill yourself? Is that how you know about a wonderful suicide?

His brown eyes looked far away yet intensely near, almost inside her head. She blinked. How did he do that?

"I didn't kill myself, but I gave my life by choice, using my own free will. I decided to die, so you can experience the ultimate death and the most fulfilling life."

That sounds like crazy talk. How can you say stuff like that?

"I think you know, deep down. Think about it. Who else knows what really happened in the closet?"

Carlie's heart began to race. The sand and ocean beat a fast retreat. Little Carlie hunkered down back in the oppressive closet with sweat running down her brow. Daddy's angry voice cursed Mommy. She stifled a cry, biting her own hand in fear, but despite her best efforts a high-pitched wail rattled her. Now Daddy would find her. She had to stop the screaming. She grabbed her mouth with both hands, but still the shrieks grew louder and louder. As she fought to breathe the humid air, she slowly realized that the screams came from beside her.

Trembling, her hands reached out to feel their way around the dark closet. The next thing she knew a sobbing and screaming toddler flung his chubby little arms around her neck.

"Bubba!" she yelled. "Noooo!"

"Carlie, open your eyes," Paul commanded in a monotone voice. "You're still in the hospital and we're having group therapy."

Wiping the sweat from her eyes, she could see the whole group staring at her. So much for relaxation techniques.

Bubba's Final Cry

After supper, visitors invaded the psych unit and paired off with various patients. Lila Mae's daughter walked her slowly down the hall while Jeffrey avoided all eye contact with his sister. Joylyn gave a young man an exceedingly passionate kiss in the hallway and paraded him down to the day room where she announced to everyone present that this prize was her husband. Carlie smiled at him and wondered how on earth he'd gotten saddled with someone ridiculous like Joylyn.

"They're kind of a cute couple if Joylyn would just sit still and keep her mouth shut for five seconds," Taylor observed.

Carlie merely snickered as her vivid imagination pictured Joylyn bound and gagged, which was the only way she'd be still and quiet, unless of course someone drugged her. A bleary-eyed Joylyn propped up on the couch next to her handsome hubby popped into Carlie's mind.

Taylor cocked her head. "What's so funny?"

"Just imagining, that's all. I can see what it would take for that gal to be quiet."

Taylor grinned. "Well, she hasn't been quite as obnoxious and loud today."

Carlie nodded. "Her meds are starting to kick in. I've seen her kind come and go. She'll get back to normal and go home, live a halfway normal life and decide to stop taking her meds. Then she'll be back, psycho as ever—maybe even more so. That's the way it is with most."

Taylor looked perplexed. "I don't mean to pry, but why do you keep coming back? I mean, you're really smart. You seem to have so much of this figured out, and you really help me, so why don't you, uh…"

"Help myself?" Carlie's forehead wrinkled and her eyes narrowed.

"Don't get me wrong. After you shared your story, I could totally see how much you've been hurt and how hard it must be to, to, uh, I guess put it behind you." Taylor fidgeted with the arm of the couch.

"I can't get it out of my head. I see it in my dreams, and it even crawled into the relaxation technique we practiced today in group." Carlie stared at the carpet. What about the new event that crept into today's exercise? It seemed like a nightmare, but could it be a memory?

"Oh, yes, it was a real memory," Dr. Emmanuel interjected as he sat between Carlie and Taylor on the couch.

"I'm sorry," Taylor said softly. "It must be difficult to live with."

"That's why I have to die," Carlie muttered morbidly.

Taylor looked appalled. "You HAVE to die?"

"Uh, never mind; just joking." But Carlie didn't look like her joking self. The mischievous glimmer left her eyes, and a hardened, quiet seething made its debut instead.

Taylor squirmed uncomfortably. She'd seen looks like that before, just prior to her husband belting her across the face or pushing her down the stairs. She grew silent and thoughtful.

"You will die in order to truly live," Dr. Emmanuel said. "It seems like a contradiction, but it's a most exhilarating and freeing experience."

Carlie glanced at Taylor, who didn't seem to notice Dr. Emmanuel squeezed in between them talking about stuff that didn't make sense. From the look on her face, she didn't know how to react to any talk of having to die.

Across the room, Craig muttered menacingly to an invisible foe. What made her hallucination any better than Craig's?

"For one thing, I brought you back from death's door. For another thing, I know you better than you know yourself. I can show you what you've forgotten, and I can set you free from what you do remember." His eyes exuded confidence and wisdom.

"Okay, let's do it. Let's just do it now. I can't keep going on with this vicious cycle. What do I need to do?" Carlie's tone, firm with determination and decisiveness, abruptly announced her intentions to the entire community of psych patients.

Taylor jerked her head up. "What are you talking about?"

Dr. Emmanuel held his hands out as an invitation. "Go on and tell her. She's your friend."

Carlie's eyes widened. *Are you sure?*

"I'm always sure." He flashed an amused grin.

Taylor looked at her face for answers, making Carlie wonder where should she begin telling something that sounded insane, especially coming from someone in the looney bin?

"Start from the beginning, when you first saw me in the emergency department, before you re-entered your body," Dr. Emmanuel prompted.

"Okay," Carlie sighed. "This is going to sound absolutely bonkers, but I have this doctor who calls himself the suicide specialist, and he's the one that kept me from dying after my last suicide attempt. I saw him in the emergency room when they were doing CPR on me. I started floating upward toward the doorway with overwhelmingly brilliant light, and this odd doctor shut the door and said I couldn't go until I learned to do it right."

From the amazed expression on Taylor's face, Carlie knew she had her complete attention—and so far, no trace of doubt. "So, you had a near-death out-of-body experience?"

"Uh huh. And Dr. Emmanuel—that's the suicide specialist— has been with me ever since. No one else seems to see him or hear him except me, so I think I'm hallucinating. He's annoying the way he says stuff that doesn't make a lick of sense, but he's also a nice apparition of sorts, not scary like whatever Craig has going on. He keeps telling me that he's going to set me free from all the junk in my past and help me know what it's like to truly live."

Carlie paused to give Taylor a chance to absorb this information. She could see all sorts of question marks popping up in her friend's mind. Crap. All sorts of question marks pinged around in her own brain.

Taylor finally found her voice. "What does he look like?"

Oh, good, she's starting with an easier question. "He has dark, curly hair and deep, piercing, brown eyes, so dark they're almost black, but sometimes they seem to glow like fiery coals. He wears sea green scrubs and a white lab coat in bad need of ironing. He's medium in build and about six feet tall with bronze skin. Oh, and he has scars on his forehead and both wrists and feet. And from what I could see of his arms and shoulders, it looked like scars covered his back side as well."

"You saw his feet and shoulders?" Taylor looked amused.

"Yeah, well, when we did that guided imagery exercise this morning, he joined me on the beach, and he was appropriately dressed for—you know—the beach."

"Is that who you called Bubba?"

Carlie held her head in her hands and groaned. "No, Bubba was my baby brother. I saw, no, I felt him and heard him in the closet with me today. I started out on the beach relaxing, then this doctor showed up, and I somehow found myself as a child back in the closet. I could hear Daddy beat Mommy before he shot her. Then I heard screaming and crying. I thought it was coming from me, but I couldn't make the racket stop when I covered my mouth. I was terrified that my dad would find me, so I tried to make the screaming stop. Then it turned out that Bubba was making that racket, and I..."

"What?"

The dark closet swallowed Carlie once more. Bubba wailed loudly. She had to silence him. Grabbing him firmly, she held her hands over his mouth. The more he wiggled to get free, the tighter she held on. She felt completely terrified. Mommy was being knocked around, and Daddy's heavy footsteps clacked past the closet, then gunshots. Little Carlie peed her pants.

She squeezed with all her might. *Please be quiet, Bubba. Please.* His little body went limp. The crushing darkness, the thick humidity, the sheer horror overwhelmed her.

Adult Carlie ran to her room, soaked with sweat, and her heart pounding mercilessly, her head filled with pressure to the point of nearly exploding. Dr. Emmanuel held her close as she trembled and cried.

"NO! It can't be true!" she sobbed.

"You saw what really happened, Carlie. I'm still with you, and I'm going to help you through this. It's important for you to remember; otherwise, you can't really die to it." He stroked her damp hair.

LaShondra barged into Carlie's room. "Hey, girl, you know you're not supposed to be in here alone." She paused to take in the scene before her. Carlie carried on strangely, even for Carlie, crying and shaking and reaching out like she was holding onto someone or something that wasn't there.

Carlie wiped her tears. "I gotta go potty. Real bad. Now."

"Okay, okay; all you gotta do is ask." The night tech unlocked the bathroom door and perched warily on the nearby chair. "Go ahead and leave the door cracked, and don't try anything funny in there. You're not going to start anything this early in the shift. Oh, no. You do your business, and then you go straight to Candace to talk about what's going on in that head of yours, you hear me?"

Carlie grunted. What choice did she have?

Her heart still pounded out of control a few minutes later when she sat in the armchair in the consult room, and her head throbbed. Candace's eyebrows raised expectantly, but Carlie's words stuck in her parched throat.

"I, uh..."

"Yes?" The concerned-nurse expression returned, etched with precision in Candace's blue eyes.

"Maybe I need a drink—some water—something to, to..." Her thoughts stubbornly swirled on her tongue without forming coherent sentences. "I don't feel well, and..."

Dr. Emmanuel rose from his seat and stood beside her, massaging her tight shoulders. "You can do this. Just get right to the point. She already knows your history, so you don't have to start from the beginning."

But it's too painful. I can't say it.

"Yes, you can. I'm with you. I won't let it destroy you."

Candace leaned forward and searched Carlie's face. "You can tell me."

Carlie took a deep breath. "You know my dream—the nightmare I have all the time." She held her aching head in her trembling hands.

Candace nodded and placed her hand on Carlie's arm. "This seems very traumatic for you."

"Yeah, I saw it again. This time I saw more. Bubba was there in the closet with me. I...I didn't know he was there. I'm so sorry. It was my fault."

Her nurse's eyes widened. "Bubba? In your dream?"

"My little brother. In my memory." Carlie's voice trailed off in uncertainty. Sweat rolled into her eyes. She still felt so hot, almost like being in that closet. She wiped her face and tried to concentrate on what she wanted to tell her nurse.

"Bubba's the one who screamed. He did it, not me," Carlie cried. "I didn't even know he came into the closet with me."

Candace nodded encouragingly. "So, you just found out that your little brother hid in the closet with you?"

"Yes," Carlie sniffled.

"And he screamed, not you?" Candace clarified.

"Yes." Carlie closed her eyes to block out the pain.

"Then what happened?"

"I tried to stifle the screams. I thought I was the one screaming, but it came from him. I didn't mean it. I really didn't mean it." Her head was absolutely killing her. She rubbed her temples and groaned.

"Mean what?" Candace patiently waited for the details to fall into place.

"I didn't mean to kill him."

Dr. Emmanuel steadied her shoulders as her body went limp and her head slumped to the left. Candace called her name loudly, but to Carlie, it sounded like someone calling from a cave somewhere deep beneath the earth, somewhere far away and forbidding. Carlie lost all awareness as the rapid response team descending upon her, loudly calling her name, rubbing their knuckles vigorously against her sternum, sticking her with needles.

Carlie inhabited a different place, even before she was lifted onto yet another stretcher and rushed down the hospital corridor.

Patty's Secret

Darkness blinded Carlie, but she knew this place well. She heard Daddy pounding and Mommy crying. Then Bubba wailed beside her. She felt his little arms around her neck and his tears fall on her shoulder.

"Please be quiet, Bubba," she whispered urgently.

But nearly two-year-old Bubba did exactly what all toddlers do--explicitly the opposite of what he was told. His screaming became louder, and Carlie grabbed him, tightly clamping her hand over his mouth.

A soft voice from the dark stopped all other noise, all movement. Everything froze in place. A light came on inside the closet, and Carlie saw Dr. Emmanuel crouched beside her and Bubba.

"You're here!" she gasped.

"I've always been here. I'll show you what stole your life, but you're going to have to trust me instead of your own emotions. This isn't going to be easy."

He reached out his hand and pulled adult Carlie from the frightened girl who held her brother. He motioned for her to sit beside him, next to her younger self, so she wedged herself in beside the vacuum cleaner and stared at the scene in front of her.

"Let's rewind a few seconds," Dr. Emmanuel said as he took her hand. "Just hold onto me."

Adult Carlie squeezed his hand in reply as the scene before her backed up, stopped, then proceeded in slow-motion.

Little Carlie's face was contorted with panic. Her own heart twisted and shuddered in terror as she grasped the doctor's arm with both hands. Rivers of sweat ran down the girl's face, and even though Dr. Emmanuel lit up the closet, Carlie knew crushing darkness gripped both the children. Maybe the utter blackness or the stifling hot humidity made Bubba shriek. Maybe he felt afraid of Daddy, too. Or perhaps he reacted to Mommy's cries. Whatever the reason, he frantically clung to his big sister, and she, wide-eyed and gasping for air, tried desperately to quieten him.

But Bubba's cries reached a new pitch, and Carlie's hand frantically searched for his mouth in the dark, found it, and covered it as best as it could, which was a difficult feat with a sweaty-slippery, thrashing tyke. The more Bubba squirmed, the tighter she clamped down. She HAD to make him stop.

That's when adult Carlie saw it. Her hand didn't just cover his mouth, but also his nose. Then the terrified, little girl leaned forward, pressing her body on him, stifling his cries, extinguishing his life.

She jumped as she heard gunshots. The front door creaked open, and Daddy's boots stomped onto the front porch. A neighbor's voice called out in the distance, asking what the hell was going on over there, and Daddy yelled back for her to mind her own damn business. The neighbor cursed and said the police were on their way.

Daddy's boots ran away from the house and a motor started, revved, and sped away.

Little Carlie peeked outside the closet. Not seeing a single soul, she figured Daddy had taken off. "Come on, Bubba, let's go get Mommy." But Bubba didn't budge. The little girl tugged and picked up Bubba, lugging him to the living room where she suddenly dropped him.

Mommy lay in a pool of blood in front of the couch, her face battered, and a hole in her chest. She ran over and knelt beside her. "NO! Mommy, wake up. Please wake up. We must go while Daddy's away. Please, Mommy."

But Mommy didn't move, and Carlie felt her insides being ripped out. Mommy's eyes, open but vacant frightened her. She shook her and cried, pleading with her to wake up.

Mrs. Stewart from the trailer house next to theirs came running through the door, half her hair still in curlers. Her eyes widened with terror as she saw the carnage before her. She reached out and held little Carlie. "Oh, baby, did your daddy do this to Bubba and your mommy?"

Little Carlie tearfully nodded.

"It's okay, baby. It's okay. You're safe now. The cops are coming."

It was the first of many lies adults told little Carlie, only to be repeated in various forms by the police officers and social workers from Child Protective Services. The sound of those hollow words echoed in Carlie's head. "You're gonna be okay now." Either they had a very perverted sense of what okay looked like, or their empty promises served only to make themselves feel better when they knew of nothing else to say. But then, what does one say to a little girl whose father just killed her mother and brother? The very same father who'd been sexually abusing her. Except, of course, no one knew what really happened to Bubba, and now that Carlie knew...she sighed, feeling her broken heart splinter into a thousand pieces.

"You're going to be alright now that you've got these antibiotics going," a voice said from afar.

Yeah, right. I've heard that before.

The scene faded, and Carlie found herself back in the medical part of the hospital. She awakened in a regular hospital bed with siderails and controls to adjust the head and feet, and she had an IV infusing into her arm. A drowsy sitter lurked in the background, propped up in a chair in the corner, her head hanging low and her eyes closed, whereas Dr. Emmanuel faithfully perched at the foot of her bed, watching her expectantly.

"Welcome back," he said softly. "You fainted, so they called the rapid response team. You ran a pretty high fever from your lacerations getting infected, causing you to become septic. That's why you're in a med/surg step-down unit; you need IV fluids and antibiotics. Don't worry, though, you'll be back in psych in a few days."

Carlie picked at the blanket, her eyes becoming watery. "Why?"

Dr. Emmanuel put his finger to his lips and nodded toward the sitter, an overweight African-American woman with orange-red hair. "She can hear you if you talk out loud."

Sure enough, she stirred, managing to assume a more upright position in the chair, and fluttered her eyes until they popped wide open. This woman had huge, bulging eyes that creeped Carlie out. She quickly closed her own eyes and pretended to sleep. In a few minutes, snores assured Carlie that she could safely to look around without engaging in any unwanted dialogue. She didn't see much in her dimly lit surroundings; it just looked like your typical hospital room filled with medical equipment.

Between the fatigue she felt at that hour of the night, being totally drained from the emotional trauma of her forgotten past, and the toll the infection took on her she quickly joined her sitter in slumber.

That morning brought the usual parade of medical personnel. A tech checked her vital signs, and seeing that she was indeed still alive, trotted off to the next patient. A phlebotomist drew her blood, and a nurse came by to introduce herself now that she had been awakened at 4:00 in the morning. The nurse pretty much repeated what Dr. Emmanuel told her about having an infection and needing IV antibiotics. She looked a bit curiously at Carlie as if thinking, "So this is what a real, live psych patient looks like," but she only acknowledged Carlie's special status by pointing out the sitter selected to stay with her at all times for her own safety until she could go back to psych.

Oh, good. I'm feeling so much safer now that I have a bugged-eyed stranger sleeping in my room!

Dr. Emmanuel chuckled. "I'm glad you still have your sense of humor."

While the nurse explained what antibiotics infused into her vein and what type of wound care she could expect, a medical student came in and started the explanation all over again. About an hour later, another intern and a resident came along, removing her dressings and reiterating the same details about her nasty infection. Then they stuck her neck with a sharp blade that brought a flow of pus onto the gauze they held next to her laceration.

If you'd let me go on and die, we wouldn't have to be going through all this. She kept her eyes on Dr. Emmanuel.

While the staff came and went, explaining this, giving her that medicine, cutting her throat and irrigating her wound, she noticed that only he dared to really make and keep eye contact with her. The others read their notes or checked her wound or fiddled with her IV pump. She almost felt like she just incidentally happened to accompany the wound, who was obviously the real patient.

Then Dr. White showed up. As usual, he'd dressed for success in a charcoal suit, a crisply starched lavender shirt and a striped tie that went perfectly with his shirt. His leather shoes were neatly polished and spotless, and his mannerisms seemed as precisely put together as his wardrobe.

He recited what had happened (she'd passed out) and why (she apparently had a bad infection that went from just being in her wound to being in her bloodstream), and what he planned to do about it (let the internal medicine doctors give her antibiotics and stick holes in her neck to drain pus as they saw fit while he would continue to manage her psychiatric meds). There. Did she have any questions?

She couldn't think of any—at least not any that she wanted to ask him, but she wondered if all these medical people read the same script.

He headed toward the door and stopped. Slowly turning, he asked, "Did you do anything to your laceration?"

Carlie lifted her eyebrows. "What do you mean?"

"Did you put anything in the cuts on your neck? You know, to make it get infected?" He pursed his lips together and narrowed his eyes.

"So, you think that somehow this is my fault? I must have done something wrong? How could I? I'm always on camera or staff is with me if I go to the bathroom. I haven't done anything, not since I cut myself anyway. I used an old, rather dirty razor, but I wasn't exactly planning to be around long enough for any infection to set in." Carlie's voice grew a little more tense than she intended, but just where did he get off accusing her?

"Okay, just wondering." He exited without another word.

The day tech checked her vital signs again and announced her fever went down a little, which made her new sitter exclaim, "Praise the Lord!"

Jasmine, the day shift sitter, had eyes that looked more in proportion to the rest of her head. She also seemed a lot more alert and ready to proclaim extreme thankfulness for every stretch-of-the-imagination bit of goodness she could find. She especially showed interest in the contents of Carlie's breakfast tray.

"French toast. Girl, that's a fine-looking start to the day. And you got you some eggs and sausage and juice. If you eat right, and the good Lord blesses, you'll be back to your old self in no time flat."

Apparently, the only thing I need is good food. So, I could just ditch the antibiotics. Carlie grinned at her private joke and took a bite of French toast dripping with syrup. *Not bad.*

The door opened and a familiar face wearing thick glasses and framed by gray, frizzy hair appeared. Patty. *What's she doing here?*

Patty glanced at the sitter and nodded. Then her eyes swept the room, hesitating a second where Dr. Emmanuel sat. A slight hint of a smile played with the corners of her lips, and her stooped spine straightened just a tad.

She sees you! She sees you, and she knows you!

Dr. Emmanuel grinned.

Patty stepped around the sitter and greeted her. "Good morning, Carlie. How are they treating you here?"

"They're doing just fine. They've stabbed me in the neck to drain me, and they're pumping me full of antibiotics, but you probably already know that. What's way more interesting to me is that you saw Dr. Emmanuel, didn't you?"

"Huh? Oh, yeah." Patty turned to the sitter. "I tell ya what, I'm going to be here a bit if you need a break."

"Long enough for me to grab some breakfast from the cafeteria?"

"Yeah, sure. Just go get it and bring it up here."

"Thanks." Jasmine gathered her books into a large bag that she slung over her shoulder.

As soon as Jasmine shut the door behind her, Patty pulled the chair closer to the bed and made herself comfortable.

"Come on and admit it, Patty, you saw him. You looked right at him and your face changed."

Patty nodded reluctantly. "Yes, Dr. Emmanuel has been a great help in my own life." She scrunched up the left sleeve of her scrub jacket to reveal a thin scar across her wrist. "You see, you and I aren't so different after all. I was once young and depressed and couldn't see any hope for my life."

"So, you tried to kill yourself?" Maybe Patty was human after all.

"Once, as a teenager."

"And Dr. Emmanuel was around back then?" Carlie stopped chewing and studied the doctor's face. He couldn't be that old.

"He's always been around, and He's the best thing that's ever happened to me. He's the best thing that could happen for you, too. Let him do what he does best, even if it hurts. Just remember that the pain is temporary; the results are permanent."

Truth be Told

Carlie's mind reeled from the revelation that Nurse Patty knew Dr. Emmanuel, but before she could ask all her burning questions, Patty dropped a major bombshell.

"There's news about your dad. I thought you should know." She held up her smart phone meaningfully.

"Oh, great!" Carlie moaned. She never liked hearing anything about her dad under any circumstances, and her latest visits to the old closet didn't make her feel particularly warm and fuzzy toward him.

Patty swiped her phone a few times and angled it so Carlie could get a good look. To tell the truth, Carlie felt a bit shocked that an old codger like Patty had a smart phone or knew how to use it. But whatever news report she found must be important, so she squinted at the small screen and gave it her undivided attention.

The Fox 4 News reporter stood in front of a large, off-white brick sign that read "Allen B. Polunsky Unit". Behind her towered a chain link fence topped with razor wire and an ominous cinder block fortress that Carlie knew as death row, also home to none other than her very own dad. The reporter crisply introduced her story outside in the blazing one hundred- and seven-degree Texas heat, trying to look cool while sweating bullets.

Carlie's stomach twisted at the next shot. There he sat, wearing white prison garb and talking behind a glass window about his appeal. "I have excellent grounds for my appeal based on how I received my sentence. I'll admit that I got drunk and went into a fit of rage from being provoked by my wife. It's also true that I shot and killed her after she came after me violently. But according to the law as the judge explained it, in order for it to be a capital offense, I would have had to killed more than one person or killed someone under the age of ten. Now, as I've always said, I didn't kill my son. Why would I kill him? I'm not a monster who kills babies. My wife, however, drove me to drink and nagged me senseless every single day of my life. And, sure, I regret killing her, but again, I was drunk out of my mind and just snapped."

At this, the reporter asked about how he could be sure he didn't kill the little boy if he was out of his mind drunk and snapped.

Kyle rambled on about why he'd snapped in the first place being that his wife had killed the baby. "What that mean, selfish woman..."

Carlie covered her head with her blanket, holding her ears, not wanting to hear any more lies.

Patty took the subtle hint and turned off the phone. "I'm sorry," she said softly. "I just thought you should know about his appeal, especially since you're the only witness."

Nobody spoke again for several moments. Carlie's heart turned somersaults and her eyes gushed like Niagara Falls. She kept the blanket over her head to hide her face from Patty. *How much more can I stand?*

Dr. Emmanuel touched her arm. "Remember, don't trust your feelings; trust me instead. This is where you die. Die to all you are. Die to the shame, the fear, the anger, the guilt. Die to everything you know and start again with me."

"What are you talking about? No, you're not making any sense." Carlie threw the covers back to glare at the so-called doctor.

Patty cleared her throat. "Carlie, he knows exactly what he's talking about, and it's the only way for you to get through this...this tragedy without...without totally losing it. Don't you know who he is?"

"Uh, he claims to be Dr. Emmanuel, but he's like the weirdest doctor I've ever seen, and I've seen quite a few."

The doctor gently placed his scarred hands beside Carlie's crisscrossed left arm. His eyes, moist and sad, showed no sign of despair. In fact, Carlie saw more strength in his eyes now than ever before—even when he slammed death's door in her face.

"I carry your scars," he said, "your guilt, your sorrows. I'm inviting you to die to all that and live in me."

"How can you? What does that even mean? And why did you have to show me what really happened right before all this blew up with my dad's appeal. You seem to know everything under the sun; how can you have such cruddy timing?"

"What really happened?" Patty asked.

"Oh, no!" Carlie groaned as her thoughts swirled out of control. "My dad's right about one thing. He didn't kill Bubba. But that doesn't mean he should get off scot-free. He killed my mother, and he has no right to lie about her killing Bubba. She should be declared a saint just for putting up with all his crap, and she wouldn't hurt anyone—especially her own baby boy. She loved Bubba." Carlie desperately searched Dr. Emmanuel's face for answers. "Why are you doing this to me?"

"Trust me. Tell the truth and trust me. I will set you free from everything that has entrapped you."

Carlie's mind and emotions felt like a tornado, ripping her apart, threatening to completely blow her out of existence. She grabbed Dr. Emmanuel's scar-laden wrists and cried, "I can't take this anymore. I can't do this by myself. You may be my only hope; God knows I don't have anyone else. But please don't make me tell what I did. Do something to keep me off the witness stand, please."

"The truth will set you free," he whispered.

Patty gently rubbed Carlie's shoulder. "Tell me what you did, Carlie. You can practice on me."

Carlie couldn't bring herself to look at Patty. Instead she kept her eyes locked on Emmanuel. It seemed safer that way. After all, this guy had already been in the closet with her, so he knew the story, seemingly better than she did herself, and he still stood at her side offering help. Strange peace stilled her soul, blocking out the tornado that threatened her just a few seconds earlier. Maybe he really meant what he said about not leaving her to fend for herself. Besides, what choice did she have? Go completely stark, raving mad, or give this guy a chance. She'd tried so many other things.

She took a deep breath, held onto her Life Line's scarred arm, and said. "I'm the one who killed Bubba. It was an accident. We were in the closet together when Dad beat Mom within an inch of her life. Bubba started screaming, and I tried to keep him quiet. I didn't mean to hurt him. I loved Bubba; he was so cute and innocent and..." She went silent. How could she put the horrible truth in words?

"What happened?" Patty asked softly.

"I tried to cover his mouth to keep him from screaming, but he wiggled, and I couldn't get a good grip on him. So, I tried harder, grabbing and holding his mouth with all my strength. The thing was, I didn't know I covered his mouth and his nose. He couldn't breathe. Then I leaned on top of him, trying to keep him still. When I heard Dad leaving the house, I carried him out of the closet, but he didn't move at all. Then I found Mommy dead, and the lady from the trailer next to ours came in and stayed with me until the police came."

"How did you recover this memory?" Patty's forehead wrinkled.

"Dr. Emmanuel showed me."

"Then you can trust that it's real, and you can trust that he showed you for a solid reason, not just to bring you more pain." Patty paused, and they all sat in silence until the door opened and the sitter came in carrying biscuits and gravy.

Patty gave Carlie's arm a reassuring squeeze. "Thank you for telling me."

Carlie nodded and watched Nurse Patty leave. *Weird. You, me, and of all nurses—Patty. It's like we're in this together, like I'm not alone anymore.*

"No, you're not alone." Dr. Emmanuel agreed.

And Patty knows and trusts you.

He smiled, and his eyes seemed to travel through space a time. "We do have quite a history together."

And you were around—what—forty or fifty years ago?

He nodded, and Carlie felt she'd discovered an impossible clue about his true identity, but she couldn't exactly figure out what to do   with   it.

Descent to Hell

Three days on the medical unit passed by quickly. Besides all the poking and prodding by doctors and being stared at by various sitters, Carlie got to spend a lot of time getting to know Dr. Emmanuel better. Seeing as how she was stuck with him, she thought it might be a good idea.

So, she asked questions, all sorts of questions, like how he knew so much about her and how he could shut the door to death and how he could possibly have been around when Nurse Patty was a teenager back in the Stone Age. But his answers remained cloaked in mystery, and she kept coming back to the one insatiable question that wouldn't give her a moment's peace: Just who was Dr. Emmanuel really?

He laughed as he recounted the story of the kitten she found and smuggled into one of her foster homes. He described the little tortoise shell and her green eyes down to every minute detail. She'd huddled in some shrubs in front of the house, meowing her little heart out, lost and alone. Carlie had to crawl through the bushes to reach her, and the poor baby rewarded her with purrs and snuggles. Carlie managed to sneak in the back door and make it clear down the hall to her room without getting caught.

Carlie smiled. She enjoyed this singular memory. Then he talked about Mrs. Petty and her silk blouses and pencil skirts. Carlie preferred sticking with a happier memory, but he plunged right into the pictures and the dolls and how Mrs. Petty tricked her into talking about things she didn't even want to think about as a traumatized five-year-old.

She hit the brakes on the conversation immediately, but he simply took her down another path. "You remember that kid, Michael—the one you saved from drowning. None of the adults saw him go under, but you were there in a heartbeat. That boy is alive and well today because of your quick response."

I feel like we're playing some dumb game show of This is Your Cruddy Life. I don't know how you got all this information, but it's kind of creepy.

"Your deepest need is to understand the meaning behind your loss of faith," he replied matter-of-factly.

She knew where that conversation would lead, and she didn't have one iota of desire to talk about the aftermath of her baptism. *Why do you have to bring all this ancient history up? Why can't you just leave it alone?*

"Because we have to deal with some of your issues together for you to make progress."

Carlie pushed her mousy brown hair behind her ear. "So, okay. What's the deal? You're my therapist, and you think you can fix me?"

"I'm the only one who can," he answered flatly. "I am your ticket out of this hell."

My ticket out? I thought that was my gun—but no—Emily took that from me. Then the razor called my name, and I latched onto it as my one great hope. And of course, I got proven wrong again when you came barging in. Just who do you think you are? What makes you the one and only great answer to all my inadequacies? Her words may have sounded accusatory, but she truly felt mystified.

He seemed to sense her heart and only smiled. "Think about it."

The closet might be a clue. How could he know what happened with Bubba? She asked the same question in about ten different ways, and he consistently assured her that he was always with her, always acutely aware of everything about her, even the tiniest detail. Once again, she felt she must be overlooking something obvious, especially when he commented that he even knew how many hairs she had on her head.

"Yes, I know about the altar call and your baptism at a summer camp in Athens. At the age of fourteen, you'd had your fill of heartache and disappointment and longed to be loved. In fact, you wanted to be someone else—you longed to be the new creation that Brother Phillip preached about. So, right then and there you asked God to forgive your sins and change your life. Brother Phillip smiled warmly and invited you to be baptized the following day."

Carlie hung her head. Why must he go there? But, then again, it wasn't worse than what she'd done to Bubba, and she still hadn't figured out how she could go on living with that horrible memory. She sighed. *The devil's in the details, for sure.*

"Yes, these are painful memories. Being baptized felt like a wonderful cleansing to you, but..."

How do you know how I felt? Carlie bristled internally.

"When you came up out of the water and walked up onto the shore of that beautiful lake surrounded by pines, all the wonder of that place and your decision was snatched away." Dr. Emmanuel didn't miss a beat, but his voice grew softer. "Some immature girls snickered at you, saying that you looked like a beached whale."

Yeah, I was some "new creation" alright. I wanted to punch their lights out. I thought saved people, born again Christians didn't feel like that.

"So, you approached Brother Phillip the next day to talk."

It didn't work for me. Tears welled up, forbidding any other words from betraying the hurt. *And this isn't something I want to talk about. It's a closed chapter in my life, so don't go there.*

"And don't answer the question you've had all these years?"

I don't have any questions about what happened, Carlie lied. She twirled a strand of her unruly, wavy hair and thoughtfully studied his face, trying to memorize every kind crinkle in the corner of his eyes, the slope of his brow, the lines etched beneath his tousled hair. Maybe his scars hid clues about his identity, and she'd rather talk about that than the pesky pastor who molested her.

Okay. So, tell me what happened to you. She ran her finger across his wrist and hand. *Did you do all this to yourself?*

"Yes and no. No, I didn't cut myself like you, but yes, I chose to die for you."

But you're alive.

"Yes, and I'm your source of life, too."

Yeah, you brought me back...Hey, I died! My suicide succeeded—at least until you stepped in. I'd finally done it right and was home free. They did CPR on me, so that means I died, and you brought me back. So, you also died, and someone brought you back?

"Sort of but not exactly. You subsisted so far removed from real life, and I am the only way for you to understand what you'd never experienced or seen in anyone else. So, I came to show it to you—and having shown you a much better way—to give it to you. It's a gift, something you couldn't get on your own."

What is this gift?

"True life. Not just existing, not just putting one foot in front of the other, but truly living, having a purpose, a joy that can't be taken from you no matter what happens. You were created for that kind of life. Life with me and through me."

But this isn't medical talk. This is, uh, like some sort of, I guess, a spiritual or philosophical train of thought. I mean, no one can just give someone else life.

"I can." His eyes sliced right through her questions and into her heart. "I'm the one who loves you, just as you are, but in my mercy, I won't leave you as you are. I will hold your hand and guide you in ways you can't possibly imagine. I will accomplish so much through you, that you will be amazed."

So, what do you want from me? Carlie fidgeted with her blanket.

"Love me. Trust me. Follow me."

A knock on the door interrupted their conversation. The sitter glanced over the book she'd been reading and called out for the visitor to come on in.

Carlie felt surprised to see Taylor's face peering timidly around the corner. "I'm not bothering you if I visit, am I?"

A broad grin planted itself firmly on Carlie's face. "No, please come have a seat. How'd you get up here?"

Taylor carefully sat on the foot of Carlie's bed. "I've been discharged, so I rode the wheelchair out to the car, told my mom—yes, I called her and I'm talking with my parents again. Anyway, she'd come to pick me up, but I asked her to come back in about an hour and walked back into the front door of the hospital. I guess I looked like a respectable visitor instead of an escaped psycho, so when I went to the information desk, they gave me your room number. And here I am. I wanted to make sure you were okay." She held her hands out to indicate how easy it was.

"I'm so glad you're here. You're looking good. The bruises are starting to fade, and I'm glad you talked with your parents. So, do they know everything now?"

"Yeah, well, I told them about the abuse, but I didn't go into every detail. And—get this—they suspected something was wrong when I shut them out but didn't know what to do about it. They decided to give me some space and wait to see if I needed them. Dad was very upset about Brad, but I know he just wishes he could have protected me.

"All in all, I'm doing pretty well. Therapy helped with my off-the-charts anxiety level, and you helped, too. At least I had one person I could relate with here. Now I'm going to follow up with some therapist at the battered women's shelter. But, you know, I sure missed you after you left. I missed your wit, and all the stuff you'd tell me, even the hard stuff. Besides, Joylyn never gave me grief while you were around."

"Yeah, well, she probably didn't want to mess with someone crazy enough to slit her own throat. Besides, I may be short, but I'm as wide as I am tall. She probably figured I'd snap her skinny frame in half if I sat on her." Carlie chuckled at her own depiction of herself. Chunkiness had its advantages.

They both stared at the sitter as if willing her to disappear. Unfortunately, she didn't take the hint primarily because she remained too engrossed in her novel to notice a lull in the conversation.

Taylor lowered her voice to a near whisper. "How are they treating you?"

"They're not bad. I'm just having a hard time shaking this infection. But it's given me time to get to know more about Dr. Emmanuel."

"Oh?" Taylor scooted closer for the full scoop. "So, what have you learned?"

Dr. Emmanuel grinned. "Yes, what have you learned? Feel free to share."

"Okay, so he's not just a doctor. He apparently helped Nurse Patty during her teenage years, though he looks like he's barely thirty, and he seems to know everything—and I do mean everything—about me. He even knew what really happened the night Daddy killed Mom. It was something so horrible, I'd like just blocked it from my mind, but he showed me every terrible detail."

You mean something even worse than what you remembered happened? What could be worse than that?" Taylor looked genuinely puzzled.

"Go one and tell her. The truth will set you free," Dr. Emmanuel prompted.

Carlie looked at him and sighed. The whole story of how she accidentally suffocated her darling baby brother came tumbling out. "It wasn't Daddy," she concluded. "I did it, but I let Daddy take the blame."

Taylor's mouth hung open, and her eyebrows scrunched upwards like unbelieving witnesses. "But how did this doctor know all this?"

Carlie twisted her lips and shook her head. "I don't know. He seems to really know EVERYTHING about me. He told me about what happened when I lived with the foster family that moved to Tyler, including what the youth pastor did with me at summer camp. He knew about the kitten I found and hid in my room for a couple of days until my foster mom heard it meowing. He even knew about the therapists I'd seen, and he told me how I got confused and blamed Bubba's death on Daddy.

"Taylor, he knew such detail! I'd forgotten how that first therapist talked with me, asking me to draw pictures and point to a doll and tell what Daddy did to me. Then she had a boy doll that she gave me, and she even called him Bubba. She handed him over to me and asked me to show her how he died. I'd blocked it from my memory, so I kept telling her that I didn't know. Then..." Carlie held her face in her hands.

"Then what?" Taylor asked anxiously.

"She reminded me of all the horrible sounds of Daddy beating Mommy, and her screams for him to stop, and then she played the sound of a baby crying and asked if that was the sound that Bubba made. I covered my ears. I didn't want to remember, but she put the doll in my arms and asked what came next. It was like I was back in the closet all over again, trying to keep Bubba quiet. I think I automatically reacted the same way that I did in the closet. Then she took the doll and held me while I cried and screamed. Later, she told the police that I witnessed how Daddy killed Bubba, and it matched the findings of the autopsy report."

"So, you showed her how you suffocated him, but she assumed you demonstrated how your dad did it?"

"Uh, huh. And after the adults kept telling me that Daddy did it, I started believing them. And when I tried to say that it was my fault, they quickly told me that it wasn't—that I was just a little girl, and that I couldn't protect my little brother or my mom from my father. And Dr. Emmanuel knew every single detail, down to the teal blouse the therapist wore when she made me relive that terrible morning."

Taylor's eyes expanded widely with amazement. "But how could he know?"

"He says he's always with me."

"Even now?" Taylor silently searched the room.

"Yep. He's sitting on my left side listening to everything we say."

"What about his scars? Did you ask him about them?"

Carlie nodded and leaned a bit closer. "He says he died to give me true life."

Dr. Emmanuel cleared his throat. "And I died for Nurse Patty, and for Taylor, too. Go on and tell her. Taylor already knows me; she just doesn't see me."

"Uh, he says you know him even though you can't see him and that he died for you and Patty, too." Carlie stalled.

"Jesus!" Taylor gasped.

"What?" Carlie flinched.

"Emmanuel is Jesus, God with us, the Great Physician, the Son of God and Son of Man. He died on the cross and came back to life three days later, so we can have abundant life. Now it makes sense." Taylor smiled excitedly.

Carlie couldn't believe her ears. Numbly she turned to her constant companion. "No, this makes no sense. Is this true? Are you really Jesus? 'Cause I can't do some religious thing. I've been down that road before at church camp, walked the aisle, got saved, dunked in the lake and everything, just to get soiled by the same preacher who baptized me. Why didn't you intervene then with all your divine power and so-called love? If you really are

God, then I hate you, and I'll never trust you. Not after what you've put me through."

Numbness quickly gave way to irritation and anger. She gasped and sputtered.

A sharp, biting pain clamped down with fierce intensity in her throat and neck. Some unseen force pushed her backwards until she felt herself being hurled down what appeared to be a long elevator shaft. Burning needles jabbed her hands and feet, but the tremendous weight carrying her down the shaft plastered her flat against its force, and she couldn't even move her hands to see what was wrong with them. Carlie struggled to inhale and choked on sulfuric fumes. Relentless buzzing, stinging and burning accompanied her descent into the abyss.

"Oh, no!" the sitter screamed and frantically poked the emergency button. "We need help now! I don't think she's breathing!"

The room went black. Carlie got sucked down deeper and deeper, with crushing darkness compressing her in its tight embrace. She couldn't breathe, couldn't move. Searing heat scorched the soles of her feet and rose up the entire length of her body to choke out the last bit of breath in her collapsing lungs. This experience contained no peaceful levitation to a better place. Every cell of her body racked with excruciating pain, like the worst torture ever invented.

Somewhere, far away she heard Taylor pray, "Dear Jesus, save her! Please save her; she just doesn't know you yet."

A jolt of electricity pulsated through her body, jolting every square inch of her frame. Flames crackled in her ears as she felt her flesh give way to their intensity. One of her ribs cracked, but that pain proved mild compared to the burning. Her mind began to shut down, but not in a quiet, soothing way. Instead, it exploded into a thousand dying embers, each neuron flooded with fresh waves of agony, and each new wave of pain brought demonic howls and screams that pounded her ears. Soon the explosions drowned out anything that might be happening in the hospital room.

Somewhere in the darkness, one of Carlie's ravished neurons screamed for Emmanuel to help. It wasn't something she could articulate; it was just there, in the core of her melting being. Nowhere else to turn. No other name upon which to call. No time to consider any other options. In fact, there were no other options, and time was running out.

ICU--Again

Carlie groaned and struggled to open her eyes. Her raw throat and every square inch of her body ached. Her eyes fluttered, and she felt shocked to see light. She tried valiantly to raise her head, but she found herself to be as weak as a newborn.

A woman's voice called her name. Carlie pried her eyelids open once more and saw a nurse who looked vaguely familiar standing beside her with a syringe.

"I see you're awake, and—from the grimace on your face—I assume you're in pain. Are you hurting?"

Carlie slowly and gingerly nodded, her eyelids heavy as lead.

"I've got something that will make you feel better," the nurse continued as she gave Carlie a dose of pain relief through her IV tubing. "There now," she said, having completed the task. Carlie sank back into oblivion.

The next time she came to, a young man wearing royal blue scrubs called her name. He flashed a light into her eyes and asked her name and where she was. Her voice scratched her throat and cracked as she made pathetic sounds, but somehow she managed to squeak out her name, and, looking around, asked if she was at Parkland.

The young man smiled and assured her that she was. Then he introduced himself as Jonathan, her ICU nurse, and asked if Charlie Sweetwater could possibly be related to her.

"Ah, yeah, my grandfather," she croaked, feeling a bit irritated at the question. "Did you say I'm in ICU?" She squinted into the light. "What happened to me?"

"Long story, young lady, a very long story. You've been here almost a month with one complication after another following your suicide attempt."

Carlie's eyes grew wide. "A month? You mean after I left the psych unit?"

Jonathon patted her arm. "You haven't been stable enough to go to the psych unit yet. After you first came in, you needed a surgeon to patch up your mangled neck and a lot of blood transfusions. I mean lots and lots of blood. Unfortunately, you had such a bad reaction to one of the transfusions that we thought we'd lose you. Then you became severely septic from an infection that started in your neck wound, and once again you slipped into unstable critical condition. You had multiple vital organs that started to fail, but you managed to pull through. And then—you won't believe it—just as you started to stabilize, you got tetanus and had to go back on the ventilator. It's really a wonder you're still with us."

"So what date is it now?"

"It's the second of August, and it's a bright and sunny, terribly hot day outside. Now squeeze my fingers and smile." He held two fingers out on each hand for her to grasp. "Good, good. Now hold your arms up like this, and lift your eyebrows," he instructed with gestures to illustrate what he expected of her. "Yes." He methodically counted to ten after asking her not to let him push her arms down.   Carlie tried valiantly to resist his gentle downward push, but her muscles didn't cooperate very well, and her arms hit the bed.

"Very good," he said, not at all phased by the fact that she'd failed the test. "You've just lost a lot of muscle tone lying in this bed for so long. It'll come back; you'll see. You're actually doing well—very well."

Carlie had never encountered a nurse so pleased with such simple performances. *He must be new*, she mused. "I can also rub my tummy and pat my head at the same time," she offered.

"Ha! Oh, that's a good one! You wake up with a good sense of humor. That's great, especially after all you've been through. Now hold up this leg until I count to five." He held up his fingers as he counted. "Keep it up." He pressed down, and her leg dropped. "That's okay, now right leg. One, two, three, four, five. Great. Okay, don't let me push this leg down." He applied gentle pressure to her ankle.

Carlie blushed.   Here stood a good-looking guy holding her legs, and—just her luck—she'd been unconscious for a month and probably looked like a hairy gorilla by now.   "Okay, are we through with the circus act now?" Her voice had a bit more of an edge than she meant to have.

"Yeah, just finishing your neuro checks. Now I'll listen to your lungs." He held his stethoscope to her chest. "Take some deep breaths."

Carlie's lungs inflated, along with all sorts of bells and whistles inside her. Touch by the opposite sex brought confusion; it never seemed to lead to anything good. She closed her eyes. What would he do next? She'd already proven herself too weak to launch any meaningful self-defense. Her heart began to race ominously. She felt the old fight or flight syndrome kicking in, but she could do neither. All sorts of medical tubes limited any movement in addition to her generally debilitated condition, leaving her at his mercy.

Jonathan hesitated. "Are you okay? Your heart sounds like it's about to jump out of your chest."

"I, uh," Carlie grimaced. "I'm just hurting and feeling really nervous."

"I can get you some pain medication. What's making you feel so nervous?"

"I don't know. Something seems wrong; I just know it, but I can't put my finger on it. How could I have been unconscious for a whole month?" Sure, that question swirled around in her head along with her conflicted thoughts about Jonathan, but she wasn't going to blurt out her sexual issues.

Jonathan looked confused. "Well, do you remember the complications I just told you about?"

Carlie began to hyperventilate. He must be hiding something from her, something they didn't want her to know about. Maybe they performed some experimental operation on her or pumped her full of some dangerous medications that had powerful psychotropic effects. Something happened during this past month, something important, something traumatic that she just HAD to remember.

She vaguely recalled someone spooky, someone following her around and interfering with her life. Someone who planted things in her mind. That was it: they used her as their guinea pig. They'd put her through a horrible ordeal; no, HE did it. That dark-skinned stranger in crumpled scrubs. The one with the scars.

A whole month's worth of memories, jumbled and in no particular order, came crashing into her consciousness in a flash of faces and emotions. She sat up in bed and let out a shriek. "No!" She held her head in trembling hands.

"What's wrong?" Jonathan asked again. "Do you need some medicine now before I continue with my assessment?"

"No, no, I need clarity. I need to think. Go on and assess me; I'm just freaking out about being out of it for a month. It seems like...I don't know. I think I had this nightmare experience somewhere else this past month. It seemed so real, and this doctor who..."

"Yes?" Jonathan stood back away from the bed as if unsure about approaching this psychologically challenged patient.

What about that doctor made him stand out? What made him different than the rest? He'd done something to her, and it confused her. She searched the room to no avail. She tried to brush the cobwebs from her mind. Where did she meet this strange physician? In a different admission? During a dream? And the images of Bubba that she couldn't get out of her head seemed too awful to be true. Of course, the medical staff didn't know about Bubba—only the psych staff. But Jonathan said she hadn't been to psych, so how did she meet Taylor? She had a friend named Taylor Whitehouse, and Carlie maintained with one hundred percent certainty that she didn't just dream her up.

"Who's my doctor?"

Jonathan, the hunky nurse, studied her closely. "You have whole teams of doctors—surgery, internal medicine, infectious disease, psych, critical care—you name it. Which doctor did you have in mind?" He slowly resumed his assessment and gently pressed her belly fat. "Does this hurt?'

"No. That's odd. That doesn't look like my usual fat—I mean, I look like I've lost weight." *Like a ton or so, with only a couple more tons to go.* She scanned her smaller girth and then her arms. A month without eating could do a body wonders. But then she spotted a tube protruding from the left side of her upper abdomen. "What's that?" She traced her attachment to it all the way up to a pump with a plastic bottle holding tan colored liquid.

Jonathon pulled out the largest syringe she'd ever seen. "That's your feeding tube; it's called a PEG, and I'm going to flush it every four hours with sterile water, though to be truthful it's not really sterile by the time it enters your GI tract. We had to keep some nutrition in you for this long, and flushing the tube keeps it patent so we can keep feeding you."

Besides being skinnier and having a strange tube sticking out of her gut, Carlie felt something else had changed deep inside her, something more meaningful than all her medical ailments. She gingerly felt her neck and ran her fingers down all sorts of lumps and bumps. Surely, she must look like Frankenstein's creation to match the monster that she knew lurked within.

Her handsome nurse asked about her pain level on a scale of zero to ten.

"Twenty," she croaked automatically. She never wanted to turn down some good narcotics. While Jonathan left to get her medicine, she surveyed the room more carefully. It looked very familiar, everything from the blah shade of green curtains and the telemetry monitor to the dripping faucet on the corner sink. Somehow it still didn't feel real, like something from a movie, or maybe an experience she'd had a long time ago, or a dream that had no beginning and no end—just snippets of useless hospital scenes. But something, no someone, was missing—that strange doctor.

"Is there a Dr. Emmanuel seeing me?" she asked when Jonathan returned bearing hydrocodone.

"Hmmm. Don't recall the name." He scanned her bracelet and the pills. "Oh, wait, the surgeon who put you back together the day you came in. You've had a team of surgical residents and interns seeing you, but I believe he operated on you." He pulverized the white tablets and mixed them with sterile water. "I'm going to give this through your tube. It may still be a while before you're up to swallowing."

As a rule, Carlie generally didn't like nurses, and she had no doubt that she'd eventually get a glimpse of Jonathan's dark side—all nurses had one—but so far he acted friendly and didn't boss her around, so she let him turn her and prop her up on all sorts of pillows like an invalid without even putting up a fight.

"Now this Dr. Manuel—is there something you wanted to ask him?" he asked before stepping out of her room.

"No. He's Dr. Emmanuel, and I saw him in the emergency department when they brought me in."

Jonathan paused in the doorway. "But you couldn't, uh… They performed CPR on you when you came in."

"Yeah, I remember floating toward the light. I felt very peaceful, but I could see the doctors and nurses working on me down below, and he stood over by himself close to the wall. In fact, he brought me back with a simple command."

"You had an out-of-body experience? Just when they brought you in?"

The memory of crushing darkness flooded her mind with a vengeance. "No, I spent time on the psych unit, and this creepy doctor followed me and—I don't know—totally freaked me out by saying weird stuff. Like he told me things about my life that no one could possibly know. Then this friend I met on the psych unit told me that he was Jesus, and I got mad at him for letting so much crap happen to me.

"Ugh, that's when everything went wrong. I experienced another weird sensation—totally different than floating to the happy light. It was horrible, filled with so much pain and falling deeper and deeper into the hottest, blackest pressure cooker ever. It had to be hell. I mean a literal hell with eternal torment. At least that's what it felt like. Then I woke up here."

Jonathan's face registered sheer amazement. "I don't know what your personal beliefs are, but I'd say God's not finished with you, Carlie Sweetwater. We did CPR on you in this very room just last week. It's a miracle you made it."

Back to Psych

Over the next few days, Carlie anxiously scanned every face that entered her room without finding any tousled head of hair framing scars above piercing yet inviting eyes. A whole hospital full of crumpled lab coats and various colors of scrubs came and went, but none on a strange doctor who claimed to be the Son of God.

"If you search for me with all your heart, you'll find me. I promise." It wasn't an actual voice, but she could hear his words in her heart.

She sighed. *Just how am I supposed to go looking for you? I'm kind of tied to all these lines. I've got IV fluids, and antibiotics, and tube feeding, telemetry leads, and heaven knows what. Besides, where would I start? Where does one go to find Jesus? To church? Been there; done that; got molested in the process.*

"No. Look for me with all your HEART."

Carlie frowned. *Does that even make sense? This whole out-of-body experience thing apparently didn't mean anything. My brain became compromised from not getting enough oxygen; that's all. I didn't really have an encounter with God; it was a crazy hallucination. All of it. The floating feeling, the excruciating plunge into hell. None of it presented any form of reality.*

She felt her old anger bubble up. It wasn't fair that she'd come that close to ending all her pain, only to be brought back to face it all again. What kind of cruel trick did her own mind play on her that she would have this close encounter with Jesus while unconscious, find him to be absolutely awesome, then lose him? She sank into a whole new level of loneliness, craving constant companionship with the One who understood her so much better than she understood herself. It would be nice to know the One who provided calm in the middle of her constant storms.

She managed to conjure up a bang-up case for wallowing in self-pity, feeling generally cranky and out of sorts by the time a perky young face introduced herself as Amanda, her day nurse. Aw, yes, Amanda, the one who sent her to psych in her dream. Carlie scowled. "So, what wonderful treatment will you torture me with this morning?"

Amanda's smile faded. "I just got word that we'll be transferring you to the psych floor in about an hour, so we've got to remove these tubes and get you ready."

"And—let me guess—I get no choice? All you medical people get to decide what's best for me, and I just have to go along for the ride?" Carlie rapidly worked up a full pout, shooting daggers with eyes full of fury. "Of course, what do I know about my own life? I'm a crazy psych patient."

"Well, your suicide attempt was what you'd call very lethal, so the mental illness court..."

"Yeah, I know, I'm going on an OPC."

"OPC?" Amanda worked quickly to free Carlie from her lines and tubes, not letting a little thing like a conversation slow her down.

"Order of Protective Custody, you idiot," Carlie snarled. "What kind of nurse doesn't know what OPC means?"

Amanda didn't bother answering, but her face turned to stone while she dumped the nearly-empty IV bag and attached tubing into a large, red biohazard container.

"That wasn't nice." It sounded like Dr. Emmanuel, and it sliced through her anger. "I love you so much, that I've given my life for you. Can't you just accept my love and share it with others, like this poor lady whose great crime is that she's trying to help you?"

Carlie choked on her own silence. She sensed the power of the L word again, rattling her very soul. She bit her lip and did a quick survey of the room without finding the source of the voice. She ached for him to be real, wanting him to fill her up where she was empty. And, boy, did she feel empty!

Yet there might be a glimmer of hope. The connection she'd felt had touched her on a deeper level than anything else in her life. Even in a coma, something real must have happened deep inside. She succumbed to a terrible emptiness, a longing she couldn't explain, like she'd just lost something that she'd never really had but had somehow sampled what it would be like if it existed.

Amanda avoided eye contact while completing her tasks. "Do you need anything else right now?" she asked crisply as she headed toward the door.

Carlie couldn't say what came over her—maybe the memory of Dr. Emmanuel and his free use of the L word prompted her, but to her surprise she could hear herself reply, "Uh, yeah. I need to apologize. I've been an absolute jerk to you. You didn't deserve that. Thanks for taking care of me."

Amanda stopped in her tracks and eyed her warily as if fearing that Carlie's change of heart merely disguised a trap. "Oh. Okay. I guess you're having a bad day."

The wayward patient wiped a stray tear from her cheek. "More like a bad life, but it's not your fault."

"That's a start," came Dr. Emmanuel's encouraging words. "Now tell me about your anger instead of taking it out on random people who cross your path."

I'm angry at you, because I can't see you. I thought you were real when I saw you.

"Uh, no, you thought of me as an intrusive hallucination."

Oh, yeah. But there at the end, we were getting close.

"But you still didn't trust me. I showed you what happened in the closet, so I can bring healing. The truth will set you free only if you let the truth be known. Your reaction showed that you weren't ready to trust me enough to follow my lead."

The closet—oh, that again.

"You don't want to remember, but you can't act like it never happened. That's just not working for you."

So, what do you want from me? My whole life has been one round of torture after another, and you didn't protect me from the abuse when it happened. You said you were with me, but if that's true, why didn't you stop all the stuff with my dad, and why didn't you protect Bubba? I don't get you. I don't get you at all. How can you claim to love me and let me suffer like this? Her anger returned full throttle.

"Because I see the big picture, and I'm able to turn your suffering into something beyond what you can imagine."

So, did the thing in the closet really happen like I saw it? And you just let it happen for some greater good, and poor Bubba and I are merely little pawns in your chess game with the devil. My problem is I don't see that much difference between the two of you—that is, if the two of you actually exist.

"I think you already know the answer to that. And, by the way, this habit of desperately needing someone and then quickly pushing him away doesn't seem to be working very well for you, does it?"

What do you mean?

"A moment ago, you wallowed in self-pity, so bitterly empty and lonely and yearning for me. I show up and you try your best to get rid of me. And just where does that leave you?"

Carlie's eyes widened. As usual, her emotions ran rampant and her thoughts raced faster than she could keep up. Was she on the verge of pushing Jesus away for good? What if she did? Her lifetime of anger and pain and abject loneliness would surely overtake her. But what if she got on board with this whole Jesus thing? He'd already proven to be nothing like what she expected. Her head ached from trying to sort it all out.

So where do we stand? You know, with each other. Before I woke up you were sending me to hell.

"That—by the way—was your choice, not mine. It's the one place where you can get away from me. I won't force myself upon you; I'm not like your father and pawpaw, you know."

So, if I choose you, you'll stay with me and help me?

"The entire time. I'll never leave you nor forsake you if you choose to put your trust in me."

A police officer arrived with a document in his hand. "Miss Sweetwater, we've met before. I'm Officer Warren, and I've come to escort you to the psychiatric unit, so you can get the care you need."

Carlie nodded. "And that's the OPC?"

"Yep, and this gentleman in the hall is gonna give you a ride in a wheelchair providing you come along cooperatively. You know what the alternative is, don't you, Miss Sweetwater? It will be much easier on you this way. Are you ready to go?"

Carlie's stomach twisted into several knots. *This wasn't going to be easy.*

"I'll be with you. Remember that all things are possible through me. You won't be relying on your own strength unless you choose to do so, and I wouldn't advise putting yourself through that grief."

The reluctant patient sat on the side of the bed and cooperated with Griffin, the transporter. In a strange way, a weight seemed to fall off her chest. She took a deep breath.

I trust you, Emmanuel. Okay? I really trust you. Or at least I don't trust myself anymore. And even though I get all worked up and angry at you, I don't want to ever be alone again. I...I want you in my life.

"Okay, I can work with that—anger, questions, distrust and all."

His words sounded kind and inviting—something she desperately needed seeing as how she'd rebounded back into the land of "Tell-Me-About-Your-Coping-Skills". Carlie closed her eyes and imagined her personal doctor walking beside her wheelchair, holding her hand, giving her strength to face the dreaded nurses on the psych unit. Somehow, she felt calmer with her eyelids shutting out the outside world, alone with her new friend. If only she could stay right there, enjoying solitude with no expectations, no pressure, just someone great who truly loved her. She almost smiled at the thought. With emotions that changed with the wind, she'd already transitioned from wanting to scream at Jesus to enjoying his company. Go figure.

"Welcome back to the psych unit," announced an irritatingly familiar voice. Carlie opened her eyes. Sure enough, Patty stood in all her nurse-imbued glory, taking the forms from the police officer and waving the transporter through heavy locked doors.

And so, it begins. She closed her eyes again. *So, everything I thought I went through since coming to the emergency room really didn't happen? The stuff about my dad's appeal, and Taylor being my friend, and Patty knowing about me accidentally killing Bubba?*

"You saw some things that could become reality if you choose me, other things that would become reality if left to your own devices, and other bits of eventual reality."

So, the crushing darkness?

"Hell is quite real, but it's not what I want for you."

The sensation of floating toward the bright light?

"Just a sneak preview of what I have for you."

And the other patients like Taylor, Joylyn and Lila Mae?

"You're being awfully quiet," interrupted Patty, who marched beside Griffin, the transporter. "Here, room 807." She pointed to Carlie's new home. "Remember that you're on camera, and you'll remain on suicide precautions until Dr. White determines that you can give us a credible contract for safety. Until then, your bathroom will remain locked, and a staff member will have to be here whenever you need to use the facilities. This is, of course, for your own protection. Also, Dr. White has decided to restrict you from staying in your room except at bedtime."

Carlie just stared at Patty. "Just what I expected," she mumbled. A bit shaky, she barely managed to rise from her wheelchair and deposit herself on the bed, taking a sneak peek at her room in the process. No, Dr. Emmanuel didn't sit on the windowsill or lean against the wall. She sighed. At least she'd heard his voice. That would have to be enough.

"I'll be back with a computer to complete your assessment. Meanwhile Liz will inventory your belongings."

"Unless you're going to count how many stitches are in my neck I have absolutely nothing."

Liz pulled out the appropriate form, "No contacts or glasses?"

"Nope."

"No dentures?"

"Give me a break."

"No clothes?"

"Again, not a stitch except the ones in my neck and this fancy hospital gown."

Liz handed her a pen. "Okay, then sign here."

Carlie dutifully did as she was told. "Hey, Liz, I'm glad you're my tech today. You bring me good luck. We always have brownies when you're on."

Liz chuckled. "We're supposed to have a discharge before lunch, so I'll see what I can do about securing that extra chocolate therapy for you."

Carlie grinned. "You're the best. It's like you're the only one here that doesn't hate me."

The tech's face scrunched up like she'd sucked on a lemon. "Now, Carlie, you wouldn't be trying to play me, would you? You know Miss Patty takes a special interest in you, and she's the most experienced nurse we've got."

"Oh, she takes a special interest in giving me pages of assignments."

"They're to help you."

"Right."   Carlie's   tone   didn't   sound   convinced.

Ready for Work

Nurse Patty breezed into Carlie's room like a nurse on a mission. She pushed the same computer on wheels that she'd used on previous admissions and plopped herself down in a chair beside the bed just as she'd done in Carlie's "dream", immediately bombarding her with questions.

Carlie groaned and hoarsely whispered, "Do we have to do this? I don't feel like talking. Besides, you already have all my information on file. I thought the hospital's electronic records made repeat questions like these a thing of the past." A distinct feeling of déjà vu crept over her.

Patty cocked her head and scrunched up her face, tapping her finger on her computer's keyboard. "Uh huh, yes. I've got your history, but I still need to know if anything's changed since your last stay. You're still at the same boarding house?"

Carlie nodded.

"Only new medical issues would be the lacerations on both sides of your neck, your bout of blood transfusion reactions, sepsis, and tetanus?"

Another nod. Pretty much like last time, minus Dr. Emmanuel perched on the windowsill.

"Okay, but some things I have to ask now. Are you still suicidal?"

"No more than usual," Carlie whispered.

"You don't have to do the exact same dance that you saw yourself doing; it will only produce the same outcome," Dr. Emmanuel's voice rang out as clearly as if he stood beside her.

"How do you feel about being saved from your close brush with death?" Patty inquired.

So, I can change the outcome?

"By changing your behavior. Yes."

"Confused," she blurted the truth.

"Oh?" Patty's expression told Carlie that—for once—Patty believed her. "Tell me about your confusion."

Carlie pushed down a surge of impatience that threatened to impede her ability to talk civilly. After all, Patty hadn't already lived this episode of "What's Wrong with Carlie Now?", so a thorough explanation was in order. She took a deep breath and began reciting the events beginning at the lake on the Fourth of July which naturally triggered a tirade against Emily for her conniving, thieving ways.

"Okay, so you felt angry at your roommate, Emily?"

"Angry, desperate to end my pain, and determined to make it happen that very day."

Patty's silently attentive face spoke volumes. Carlie thought she detected a hint of relief that they weren't engaged in the usual verbal cat-and-mouse games, curiosity at why Carlie was

genuinely talking to her, and what was that other look? Hope?
Yes, Patty looked hopeful in a professionally reserved way.

Carlie charged on. "Well, the really confusing thing is what
happened in the hospital. They did CPR on me in the emergency
department, and I saw a doctor—at least I thought he looked like
a doctor. And I floated above my body toward a door with
wonderful light. It was a peaceful, happy feeling. One of my ICU
nurses by the name of Jonathan said it must have been an out-of-
body experience, but it didn't end when they resuscitated me. I
woke up in the ICU with this strange doctor telling me all sorts of
weird stuff, and he followed me here to psych where we went
through some amazingly intense events. Then I got transferred to
a medical floor because of being septic, and you came up to visit
me, and it turned out that you knew this doctor, who happened
to be..."

Carlie stopped to consider how her next words would be
received. If her experience proved true, then the best way of
getting through all the background would be to tell the whole
truth. If delirium produced this very complicated dream or
hallucination, Patty would promptly categorize her as a nut case.

She searched Patty's face for her reaction and saw wide-eyed
wonder. This experienced psych nurse who'd probably seen every
type of psychosis and every form of dysfunction under the sun
appeared mesmerized by what she heard.

"Who did he turn out to be, Carlie?" she asked softly.

"Well, he called himself Dr. Emmanuel and said he specialized
in suicidal patients. He promised to always stay with me, said he
loved me, and he'd give me real life. He told me that you knew
him, too, and that as a teenager you tried to kill yourself, but he
intervened."

Patty's eyes fell to the floor, and her shoulders drooped an inch or so. "Oh, that."

"Can I see your left wrist?" Carlie was dying to know how much of her story was real.

To her amazement, Patty pulled up the sleeve on her white lab coat to reveal a faint scar. "Clearly Dr. Emmanuel is…"

"Jesus. And you're a believer?"

Patty nodded slowly, looking like her day had taken an unexpected turn. "And you? What became of your experience with Jesus?"

"Well, it gets even more…more intense. He showed me what actually happened the morning Daddy murdered Mommy." The words seemed to back up in her throat, and an urge to vomit twisted her stomach violently. Tears threatened to overflow her watery eyes. Carlie sniffled not so bravely and groaned, "It was horrible. I saw it. Bubba, my sweet baby brother—I saw what really happened."

Before she knew it, she'd spilled the whole terrible story and went through an entire box of Kleenex in the process. Patty didn't say a word. She just took Carlie's hand and let her cry until there were no more tears and Carlie felt completely drained and dehydrated. Together they sat in thoughtful silence for what seemed like a decade. Carlie feared saying another word; in fact, she felt sure that no words that could possibly describe how twisted her guts became after baring her soul.

"There's just one more thing you have to tell her. Tell her about hell," Dr. Emmanuel urged.

Carlie swallowed. "As bad as all that was with Emily and Bubba, something even worse happened." She paused to sort her thoughts.

"Worse than the death of your brother?" Patty asked.

"Yeah, even though I wanted to crawl in a hole somewhere and die along with him when I found out that I suffocated Bubba. I suffered a fate even worse than that. You see, I started getting to know Jesus, and I began to enjoy his company, but I just couldn't get my head wrapped around him having all this power but not sparring me from—you know—everything I'd been through." Carlie rubbed her forehead.

"I, uh, I argued, no accused Dr., uh, Jesus of not helping me when they started CPR on me the second time. That time I went to hell. At least I was on my way. I fell into the most horrible dark, burning, excruciating place I've ever been. I can't put into words the level of suffering I felt. Mental and spiritual anguish unraveled me and proved to be more crushing than the physical pain. My total depletion of anything fulfilling like his love made me realize that I needed him, and the worst pain of all came with the realization that I turned him away. Then I woke up in ICU, and I couldn't see him anymore."

The quiet nurse gently patted Carlie's shoulder. "It sounds very traumatic. How are you now?"

"Confused. I still hear his voice—I don't mean an audible voice like yours or mine, but like someone talking inside my head...or my soul. Am I hallucinating or delusional? If I am, why does it give me hope? And if it gives me hope, why am I scared of it—of him?"

Nurse Patty sat back in her chair. "No hallucination knows what happened to me during my teenage years. Or what really went on in that closet during your childhood."

"So, it's really Jesus?"

"Well, there's a way to know for sure, but it's going to take some effort on your part. How interested are you in finding out?"

Carlie looked up at the ceiling. "This is going to require brutal honesty, isn't it?"

"Uh huh."

"Like all those assignments you always give me."

"More demanding than that. You can't bluff your way through this."

Somewhere in the depths of Carlie's troubled soul the familiar voice spoke. "Come to me if you're burdened and worn out, and I will give you rest."

She wanted that voice to keep on talking and closed her eyes as if to soak up his words. *I need some rest...your kind of rest. I am past worn out, and I can't go on without you. That much is for sure; I just need to know you're for real.*

"Then do what Patty says."

She opened her eyes and nodded at her nurse with resolve. "I'm   ready   to   do   the   work."

Carlie's Rewrite

Jason tentatively knocked and stuck his head into Carlie's room. "Sorry to interrupt," he said softly, looking to Patty for permission to continue.

Wow. Even the staff here finds Patty intimidating.

"Or they respect her," Dr. Emmanuel whispered.

"That's okay, Jason, what's up?" Patty asked.

"Well, lunch is almost over, and I thought you might want Carlie to eat before OT."

Patty looked at her watch. "Oh, my goodness! Time got away from me. Uh, I know you've received your nutrition through your PEG tube up until the last couple of days on a bland diet, but now we're going to get you some real food. Do you feel up to walking to the cafeteria, Carlie?"

"Let's see." Carlie tried to stand, but her legs felt strangely weak and useless after a month of lying in bed, and her head started to spin.

Patty steadied her and seated her safely on the side of her bed. "Jason, let's use a wheelchair until PT works with her and declares her safe to ambulate."

"PT?" Carlie was used to some hospital abbreviations like OT, which stood for occupational therapy. Of course, she never understood why they called it occupational therapy because as far as she could tell, all their goofy little activities had nothing to do with any occupation she'd ever heard of.

"Physical therapy," Patty explained. "They can help you build your strength and get you back on your feet again." She paused as if still immersed in the bizarre story Carlie just told her. "Hey, I appreciate you opening up and telling me the truth about everything. That took guts. You've been through so much, that I can't imagine how tough it's been for you. I just want you to know that I'm really impressed by your honesty and will do whatever I can to help you. In fact, I'll start by getting you a Bible, so you can find some of the answers you're looking for."

"A Bible? I wouldn't know where to start...I mean, crap, how on earth could someone like me begin to understand the Bible?"

"But you want to know if what you experienced was genuine, right?"

"Yeah."

"And there's one source of truth that will reveal what you can believe and trust."

"And so, the hard work you talked about begins?"

Patty grinned. "I'll get you a modern version, and I think you'll be pleasantly surprised by what you find. I'll be glad to help you get started, and you can bounce stuff off me if you'd like."

It was Carlie's turn to look amazed. She didn't know what exactly she'd expected from Patty after getting real about her internal conflicts, but this didn't show up on her radar. Sure,

Patty could pull off holding her hand and letting her bawl her eyes out, because that was stuff psych nurses seemed to live for. But offering to go the extra mile and bring her a Bible? Could Patty be a real, live human somewhere deep beneath her crisp lab coat and blue scrubs? Unless, of course, her so-called kindness secretly presented a trap, a ploy to keep her talking so they could use her own words against her. Distrust of psychiatric services ran deep.

"That's your old thinking pattern flaring up again. And right after she graciously supported you through all your tears and emotional turmoil. Let it go," Dr. Emmanuel declared. "Release the paranoia."

Before she had a chance to decide how to react to Patty or to Jesus' comment, Jason arrived with a wheelchair and whisked her away to the cafeteria and back to the old version of the psych unit. She saw Craig, tightly holding onto his tray and staring into space, rocking back and forth from one foot to the other with Liz gently offering to relieve him of his burden so he could flee from his unseen danger. Carlie parked across the table from Lila Mae, who mumbled something about not getting breakfast. Meanwhile a very manic Joylyn paced and snatched any leftovers she could find on various deserted trays. So much for any extra brownies today. But—hey—she expected this sort of normal psych stuff. Except for the part about her living through it all before.

Carlie lifted the cover from her plate. "Mmm. Brisket for breakfast Ms. Lila Mae."

The old lady frowned curiously over her glasses that slid precariously down her nose. "How do you know me, dear? I don't believe we've met."

Carlie stopped mid-chew, barbecue sauce running from the corner of her mouth. She grabbed her napkin. "Uh, I think Jason told me your name. I'm Carlie, and I just transferred here from ICU this morning."

Lila Mae appeared relieved. "This is what they call breakfast now?"

Carlie couldn't help but grin. "Hey, they can serve me brisket for breakfast, lunch, and supper. It's my favorite hospital meal."

Lila Mae smiled merrily. "It IS good," she admitted. "The only thing that would make it better is some old-fashioned vanilla Blue Bell ice cream on top of that brownie."

"I like the way you think, Ms. Lila Mae." Carlie waved at Liz. "Could we get some ice cream to go with our desserts?"

In no time at all, Ms. Lila Mae inhabited Blue Bell heaven, and Carlie got to be something of a hero. Maybe having a do-over offered certain advantages. *What happens next? Oh, yeah, Craig's meltdown in the hall.*

"Ms. Lila Mae, I think we should relax and enjoy our treats. No need to hurry. They'll come get us when it's safe."

The elderly woman pushed her glasses up on her nose. "It isn't safe?"

"I mean when it's time." Maybe *I shouldn't act like I know what's going to happen. That would be too much to explain.* Carlie tried to picture telling a group of psych patients that she met Jesus and saw the future.

The next few days, Carlie tried her best to learn from the mistakes she'd made in her coma vision. She found that keeping from losing her temper and flying off the handle at the staff and their irritating ways posed the main challenge. Every time she felt her blood coming to the boiling point, that quiet little voice reminded her that a different choice would bring a better outcome. Jesus kept telling her that the old Carlie died, leaving nothing but a memory that she was free to reinterpret, but she often countered by telling him that she didn't know this new Carlie yet. Then he reminded her that didn't matter and encouraged her to simply keep listening to him and following his lead.

Some of Carlie's vision replayed right on cue, like when a very battered Taylor came into the dining room and Joylyn launched into accusations of corporate espionage. Carlie found herself rolling her eyes and standing to face the loud mouth. "Joylyn, lay off her. She's obviously injured and no threat to you. Since you've got so much on your agenda, why don't you go take care of your business, and I'll keep an eye on her."

Carlie slid into an empty chair opposite the bruised girl. "Hi, uh, I'm Carlie. Mind if I eat with you? I promise not to press charges against you for spying on my ultra-secret, sure-to-make-me-rich-quick, corporate structure that I don't even have except in my own mind. What's your name?" Carlie grinned, because she already knew Taylor's name.

"Taylor Whitehouse. I just got here about an hour ago." Taylor looked relieved to see a friendly face.

"So, how's it going so far, besides being accused of all sort of nefarious acts by our resident maniac?"

Taylor smiled weakly. "I like you. You're funny."

"Yeah, I'm just here for comic relief. In fact, I'm so wildly popular at the nut hut that I hang out here a lot. They call me the queen of good times." Carlie enjoyed this replay and the realization that this friendship would blossom. *Thanks, Jesus. I know you're the one who prompted me to get to know Taylor, and I just want you to know that I appreciate it. I'll try not to wig out when I have to tell her my story in group.*

However much she meant those words, she soon found that just because she knew she **should** avoid certain reactions didn't mean she knew **how** to avoid repeating her old patterns.

When it came time for her to share her story with Taylor upon Nurse Patty's prompt cue, Carlie felt her eyes glaze over, and her heart did a couple of somersaults. *Uh, oh. Help, me, Jesus, I haven't even said a word yet, and I already feel panic setting in. This didn't happen last time until after I'd finished spilling my guts.*

"But now your story includes a very stressful bit of information you didn't remember before. Think about me. I'm here with you; let me help you."

The group sat expectantly, all eyes on her, waiting for the Carlie show to begin. Carlie's right leg started bouncing, soon followed by her left, and she gripped her chair as if it threatened to toss her into space. *Where do I start?*

"With your suicide, your death." Funny how Jesus never sounded nervous, but then, he had that whole God thing happening.

She took a deep breath and took the plunge, reciting in vivid detail the events leading up to Emily's suicide at the lake, including her raging emotional state.

"That's terrible!" Taylor exclaimed.

Carlie's whole body was vibrating from a bad case of nerves. "Uh, yeah, I freaked big time. So, anyway, I got another girl who had a car to bring me back to the boarding house, 'cause she wanted to hurry up and get away from the lake about as much as I did. The picnic became like a crime scene or something with the police and an ambulance, and everyone going crazy. Way more drama than I could deal with."

No one moved or made a sound, so Carlie took a deep breath and continued the story of her gory suicide attempt. "By the time they got me to the hospital, I'd lost a lot of blood, and they were doing CPR on me, so that technically made me dead. Have y'all heard about those out-of-body experiences that people have when they're dying?"

Several of the patients nodded. "Well, I had that floating feeling and was in the process of heading up toward a light. I'd never felt so peaceful and happy, but this strange doctor intervened and told me I'd have to come back and learn to do it right. From there he began taking me through, uh, I guess something like a vision where I saw more clearly what really happened when during my childhood."

Her stomach violently twisted, and Carlie bolted for the bathroom but only made it to the door before vomiting. Patty summoned Jason's help in producing a wet washcloth for Carlie's face while she fetched a pill that dissolved on Carlie's tongue to settle her nausea. Jason assisted the trembling girl back to her chair and began cleaning up the mess on the floor. Patty pulled her chair over to sit close to Carlie.

The rest of the patients chatted in several mini-groups until Paul called the meeting back to order. Carlie closed her eyes and held her stomach.

"I'm still with you." In her mind's eye, she could see Dr. Emmanuel's eyes, kind, yet powerful.

And she could see the dark, humid closet and hear Bubba's cries. The truth sprang out of her mouth as if it had taken on a life of its own. Every horrible detail, every fear, every pounding beat of her heart came tumbling out. The sexual abuse. Her mother being battered and her terrified cries for Daddy to stop. Smothering Bubba in a frantic attempt to silence him. Hearing Daddy shoot Mommy. Carrying Bubba's lifeless body out of the closet.

Then sobs and shrieks came from a totally wigged out Carlie. The room full of horrified patients and staff faded into the background while gentle hands guided her to the quiet room, and she mercifully received a shot of tranquility. Then all went quiet.

Progress

Morning came, along with scrambled eggs, sausage, and French toast. Lila Mae looked positively euphoric as she sampled every item on her plate and pronounced it good. Taylor quietly studied Carlie for any traces of a potential repeat of yesterday's melt down.

Carlie had slept soundly through the night, a remarkable feat considering that apocalyptic-type therapy sessions generally created marathon nightmares only ending after she peed the bed and woke up wet and terrified. Last night no nightmares, no blood-curdling screams, and no visions of her dead little brother disturbed her sweet Haldol-Ativan-Benadryl rest. She moved a lot slower than most mornings, but overall, she made progress, just as Dr. Emmanuel reminded her when she crawled out of bed still dry.

Taylor timidly bit into her sausage. "Sleep well?"

"Yep. You?" Cobwebs still needed to be swept out of her drowsy mind.

"I slept okay. Just kind of worried about you."

Carlie blinked and swallowed her orange juice. "You worried about me?" Then it hit. *Of course, dung for brains, you acted like a raving maniac in group therapy.*

Taylor wiped her lips with a napkin. "You seemed pretty upset, and the staff took you off somewhere, and I didn't see you the rest of the day…or evening. I just wanted to see how you were."

"Oh. About that—I, uh, I don't know." Her appetite suddenly disappeared. "Sometimes the stuff from my past is just beyond what I can take. Especially the new stuff."

"New stuff? You mean about your roommate killing herself with your gun?"

Carlie winced. *I seem to be one layer after another of misery and horror. There's enough junk in my life to fill up at least three lifetimes.* Her stomach twisted, and she pushed her tray away. "I really don't want to talk about it now. I mean, it wouldn't be good for me to puke all over breakfast, would it?"

"Oh, I'm sorry." Taylor looked down and picked at her food.

Dr. Emmanuel's unmistakable voice said, "Here's someone who cares about you. Don't push her away."

Carlie nodded. He was right, as always. "Thanks for asking though. Maybe I can talk with you later when there's no food around for me to hurl. Is that okay?"

Taylor brightened. "Sure, if you want to talk, that is. I, uh, I just want to be there for you like you've been for me. You seem to get me, and that means a lot. You'd be surprised how many people act like I must enjoy letting my husband smack me around."

Just then Anna wheeled a computer over and began scanning Carlie's bracelet and the assortment of pills that looked like the same cocktail Carlie got every morning. Anna exhibited extreme efficiency, asking all the routine questions while she opened the individual medication packages. Carlie responded with correct answers: her name and date of birth, that she was on Parkland's psych unit on August the 11th, and—no—she didn't hear voices *except Jesus* or have any visual hallucinations and didn't feel a bit suicidal and would be glad to verbally contract for safety. Having completed her initial interrogation of the day, she obediently gulped down the pills and opened her mouth to prove she'd swallowed them.

Anna smiled approvingly and tossed a strand of her jet-black pony tail back over her shoulder. "Dr. White called and will be in to see you in approximately ten minutes."

Carlie's stomach settled sufficiently by then, so she hastily finished her French toast and promised to join Taylor in OT before making a beeline for the consultation room. She plopped down comfortably in an armchair, feeling strangely pleasant for a change. Having a friend, someone to do stuff with, even mind-numbing, gut-wrenching stuff like therapy gave her comfort. But pleasant emotions had always been in short supply in Carlie's life, so she didn't want to get too comfortable, because feeling good about anything never lasted long for her. She wondered how long she could remain in this foreign state of mind.

Dr. White bustled in quite importantly in his meticulously starched long-sleeved shirt and deep red tie. He glanced at his obviously expensive watch as he sat and lifted his eyebrows inquisitively, carefully analyzing Carlie's facial expression.

"I've heard some incredible stories about your stay in the hospital," he announced.

162

The puzzled patient returned his stare. *He's actually looking at me. And all it took to get his attention was to finally succeed in killing myself, then get resuscitated and stay in a coma for about a month.* Of course, her mouth gave a different reply. "Yeah, it's been crazy, I mean, in a good way, not an insane way."

He leaned back and tilted his head thoughtfully. "Uh huh, so tell me about this crazy good thing that you've gained from your experience."

"Okay, well, it was so peaceful—dying, that is—until Dr. Emmanuel, I mean, Jesus, brought me back and told me I had to learn how to do it right."

Dr. White pursed his lips together and scrunched up his forehead. Carlie didn't know if he was constipated, in deep thought, or just disapproving of her story. She didn't have long to guess.

"Let me get this correct: you met Jesus?" His tone betrayed his disbelief. "And now your life is changed." He snapped his fingers. "Like that. Something years of therapy couldn't do is somehow accomplished while having CPR or maybe while you were in a coma?"

It felt like a kick in the stomach. Carlie puckered her lips. "Why do I bother talking to you? You don't believe anything I say. This ends now. I'm out of here."

She stormed out of the Consult Room and slammed the door for good measure. The harsh thud behind her made her grimace. *Oh, Jesus, I blew it again. Just like always. I never seem to get it right with these people. They make me so mad!*

"Just say you're sorry." That inner voice prompted reasonably. *Like that will do any good.*

"You're either going to follow me or not. Trust me or not."

Staff started to gather, and Dr. White stood in the doorway staring at her disdainfully.

Carlie held her hands up in surrender. "I'm sorry. I let my anger control me. I didn't mean to; it just happened. Can I just have some time alone in the quiet room to sort it out?"

Dr. White nodded. "Maybe you've made progress after all."

Carlie stretched out in the seclusion room and looked up at the ceiling, smiling rather insincerely at the camera mounted overhead. Then, for good measure, she waved and turned over to face the wall. *Sorry, snoops, no fireworks today.*

She couldn't remember ever being in the seclusion room without being heavily medicated, restrained, or locked in. It didn't seem like the same place. It was fairly nice and quiet, not as scary with the thick, wooden door open. For all her past drama here, her brain conducted itself quite well this time around. In fact, despite all the torrential emotional storms she's weathered there, she sensed something strangely calm...even relaxing.

In her mind's eye she could picture Jesus dressed as Dr. Emmanuel, sitting cross-legged on the floor grinning at her. "I told you that you could trust me. Apologizing has its rewards."

Yeah, they never saw that coming; it totally threw them off.

"And it gives us some time to kick back together."

Carlie smiled for real. *Is that something God does? I never thought of you as kicking back, hanging out with anyone...especially me.*

"Remember that I'm the one who invited you to come abide in me, feast with me, find yourself in me."

Hey, I'm learning. I didn't punch a wall or kick a staff member or get held down and medicated. Dr. White made me mad, but I didn't go crazy Carlie on him—except for that whole door-

slamming thing. Maybe he's right. Maybe I've made progress. And it feels...good. Well, strange, but good.

Speaking of feeling good, why waste her chance to entertain the staff? They'd be expecting something more from her than a single bang and an apology. Carlie got on her hands and knees and wagged her tail, which looked a lot more like wiggling her butt in the air, seeing as how she had no tail. Then she pounced with a loud growl and hiss, shredding the air with her imaginary claws.

"What on earth are you doing in here?" Jason stood in the doorway looking amused.

"Just giving y'all exactly what y'all want. It's the Carlie Flew Over the Cuckoo's Nest edition of craziness."

Jason shook his head. "You're not crazy. I know real crazy when I see it, and you're not it. So, now that we've gotten that out of your system, how about going to group?"

A few minutes later, Carlie found herself wedged between, the wilted mute, and her friend, Taylor. Each patient had the task of setting a goal for the day. Mrs. Lila Mae said she would fill out her breakfast menu. Several depressed patients jumped on the same bandwagon and committed to write down five good traits about themselves. Taylor's goals made Carlie clap for joy. She would check into getting a divorce today, and she would make a few calls to set up the process, including calling her parents. Solid goals, and they might just save her life.

Next came Carlie's turn. She'd already managed to navigate rough emotional waters this morning with Dr. White, but she knew that more would follow, so she quickly offered up the goal of refraining from any meltdowns today. Paul smiled and asked her to clarify her goal a little more, so with his help she agreed to recognize the signs when she first started becoming overwhelmed and ask for time in the quiet room or medication, depending on the severity of the internal storm at the time.

Jeffrey tilted back and glanced at her quizzically but had nothing to say when his turn came. As usual. His expression went blank again as he stared straight ahead.

Craig rambled about his goal to stop the CIA from tapping into the electrical current of his neurons using uranium and waves from deep space. Somehow—Carlie couldn't quite follow his train of thought—they wouldn't be able to control his thoughts with ultra-red screening. Not ultra-violet; that mistake never worked. With Patty's prompting, he agreed to take the medication that would deter CIA-initiated impulses.

Joylyn had been caught trying to cheek her meds, so the staff made a big deal in the goals group about the benefits of taking one's medicine. Joylyn didn't buy a word of it, insisting they just wanted to stifle her creativity. Paul asked her how she felt the medicine did that to her, and Joylyn started hurling accusations, quickly followed by airborne couch cushions.

Craig started rocking, and Carlie leaned forward, covering her ears. *Can she get any louder or more irritating?*

Then she felt something and looked over. Jeffrey's hand rested on her shoulder. She froze.

"Peace, be still," the familiar voice whispered.

She closed her eyes to block out the craziness around her. The surrounding vortex of craziness and confusion threatened to suck her in. Her heart pounded as she panted for breath, and light-headedness settled in. She grasped her head with one hand and her chest with the other. *I'm going to explode.*

"No, you're just hyperventilating. Slow your breathing down. Like this." She could hear Jesus taking calm, deliberate breaths, so she inhaled. Slowly. Deeply. Some sweet aroma greeted her nostrils, and she could see a majestic throne surrounded by fiercely attentive guardian angels. Jesus sat on the throne with his legs crossed and sipping a colorful beverage. He smiled and motioned for her to join him. She timidly stepped forward, and the next thing she knew, she felt his arms around her while he cradled her like a baby in his lap.

Joylyn's shrieks and staff rushing in got relegated to some distant space. It faded into the background like a TV left on in the back of the house. It had no relevance to her, no power to suck her in—no power at all.

Carlie relaxed in her peaceful place for once. Almost like her first out of body experience, she felt very much alive, greatly loved and mightily protected.

She could have stayed there forever, but hands on her shoulders gently shook her. "It's over. Time to go," Taylor announced.

She opened her eyes. Taylor and Jeffrey watched her carefully. *Wait. Why is Jeffrey making eye contact?*

How many times had she witnessed his two sisters and one reluctant brother sitting on the sofa beside him trying all sorts of strategies to get him to open up with them? They'd brought Chinese food, pasta, pizza, fajita nachos—you name it. He wouldn't eat, wouldn't talk, wouldn't even look at them. He only slumped a little more and looked even more dejected. But now he'd reached out and touched her.

"Are you okay?" Taylor asked carefully.

"Uh, yeah, just wondering about Jeffrey. What's going on, Jeff?"

The somber guy just shrugged and looked away, but a different glimmer briefly flickered in his eyes—like someone waking up from a long slumber. He slowly took in the room and his two companions, rubbing his forehead thoughtfully. "You're getting better."

Through Jeffrey's Eyes

Jeffrey silently groaned to himself when Carlie sat beside him. *There are too many drama queens in this place,* he mused. *Why do they get to carry on every single day with their violent mood swings and insatiable desire to die? Why do they continue to live but not HER?*

Jeffrey slumped deeper into the cushions of the sofa. His head hurt so badly; his stomach clenched in perpetual knots; his chest ached with each breath. His family wondered why he didn't talk, but who had words adequate for describing his utter nothingness? Who could understand what his beloved Leah meant to him? Grief and bitterness hit like a cannonball in his gut while being forced to sit and listen to the nonsense being uttered by this host of fools surrounding him. Carlie and Joylyn easily topped his list of least favorites with their copious babbling.

Carlie's volatile nature and horror stories contrasted with his sweet and brilliant Leah. Here was someone so bent on self-

169

destruction that she lashed out at anyone who tried to help her. He'd witnessed her verbal and physical abusiveness toward the staff and didn't understand why they didn't just lock her up in solitaire and be done with her. Maybe they could put medicine in her food and simply slide it into her cell. Wait, no, that would be a prison instead of a hospital setting.

Still, she'd probably end up there some day like her father. He could easily see her killing anyone who stood between her and her next suicide plan. She couldn't be anymore screwed up if she tried, but, then again, the story about her childhood was enough to make anyone cringe. How could there be that kind of abuse out in the world?

Jeffrey begrudgingly admitted to himself that Carlie had good reason to be seriously messed up, but even so, couldn't she be a little nicer about it? He didn't want to admit it out loud, but deep inside loomed the perception that everything she did was a grab for attention. She certainly didn't suffer in silence at all. Nor did she seem to have any concern about anyone besides herself. So, yes, she might be a nutcase for good reason, but he found her easy to hate. She presented the polar opposite of his wonderful Leah.

Of course, there could never be another Leah, not in a million years. He sighed. *Only the good die young.* And Leah had to be the very best. She'd been through her share of problems in her childhood, too, but she didn't take it out on others. She grew up in extreme poverty and lived with her mother on the streets of Dallas, getting their meals from a soup kitchen and bunkering down in a homeless shelter at night. Still her life centered on helping others, not lashing out willy-nilly. Her desire to help impoverished children better themselves fueled her drive to pursue a degree in elementary education. He admired her for her goodness and strength.

Jeffrey's thoughts naturally centered on Leah: all the little things that she used to say, her warm, brown eyes that danced with enthusiasm, and the way her lips dipped and curved into the sweetest smile known to all mankind. When he thought about her, he could leave this cruel reality behind and breathe her fragrance one more. Of course, reality would rear its ugly head from time to time, and all his emptiness would come crashing in on him with a fresh wave of grief.

He didn't have long to contemplate the meaning of Leah's short life before Joylyn started acting out. This one impressed him as a not-so-nice Energizer Bunny on steroids. He had never witnessed anyone who could turn a place upside down as quickly as Joylyn. Not only did she insert herself into everyone else's business, but she had to be intensely loud and abrasive at the same time. Plus, she buzzed around like a speed demon bent on irritating the living daylights out of everyone in her path. Between the grandiose nonsense coming out of her mouth and her complete lack of boundaries and respect for others, she had to be even worse than Carlie minus the vomit.

He internally groaned. Why did these clowns get to live and create havoc every five seconds, while Leah—who made the world a better place—had to lie rotting in a grave? Life wasn't fair.

He'd never met anyone who could make everything around her right again like Leah. Now his world would never be whole again; the gaping void from Leah's death consumed him. He closed his eyes. Nothing remained out there for him anymore. *Just shut it out. Just shut down.* It was the only strategy he knew.

The group around him got started with the therapist asking about goals. *Goals? What goals? Leah's gone, and it's my fault. I can't change what happened, so goals are useless. I'm useless... I should have insisted that fateful night. She would still be here, but now...*

Yeah, I once had goals. I excelled at a job that I found fulfilling, planned on getting married to the gal of my dreams, getting a dog and having 2.5 kids. Now? No Leah, no life, no goals. No purpose. Nothing worth talking about.

The bruised young lady sitting on the other side of Carlie had a goal to leave her abusive husband. Her moist, sad eyes caught his attention. She seemed nice. Not Leah nice, of course, but nice enough. At least she didn't carry on loudly and obnoxiously like some. How could that jerk do this to her?

The fact that he felt himself dying on the inside along with his cherished Leah while some other dude used his wife as a punching bag didn't set well with him. He felt a sudden twinge of anger. Not just a mild annoyance at an unseen stranger, but a punch of righteous indignation.

What I wouldn't do to have Leah back! How dare this idiot hurt such a lovely woman who clearly loves him? It would feel so good—if not downright therapeutic—to give him a taste of his own medicine. Jeffrey clenched his fists.

Meanwhile Carlie started giving her recital to the tune of "I'm not going to go berserk today". Jeffrey couldn't tell if Paul, the therapist, danced to the music, but he sure didn't. He'd been in the direct line of fire yesterday when she'd gone off on a dreadful tale and then made a mad dash for the door, spewing the remnants of her last meal in the process. Though most hit the floor, he'd been the recipient of some splatter, and the memory of yesterday's stench still lingered in his nostrils. And now, here he sat beside her, making him one of the most likely to go down with whatever histrionics plagued her today.

He leaned a bit to the side away from her and gaged her volatility meter to determine if a quick exit might be in order. But her speech didn't last long—which seemed a miracle in and of itself, so it looked like he might escape her theatrics for this goals group.

Then his turn came, as Paul reminded him. Since he never spoke a single word, most of the other patients treated him as if he was just an inconveniently placed part of the decor. They walked around him, sat next to him or talked over him. He didn't matter, but he took up space, and maybe a minute of Paul's time dedicated to silence. Then on to the next patient.

Craig rambled on about the government trying to control his thoughts, but Jeffrey found himself looking at Carlie again. At least she knew how it felt to have the blood of someone she loved on her hands.

Oh, Leah, if only I'd driven you home.

He worked hard at swallowing the bitter pill of guilt. He should have known better. She looked too tired to drive, and he should have protected his fiancée even though she asserted that she could get there safely. He let her down. He failed her parents, and he gave up all rights to happiness. So now he sat day after day in the county hospital's psychiatric unit.

Ha, the county hospital, and a psychiatric patient to boot. No wonder Dad doesn't bother to visit. It's bad enough that I'm his son, but to come to this loathsome place for the mentally unstable and mostly indigent to boot? Unthinkable!

Things turned out just as his father predicted: he, the baby of the family, was a colossal failure. His childhood selective mutism made him a reject in his father's eyes, a genetically defective offspring who came as an afterthought to the perfect family.

His athletic siblings excelled as rising stars in their chosen fields. Big brother, Elliot, the high school quarterback and valedictorian, made partner at Dad's law firm. Older sister and state tennis champion in her high school years—another Goldstein valedictorian, Samantha, recently started practicing as a cardiologist at UT Southwestern. Last-but-certainly-not-least, Kimberly, the lone Goldstein salutatorian, became a lanky basketball prodigy-turned-super-model who graced magazine covers and TV commercials in roughly twenty different countries. All graduates of Harvard or Yale and intellectually gifted.

Except Jeffrey. He alone brought in a less-than-stellar 3.75 GPA through his college years. And only he brandished a bachelor's degree in music education from a state university—a far cry from the ivy league schools where his older siblings soared on golden wings...at least in his father's eyes.

Joylyn's voice rose with increasing force and volume. He blinked and almost got whacked in the nose by a flying cushion. Craig started rocking beside him, and since Craig always had the potential of becoming a human powder keg, Jeffrey scrunched down as much as possible and prepared for the worst. Craig white-knuckled the sofa cushion.

Carlie leaned forward, holding her head and hyperventilating. *Is she going to explode again?* Jeffrey braced himself while the entire room came alive. Nursing staff magically descended upon the group as if on cue. The rocking beside him only intensified as the showdown proceeded.

Oh, great, Craig poised for action on my left, and Carlie spinning into orbit on my right. To his own horror, his hand reached out and touched Carlie's shoulder. *Okay. Just keep calm.*

Just keep calm. He wasn't sure if he thought these instructions about Carlie or himself.

Joylyn tried to bolt past the opposing team, but Jason quickly immobilized Joylyn's arms and lowered her to the floor while the female staff swaddled her legs and stilled her thrashing head.

Through the turmoil, he kept rubbing and patting Carlie's shoulder. It seemed to be the only thing he could do. Maybe it would help. Maybe he wouldn't get caught between three erupting volcanoes after all.

Craig leaped to his feet and out the door. *Two down; one to go.* Jeffrey peered timidly at Carlie and saw Taylor offering her comfort, also. Their eyes met, and Taylor mouthed a silent "thank you". She must not like the drama either.

Jeffrey shifted his gaze to Carlie. He didn't expect that it would feel good to be seen and acknowledged by someone, and it certainly couldn't be right. With Leah gone, how could life cruelly pretend to go on?

Carlie's breathing slowed now, and she lifted her head to see if the coast was clear. *Good; one crisis averted.*

No! Not so quick. He froze with his hand still on her shoulder. She stared at him. The object of his disdain made eye contact with him! He blinked but matched her gaze.

"Are you okay?" Taylor asked softly.

"Uh, yeah, just wondering about Jeffrey. What's going on, Jeff?" She looked like she really expected an answer.

He just shrugged and scanned the room in search for something to fill the silence, but what happened inside him? He couldn't say sure himself. He rubbed his forehead thoughtfully. *Well, she didn't go off on us today—not yet, anyway. Maybe she is changing, or at least trying. Maybe this hopeless tornado of human emotions is becoming slightly less destructive. Maybe, just maybe, if there's hope for someone as far out there as her...*

"You're getting better," came out in a hoarse voice, but the light that flickered ever so briefly in her eyes told him how much those words meant.

"Oh, uh, thanks." Her guard went up again as she wrinkled her forehead. He took that as his cue to leave.

As he trudged out of the therapy room, he could feel curious eyes staring at him from behind. Then it occurred to him. He had spoken.

Paul intercepted him by the door. "Can you come to my office for a moment?" He'd uttered one simple sentence. Did that signify that now he became an open door—or maybe a cracked door—something for the staff to pry open even more to tear up his pain in front of the world? He froze and glared at the floor while his head numbly nodded.

"Wait." Taylor made her way over to the doorway where Paul blocked his exit. "I'm sorry to interrupt, but I really need your help in figuring out what, I mean, how I'm going to accomplish my goal. Jeffrey, do you mind if I talk with Paul first since I've got to make an important phone call this morning? I promise not to keep him too long."

Jeffrey glanced up in time to see her wink at him. He nodded, this time making eye contact, first with Taylor, then with Paul.

Taylor's Perspective

Taylor spent the night before tossing and turning for good reason. She knew that she had to decide, and it had to be immediate. Her life depended on it.

She could still see Brad grabbing the bat and coming after her. He yelled at her for coming home ten minutes later than usual and accused her of being unfaithful. Even though she tried to explain that a wreck on the road home caused the delay, he wouldn't listen. His first swing of the bat broke a vase her parents gave her. He laughed and smashed her cell phone as well. She flinched and ran out the front door, screaming for help.

Unfortunately, her husband ran faster and took a swing, managing to break her arm. She fell to the ground in pain while he kicked and punched her mercilessly.

A next-door neighbor yelled at Bradley to stop, and the one across the street pulled a gun, identified himself as a Dallas police officer and ordered Brad to place his hands over his head and remain very still while he cuffed him.

Everything else seemed like disjointed fragments of memories that included an ambulance ride and tons of questions; everyone had questions. The police. The EMT. Doctors, nurses, radiology technicians. She tried to answer to the best of her ability, but every part of her battered body screamed with pain.

Through swollen eyelids, Taylor cried as medical staff attended to her wounds in the emergency department. Even the slightest movement or sound caused her to jump in terror, her heart racing to the point that she had to be given heart medication to slow things down a bit. A kind nurse spoke with her about getting help for her understandably acute panic and anxiety, so she awkwardly signed the consent for psychiatric services with her left hand.

Truthfully, she didn't know what to expect on a psychiatric unit. The admitting nurse seemed thorough and genuinely concerned, so she thought that she'd made the right choice in coming there.

Then Joylyn entered the dining room and launched into the craziest tirade she'd ever heard. Taylor trembled when the accusations began, even though they were totally absurd. She'd borne the brunt of irrational allegations before and knew that it didn't matter if claims against her carried no validity. They all brought bruises, black eyes and broken bones anyway.

She felt tremendously grateful when Carlie stood up for her and sort of took her under her wing. Sure, Carlie had enough of her own baggage, but she knew what to expect in a psych unit and how to handle herself with other patients. Taylor soon learned to stay out of Craig's way, thanks to Carlie warning her about keeping a safe distance from any paranoid schizophrenic who appeared "tightly wound", as she put it. She learned to gage Craig's level of agitation by watching his behavior to know when to beat a quick retreat.

As for Joylyn, she argued with everyone, but Taylor noticed that she tended to back down a little around Carlie. That gave her extra incentive for hanging out with her. Then hearing about how Carlie's father killed her mother gave her food for thought. That story seemed to back up what the nurses and therapist warned her about as they repeated details about the necessity of making a safety plan for escape.

I'm probably a hair away from Brad doing me in for good. Each time he beats me, it gets worse. How much more of this can I take? After two years of marriage, it all comes down to one decision: end the marriage or let Brad end me.

Taylor really wanted to talk with Carlie about what she should do, but Carlie spent the evening sedated and didn't feel up to talking that morning at breakfast. She felt urgency like never before, so goals group gave her the opportunity to announce a change in her course and enlist help in making that change.

Carlie had a session with her psychiatrist after breakfast. That gave Taylor an opportunity to get to the group room early to claim a place for the two of them. She noticed Jeffrey, the mute guy, slumped as usual on one of the sofas and sat down, leaving an empty place for her friend between Jeffrey and her.

Her eyes darted back and forth as other patients filed in. She hoped for a chance to talk with Paul before group started, but one of the nurses managed to grab his attention instead. Nervously she chewed her nails.

Don't back out. Don't back out. They said they'd be glad to help you get set up with services for battered women. Just stay calm and follow through. This is your chance. He can't stop you this time. At least not while he's in jail.

Taylor kept admonishing herself to be brave, repeating that this particular group on this very day would be her turning point.

In fact, she determined in her heart to stop being a victim now. She clenched her teeth and wiped her sweaty palms on her jeans.

Paul called the meeting to order while Joylyn literally jumped over an elderly patient's legs and landed on the sofa with a thud. Jason chided Joylyn about her recklessness and sharply warned her that he wouldn't tolerate any other outbreaks. Tiffany, one of the day nurses, backed up Jason's warning after Joylyn laughed in his face and called him a few foul names. Liz slipped out the door while Tiffany put her two cents worth in. Joylyn immediately noticed and shut up.

Taylor mused to herself that when two staff members confront someone and another one leaves the room, that must signal that the troops are being rallied.

Paul stood up and started the morning meeting by talking about the importance of having goals. He brought up different kinds of goals: short term, long term, financial, health and wellness, social, occupational and personal growth goals. Taylor felt like she would burst wide open before he'd stop talking and open the floor.

Around the time he asked for the patients to set some goals for the day, Carlie walked in and sat beside her. Taylor felt glad to have her there in time to support her new plan. She was the one person most likely to understand. With her jaw clamped in determination to make her announcement, she felt her heart beating wildly inside her chest. There could be no turning back, not if she wanted to live, and the urgency she felt to get the ball rolling made her so tense with anticipation that she scarcely listened to anyone else.

When it came her turn, she blurted out, "I'm going to start the process of leaving my husband today. First, I need to get a divorce lawyer and call the people at that battered women's shelter—what's its name?"

Paul nodded. "Genesis?"

"Yes, I'll talk with them about a safety plan for getting away from Bradley while he's in jail."

"Excellent!" cooed Paul. "How do you feel about this decision?"

Taylor took a deep breath and fidgeted. "It's not easy. I believed that marriage was until 'death do us part', but lately I've awakened to the fact that if I don't leave him, I'll be the one dying. Now that I've come to that conclusion, I feel like I've got to jump on this opportunity to put lots of space between us."

Carlie started clapping, followed by the rest of the patients who were coherent enough to understand. "Good for you," she cheered.

Tiffany, who happened to be Taylor's nurse that day, spoke up. "We're all here for you, and I want to assure you that self-preservation doesn't mean you've failed. Your husband failed the marriage when he was untrue to his wedding vows. He didn't love, honor or cherish, and if he wrote different vows, I'm sure they didn't include beating you and putting you in a hospital. By making the marriage unsafe for you, his wife, he betrayed your trust."

It made sense, but the knot in her stomach didn't relax in the least. "Thank you for your kind words. I need all the help I can get, and that leads me to my next goal. This one isn't going to be easy, but I've got to tell my parents—it's been so long since we've talked. They'll help me for sure, but I dread explaining everything to them. I just feel terrible about allowing Bradley to come between us, but he threatened to hurt them if I let on in any way what was going on."

"Be sure to come by my office after group and we'll put together phone numbers and anything else you need, including a chance to role play. Sometimes it helps to practice difficult conversations," Paul promised. "Besides, I can help you with the call to Genesis to get you started."

"Okay, thanks." Taylor thought role playing might be a good idea. She could at least get some practice on how to avoid blundering her way through it all. Immersed in thought, she barely paid attention to Carlie's goal to hold it together or notice Craig's plight with secret government mind control by using light frequencies. It took a couple of flying projectiles to snap out of it.

Oh, my goodness! What's wrong with that woman? She glared at Joylyn with disapproval. *I'm trying to get my life together. This is serious business, and she's carrying on with all this tom foolery.*

Tiffany and Jason jumped to their feet and immediately a swarm of staff joined them in corralling everyone's least favorite bipolar.

Carlie, trying diligently to keep her promise to make it through the day without any explosions, held her head in her hands and pumped sprints of quick breaths in and out of her mouth without giving the air time to hit her lungs. Her legs bounced madly, and her torso rocked as if her life depended on it.

Taylor reached out to reassure her friend. As she touched Carlie's shoulder, she saw Jeffrey, the barely upright mute, also comforting her. Taylor blinked her eyes. Was she seeing right? Jeffrey's eyes met hers, so she mouthed a thank you while she tried to sort out what sparked this change in Jeffrey. Out of the corner of her eyes, she could see Craig jetting out of the room, probably to flee whatever conspiracy was at play. She could understand Craig's sudden exit, but not Jeffrey's behavior, so she found herself staring. Staring and patting Carlie's shoulder. What else could she do?

As the room calmed, she realized that the crisis was over and helped Carlie slow her breathing. *At least I've learned something from my time here. Slow, deep breaths go a long way.*

Carlie's rocking and vibrating slowed considerably, along with her respirations. Taylor could see the puzzled expression as she realized Jeffrey's hand was gently rubbing her shoulder. *Oh, no. Who knows how she'll react to a guy touching her?* Even a psychiatric novice like Taylor knew that childhood sexual abuse meant being very careful about touch; she'd read about it back in college.

"Are you okay?" she asked carefully.

"Uh, yeah, just wondering about Jeffrey. What's going on, Jeff?" Her friend's focus remained solely on Jeffrey.

The poor guy just shrugged and looked like he'd been caught robbing a bank. Even though his discomfort was apparent, Taylor thought she detected something different in his face—like someone coming back from being gravely ill, like the landscape transforming from winter to spring. Well, maybe not that drastic, but he did look alive if only for a split second before he tried to climb back into his shell.

He glanced away uneasily, rubbing his forehead as if to erase what just happened. "You're getting better," he said, his voice timid and soft, barely above a whisper. Then he headed out the door.

Paul took note of the unfolding situation and called out from across the room, saying he wanted to talk with Jeffrey. A look of sheer terror filled Jeffrey's face. Before he could respond—not that he was on the verge of giving any quick replies—Taylor decided that one good turn deserved another. She offered to speak with Paul first.

It made sense. They'd talked in group about the phone calls she needed to make and how she needed help, and since she needed to jump on her tasks, it wouldn't sound strange for her to ask to go first. That would give Jeffrey a little time and space to gather his thoughts before he had to face Paul.

When she made her offer, trying to sound both nonchalant and urgent, which she believed to be a tricky feat, Paul fell for it. Jeffrey lifted his head and once again made eye contact. Sure enough, she saw light accompanying a very slight nod. That nod might as well have shouted his appreciation. As she got up to follow Paul to his office, she glanced back with a faint grin and winked. Jeffrey's lips twitched into a transient half-smile.

Once she found herself behind closed doors with Paul, she got down to business. She would move forward now. If Jeffrey could do it, if Carlie could come out of World War III in goals group without a trip to seclusion, Taylor Whitehouse could start her new journey in life.

"Can we make the call to Genesis right now? While I still have the nerve?"

Paul slid into his chair. "Sure, have a seat, and I'll put us on speaker phone." He motioned to the chair in front of his desk and pulled his phone closer to the center of his desk. "I've got their number right here." He pulled out a sheet of paper from his top drawer that looked like the referral sheet she'd received in the emergency room.

Taylor watched and listened as he dialed.

"Genesis Women's Shelter and Support. My name is Stephanie De Leon. How may I direct your call?" Her voice sounded efficient and strong. Nothing to fear. No reason to look back.

"Hi, Stephanie, this is Paul Mason from Parkland where I'm a therapist. I need to speak with someone in intake."

"Okay, Paul, that will be Wendy Bennet. Please hold while I transfer you."

Taylor's heart amped up its beat a notch while the extension rang.

"Good morning. Wendy Bennet here. How may I help you?" Another strong, confident voice.

Paul took the lead while Taylor fidgeted in her chair. "Good morning, Wendy. I'm Paul Mason from Parkland, and..."

"Oh, yes, Paul, I remember you. We've talked a few times. What's up?"

"I have a young lady with me on speaker phone whose husband beat her severely, breaking her arm and sending her to the hospital. Her name is Taylor Whitehouse, and she's ready to leave him while he's in jail. I figured you'd be just the one to help her." He nodded to Taylor as if to signal that it was her turn to speak.

Taylor's voice suddenly wilted as the words hoarsely spilled out of her mouth. "I've got to get away from him, but he's also threatened my parents if I tell them anything about how he's been treating me. He's basically cut me off from everyone." She valiantly fought back tears. There would be time for crying later. "Can, can you help me and my parents? I'm so afraid. And they don't know yet, but I'm going to call them today."

"Oh, Taylor, I'm sorry you're going through the fear and pain of being abused. I want to encourage you, though, by letting you know that we've been able to help hundreds of battered women each year to safely get away from the abuse and learn how to avoid repeating the cycle with another man. You've come to the right place, and we'll be glad to help you. Are you up to answering some questions, so I'll know how to best support you?"

"Uh, yes, anything you need to know." Taylor felt hope welling up. If they could help hundreds every year, then she must be in good hands.

The questions turned out to be some basic information like when she got admitted to the hospital. Some were more probing and got into areas of her life that she would have to give up or alter to make a clean break. It gave her a lot to think about, stuff like her name, bank accounts and place of employment, anything that would make it easy to find her. Fortunately, Paul provided her with a pen and paper so she could take notes. The conversation ended well, and she set an appointment to meet Wendy face-to-face tomorrow.

Tomorrow. That was fast. She just made the decision this morning. As soon as Paul hung up the phone, Taylor found herself hit with emotions from every angle. Relief. Anger. Fear. Sorrow and guilt and... She started bawling like a newborn baby.

Dr. Manuel Garcia

Carlie watched Taylor rushing to Jeffrey's rescue and following Paul to his office while Jeffrey lagged behind. *What on earth is going on here? I didn't spend that long in the time out room, did I?* She shook her head as if expecting to clear the cobwebs of her confusion and sat back down on the sofa. She wanted to be alone for a few minutes to sort things out.

Okay, so Jeffrey can talk, and apparently he knows what's happening around him, but what's happening between him and Taylor? How does he know if I'm getting better? And if I am...well, what does it say that this barely functioning human thinks I'm improving, but the staff is still suspicious of me?

"So many questions. Remember that I said that if you seek, you will find. So, do you want to talk to me about your questions, or do you just want to keep doing this circular dialog in your head?"

"Jesus?"

"Do you expect another voice in your head?"

Carlie grinned. Who knew that God had a sense of humor? "Well, I'm still not really expecting any voices to be in my head, but if I'm going to hear one, I'm glad it's yours."

"I believe you have questions about Jeffrey and Taylor."

"Yeah, I've never seen Jeffrey make any contact with another living soul, so why me? And I clearly saw Taylor wink at him; what's that about?"

An uncomfortable pause followed. Gaps in conversations can make people jump in there saying the first thing that comes to mind, but at least she could see people who were silent. What was Dr. Emmanuel doing? He didn't exactly have to search for an answer and get back with her. After all, he knew everything.

"Uh, Jesus, are you still there?"

"Yes, I said I'd never leave you."

Carlie sighed and chewed her bottom lip. "Okay, you're here but not answering me even though you just told me to ask you stuff."

"No, not just any stuff. Ask me what I want you to know, what I want to you to do, how I want you to respond."

Carlie leaned back on the sofa and gazed at the ceiling. "So, there's something you want me to do about them?"

"Not exactly something to do about them as much as a way to interact with them. You've never been very good at relationships."

"Thanks for the reminder." She grimaced.

"You weren't raised with healthy relationships, so how would you know what it even looks like, much less how to engage in one?"

A slow smile tugged at her lips. "This is so true, but how am I to have healthy relationships in a psych unit? You haven't forgotten where I am, have You?"

"I don't misplace my children. I have a reason for you being here in this hospital right now just like I have a reason for Jeffrey and Taylor. I have a place for both of them in your life for a reason."

"What reason? Why?"

"Trust Me."

"So, I'm not getting any great insight into what's going on or how I'm supposed to relate to them. Maybe it's just me; I tend to be a bit dense, but could you make things a bit clearer?" She rubbed her temples as if trying to make the answer sink in.

"Trust me."

"Trust me seems to be your theme, your answer to everything." She felt annoyed and determined to make her point. "I get the whole don't trust you and go to hell in a hand basket versus the trust you and get a free admission into heaven thing, and yes, I believe that's a sweet deal, but what about the here and now? I can't just sit back and trust that's everything's going to work out magically somehow, can I?"

"Not magically, but divinely. Why wouldn't I work things out for my children who put their trust in me?"

"Because I have to take action. I have to make decisions."

"And how has your course of action worked out for you so far? Do you really trust yourself to make the best decisions?"

"Wow, it always seems to come back to this, doesn't it? Who am I going to trust?" She rubbed her forehead vigorously. "Okay. You win. Just using the process of elimination rules out trusting myself. I've seen the results of that choice. And I'm not about to trust anyone else."

"Not after your father, the youth pastor, and that one foster family."

"Oh, man! There's no winning any arguments with you, are there?"

Jesus chuckled. "I'd say you won big time just now. You came to an important realization."

"But I've come to that realization before. Why doesn't it just stick with me?"

"Because every day brings new challenges, and you have to decide all over again if you dare to trust me."

"For every little thing?"

"Yep."

"Okay, I think I've got it this time, so now we can move onto what I need to do with this unfolding situation." She giggled impishly. "And the answer is...ta da...trust you." She threw her hands up in surrender.

"Uh, your surgeon is here to examine you, and Dr. White is with him," a new tech wearing a name badge that identified her as Gabby M. smirked just a tad. "So, if you're finished with your conversation here, I'll escort you to your room."

"Don't respond. Bite your tongue and silently follow her. Trust me. The questions you have about how to relate with Taylor and Jeffrey are relevant, but right now you're about to face the unexpected."

"Okay." Carlie followed Gabby obediently. *Everything around here is unexpected. What's one more little surprise?*

As Carlie rounded the corner, she could hear Dr. White mumbling, "I believe this will clear up everything...if she will accept that it's a fact."

A doctor in crisp ceil blue scrubs nodded agreeably. "It's really a very simple misunderstanding."

Carlie paused in her doorway. Dr. White's face betrayed a triumphant state of mind as he cleared his throat. "Oh, Carlie, come on in. I want you to meet the surgeon who put your mangled throat back together. His name is Dr. Manuel...Manuel **Garcia**." Of course, he placed special emphasis on Garcia as if to point out that this surgeon was not divine.

The Dr. Manuel Garcia standing before her had straight, black hair, not wavy. No scars could be found on his forehead or his wrists. He wore stylish glasses, and he looked like a very smart man, but he wasn't the Dr. Emmanuel she knew.

He reached out to shake her hand and then beckoned her to sit on the bed while he examined his handiwork. "Hmmn. Yes." He turned her head and tilted it just so to gain a better view. "Good. Now the other side. Yes. Good. The sutures can come out. Hold still, now." He opened a suture removal kit and donned some gloves. "Just a little tug; shouldn't hurt a bit. There, not bad, huh? That was the first. We had to put in several drainage tubes because of the infection. Now we keep going, okay?"

"Uh, sure," Carlie agreed.

"I remember the night of your surgery. You arrived in bad shape, young lady. So much blood loss, so much damage. It's a miracle we brought you back. Of course, between the blood loss, being unconscious and having CPR performed on you, I doubt that you remember much from that night. We gave you anesthesia for the surgery, and that can also mess with your memory."

"You know where he's going with this train of thought, don't you?" Jesus asked. "Don't buy into it. Trust me."

The surgeon continued, "I understand that somewhere with your near-death experience and your delirious state after surgery when you became septic, you saw and heard me talking to you. I understand that you thought I was, uh, the Son of God. Perfectly understandable. You must have heard someone calling my name sometime in that frantic night when we worked so hard to save you. Somehow, I became more that who I truly am. It's funny, actually—hold still—they say that we surgeons think we're gods, but I'm here to assure you that I'm not. Okay, the other side."

He tilted her head the other direction and began snipping.

"If you have any specific questions, I'll try to answer, to fill in the gaps of what you remember with what actually happened."

Carlie grimaced slightly. "Why do I still have stitches a month after surgery?"

"Oh, that was most unfortunate. You had such a bad infection that we had to go back in to drain the pus. We ended up leaving drainage tubes in for a while. Your case became quite complicated indeed with so many problems, but here you are, ready for me to discharge you from my care, which means that Dr. White can proceed with transferring you as planned."

Carlie's eyes widened. "To Terrell?"

Dr. White nodded.

"When?"

Dr. White readily gave his planned response. "We'll probably set it up for tomorrow morning. Right now, I want to make sure we can clear up any misconceptions you may have brought out of your delirium. If you go to Terrell talking about having conversations with Jesus, you understand what they will assume?"

"You never believed me," Carlie grumbled.

"Careful, don't say what you're thinking," Jesus reminded her.

Dr. White stepped closer to Carlie's bed. "Do you realize how many patients I've treated who claim to have messages from God or Satan, or to be God or Satan? I haven't treated you any differently than any other patient. I'm concerned that the hallucinations you experienced when you were delirious with sepsis have become more real than reality to you now. My goal is for you to be able to distinguish reality and to respond to it appropriately."

"Hey, he's really trying to be compassionate," the invisible Jesus commented. "Since he hasn't seen me, you can't blame him for his perception of reality."

Yeah, he's a real jewel. So now what? I'm heading to Terrell anyhow; does it even matter what I do or say at this point?

"It absolutely does. Think of me as your lawyer. Don't say anything without consulting me."

Trust you, not myself.

"Correct."

Dr. White touched Carlie's shoulder. Both doctors stared at her expectantly. "You're so quiet," Dr. White observed. "Tell us what you're thinking."

Like that's gonna happen.

"Be civil. Stick with thinking about going to Terrell, saying good-bye to people here."

"I, uh, I thought I'd be here longer. I guess I forgot about Terrell."

Dr. Manuel raised a curious eyebrow. "Okay, you have no questions for me? I mean, about who I am or what happened?"

"No, I can't think of anything," Carlie answered somberly. "I just dread Terrell."

Dr. White shifted and straightened his back. "Well, Dr. Manuel Garcia, thanks for clearing everything up. Carlie, I'll see you again before you go. If you feel like you are about to escalate out of control, please ask the staff to help you."

Saxophone Blues

Taylor slipped out of Paul's office with slumped shoulders and red, moist eyes. Her right hand trembled ever-so-slightly as it clutched a sheet or two of paper. She took a deep breath and whispered to Jeffrey that he could take his turn.

For the second time that day, Jeffrey didn't know what came over him. He felt strangely protective of Taylor, whether to shield her from the jerk who used her as a punching bag or set straight the intrusive therapist who'd obviously distressed her. Maybe he just wanted to compensate for not protecting Leah, to somehow atone for his lack of foresight and set things right again.

Whatever the case, he reached out to her. "What's wrong?" he asked softly. "Did Paul say something to upset you?"

Taylor shook her head. "He just put me in touch with a lady from Genesis who prepared me...told me the truth about, about what I need to do, how to get help leaving my husband and getting a safety plan in place. I'm forced to give up so much to make sure he doesn't find me. It's just a lot..." Her voice trailed off.

"Can I help?" Again, his words escaped his lips before he had a chance to rein them in.

Paul stood in the doorway and announced that he was ready for Jeffrey. Jeffrey nodded at Paul and slid past Taylor. "I'll see you later." He sank into the leather armchair in front of the mahogany desk and prepared to be grilled.

Paul leaned back comfortably in his chair and laced his fingers in front of his ample belly. "How are you doing today?"

Jeffrey scowled. *What kind of question is that? He knows about Leah. He knows I'm despondent beyond words to the point of being incapacitated with gut-wrenching depression. Is that what he wants to hear? How sorry my life is? How sorry I am as a man?* He held his throbbing head in his left hand with his elbow propped on the arm of the chair. *Might as well get this over with.*

"I'm so depressed that I can't even see straight, but you know why I'm here. You know that my fiancée died in a car accident. You even know the circumstances about it being late at night after a long road trip, how she dropped me off at my house in Dallas before continuing to her apartment in Denton. She shouldn't have been driving, but I neglected to intervene. I should have insisted on driving her home. Leah was the best thing that ever happened to me, and I screwed up."

Paul stayed totally still as though he didn't want to stop the flow of words coming from his previously mute patient, but after a sizable gap in the conversation, he made some pointless observation. Jeffrey, submerged in his own thoughts, only heard Paul's voice like white noise in the background. Another five or six minutes of silence passed. They were getting nowhere fast.

That's when Paul reached over and unlocked a cabinet. "Your sister, the one who's a cardiologist, thought this might help." He reached deep into the cabinet's highest shelf. "Of course, I can't let you take it outside this office, and you can use it only with supervision." He pulled out a black case that Jeffrey instantly recognized.

"My saxophone?"

Paul nodded and set it down in front of Jeffrey. "She said music came to you easier than words."

Jeffrey opened the case and cradled his sax. Memories of playing for Leah made him sigh sadly. Sweet Leah. Beautiful Leah. He could see her smile and the twinkle in her chocolate eyes. He longed to touch her cheeks, kiss her lips and hold her tightly. He found himself in another time. And for a moment, time stood still. His wounded heart drank in Leah's love.

He automatically reached for his mouthpiece and popped it into place, closed his eyes and blew out a soulful bluesy tune that left Paul speechless. He hadn't played since the funeral three months ago, but the music flowed fluidly, proving to be just the catharsis that his soul yearned for, and he poured all his broken spirit into his song. His sorrow found its voice, crying and moaning through syncopated rhythm that caught the therapist off guard and drew anyone who could hear it.

Out in the hallway patients started to gather, spellbound by the artistic expression of emotion coming from Paul's office.

Carlie had just left her room after meeting a very human Dr. Manuel Garcia who may have been a top-notch surgeon, but he didn't hold a candle to Dr. Emmanuel. *Yeah, he knows he isn't God, but he thinks he saved my life. I know the truth. I saw the one who snatched me from the exit door.* She mulled over what he said about most surgeons thinking that they are gods, but not him. *And yet he took credit for what Jesus did.*

She stopped in her tracks when she heard music that seemed to capture her feelings beautifully. She sat on the floor leaning against the wall opposite Paul's office and closed her eyes to shut out the other patients who lingered around. *It doesn't matter what he or Dr. White think. It doesn't matter that I'm going to Terrell.* She drank in the mournful notes.

I hurt so much; I don't even know why I'm crying. I trust you, Jesus. I need you. Maybe it's just this song. Maybe it's facing the unknown. Maybe I just don't know up from down.

Well, Jesus, this seems as good as anywhere to begin figuring out how I'm going to move forward. I guess a good place to start would be learning from my past mistakes. Like how I distrusted you, thinking I was hallucinating, and was miserable, but recently I've started having faith. Truthfully it is such a relief to share everything with you and rely on you. I'm so sorry it's taken me this long to give this messed up wreck of a life over to you. Take me and do something with me. I can't make it without you.

Now Dr. White and this other Dr. Manuel have this perfectly logical explanation for everything I saw and heard. They don't know I still hear your voice...well, I don't exactly hear with my ears but inside my head...and my heart. I may be as dysfunctional as the day is long, but now I have you to coach me.

You warn me when I need to chill, and you keep making it simple for me, reminding me to just trust you. I know I'm not trusting in a delusion or hallucination or product of a delirious mind. I'm getting to know you.

The formerly forlorn melody coming from Paul's office gave way to a very hopeful hymn that Carlie recognized from her stay with some old-school foster parents who used to sing church hymns to her, trying to calm her down. This hymn was Ms. Momma's favorite. She would lift her arms toward heaven and joyfully sing "It is well with my soul." The words of the chorus lifted Carlie's mood considerably. *No matter what's ahead, it IS well with my soul.*

Carlie couldn't remember much about that foster family. It was her first placement, when Child Protective Services removed her from the murder scene. She didn't stay there long, just a few months before and during her initial evaluations—the ones that ended up with her getting put in therapy where she drew pictures of everything that happened in her life. The more she drew the more the adults pursed their lips and very seriously told her what a fine job she did, but she didn't feel good at all about her drawings. She felt angry, dirty, ashamed and worthless. Everything she drew just brought the memories back and reinforced the horrible lessons she'd learned in her early childhood. Lessons that little girls were meant to be abused. Lessons not to trust anyone.

Then she'd come home from therapy and Ms. Momma would sing, and she'd feel better for a while. After just a few months of getting settled into her first stable environment, the smart people at CPS decided that she needed to be in a big city where experts could help even more, though for the life of her Carlie couldn't see where they'd helped with all the drawings.

Carlie clutched her knees to her chest, buried her face and let the tears flow. Ms. Momma wouldn't have ridiculed her for talking to Jesus, not like the experts who once again were shipping her off to another facility.

"I know you hurt, and I'm here for you." Jesus always understood.

Then Carlie felt a hand on her shoulder and sensed someone sitting beside her. Taylor's grim, tear-streaked face spoke volumes.

"I made the first call. It's in process."

Carlie nodded and put her arm around her friend. At least hurting together wasn't as bad as hurting alone.

Taylor and Carlie compared notes. Taylor planned on being discharged to an abused women's shelter where she would continue to receive counseling and assistance getting back on her feet during her divorce. She would have to be transferred from the elementary school where she taught last year to somewhere her husband wouldn't find her. She sighed. She wouldn't even be able to say good-bye to her coworkers. Her red eyes brimmed over with a fresh wave of sorrow, and her voice wavered briefly.

"I...I have to change my name and everything while he's still in jail for beating me up. Eventually he'll get out, and Taylor Whitehouse won't exist anymore. I can't even go back to my maiden name. Who will I be? It's so crazy overwhelming. I have to find another name that I can get used to."

Carlie scrunched up her forehead. "What was your maiden name?"

"Gilchrist. Why?

Hmm. Gilchrist, Gilchrist. Maybe something similar but different?"

"Not too similar. He might figure it out."

"Gill...Jill...Jillian. Christ as in the Christ? Christine. Jillian Christine. You could go by Jill."

"Jill? Simple but kind of elegant if you don't start that whole Jack and Jill thing. Christine for a middle name?" Taylor asked.

Carlie nodded and grinned. "You could make Taylor your last name. It's common enough that it wouldn't stand out, and if someone called you Taylor and you turned around, you'd have a simple explanation. I doubt that he'd look for someone with the last name of Taylor."

Taylor smiled and brushed her tears away. "I'd get to keep a piece of me, thanks to you." She gave Carlie a quick hug. "You're so quick thinking; I like it!"

The soulful saxophone's last note drifted into silence, and the hallway audience applauded as a sheepish-looking Jeffrey emerged from Paul's office. Carlie's mouth gaped. "That was you?" She noticed tears in the eyes of some of the other patients as they thanked him for the way he touched them so deeply, but true to Jeffrey's normal form, he backed away without making eye contact or saying a word.

"That was beautiful!" Taylor exclaimed, hot on his heels, determined not to let him get away that easily. "What other talents are you hiding?"

Jeffrey hung his head and began retreating down the hall at a quicker pace. Carlie grabbed Taylor's arm. "I don't think he's up to talking. Playing like that—well—it had to take something out of him. He put way too much feeling into those songs; let him rest. We can chill in the day room for a while."

That's when a sick premonition gripped Carlie. She could see Patty coming her way, grimly clutching her cell phone and locking eyes with her. Carlie froze.

Patty summoned. "I need to show you something." She glanced at Taylor. "In private. Let's go to your room."

Carlie remembered seeing Patty with her cell phone only once, and that happened back when she was supposedly delirious hooked up to intravenous antibiotics. Still, there could only be one thing on that cell phone that Patty would show her. Her heart sank with the memory. *Help, Jesus! I trust you. I trust you.*

See, I have no choice but to trust you. Where else can I turn? She followed Patty like a condemned woman being led to the gallows.

As they entered her room, Patty tried to explain. "I just saw this. Liz brought it to my attention, and I knew I had to show it to you. Let me say that this is going to be upsetting, so if you think you'll need medication first, I'll be glad to give you something."

"I already know," she said flatly. "It's my father; he's appealing his conviction, isn't he?"

Patty looked surprised. "Did you see it on TV?"

"No," Carlie replied. "You showed me while I was unconscious. I mean, in my vision or whatever. You came to me with your cell phone, and we talked about me having to tell the truth. Jesus said the truth would set me free. I don't know how, and it certainly makes no sense to me, but I know I have to trust him because I for sure can't trust me."

Patty squeezed her hand. "I'll be praying for you."

Transition

Numbness settled in like a dense fog, muting any emotional reaction from Carlie, a much different response than the staff expected as evidenced by how frequently they crept up beside her as if walking through a mine field and asked how she felt.

"I don't feel anything...nothing at all," she replied every time. Only Patty got a different answer, because Patty—oddly enough— happened to be the only nurse who believed that she truly had a mystical out-of-body experience with God. Only Patty understood that Carlie already knew about the appeal and what she had to do.

Taylor knocked on Carlie's door the next day. "Time for breakfast," she announced, "and I have news. Paul and whoever that social worker is—I don't remember her name—already met with me this morning. They have everything ready for my discharge today. Can you believe it?"

"Oh, that was fast." Carlie emerged from her room and headed down to the dining room with her friend.

As they picked up their trays, Taylor nodded toward Jeffrey sitting alone. "Let's join him." Before Carlie could protest, Taylor hastened to his table and asked if they could sit with him this morning.

Amazingly enough, he made eye contact and nodded. Whatever happened yesterday to break through his protective shell still seemed to be in effect. Carlie strategically made her way to the chair next to Taylor to make discussion of their discharge plans easier.

"Good morning, Jeffrey. How are you today?" Taylor looked at Jeffrey expectantly.

Impatient to get on with the important stuff, Carlie opened her mouth to get the ball rolling. Just because he sat more upright and nodded in response to Taylor's question didn't mean he was ready for meaningful dialogue.

"I'm depressed, but I guess I'm better after getting to play my sax yesterday. I hope Paul lets me play again today."

"That would be great if he let you play it during one of our group sessions. Let's see after goals group we have medication review with the charge nurse followed by coping skills. Then lunch and OT, and after that, I'll be discharged. Do you think he'd let you play for coping skills? It seems like a great coping skill to me." Taylor grinned. "I believe your music touched everyone who heard it—you know—on a very deep level."

Carlie couldn't believe what she was hearing. Men were the enemies, period; no discussion. Surely Taylor, of all people, should appreciate that simple fact. Did she forget that easily? Just because Jeffrey came across as a deeply wounded soul didn't mean she should forge some sort of bond with him.

"Thank you for your kind words," Jeffrey replied.

Yeah, I bet he's eating up all the praise he can get. Go ahead and feed his ego.

"I only spoke the truth," Taylor continued. "Didn't you find his music soothing and anguished at the same time, Carlie?"

Dumbfounded, Carlie just nodded. She didn't need to say anything more. Besides, she wanted to see where Taylor went with this line of thought.

"I really want to hear you play again before I leave—if that's okay with you." Taylor touched Jeffrey's hand. "It would mean so much to me."

Jeffrey sat even more erect, looking for all the world like a normal guy. Sad, but normal compared to his past appearance as a hollow shell of humanity.

"What time do you have to leave?" Carlie almost choked on her sausage when Jeffrey spoke. How much progress could he make in one day?

"They said that I should get to the women's shelter around three o'clock, so I'll probably leave between two to two thirty."

Carlie finally found her tongue. "And I also will be leaving; they're transferring me to the state looney bin in Terrell. Lucky me." Her tone hinted at bitterness.

"I'll be here for a few more days, at least according to Paul," Jeffrey offered.

"Let's stay in touch," Taylor blurted, "the three of us. I'll have to get a new cell phone number so my ex can't call me, and Carlie won't have access to hers while she's in Terrell."

"I'll give you my number for when I'm out on the streets again," Carlie commented.

JeffreJy found himself once again feeling the need to protect, to atone for past negligence and willingly wrote down his cell number after borrowing a pen and paper from the staff. They finalized the arrangements. Both Taylor and Carlie would keep in touch with Jeffrey, who would pass their new phone numbers on to each other. Only their little circle would share any information. They would have each other's backs.

That afternoon Jeffrey held his head a lot higher as he waved good-bye to Taylor. She cried a river as she headed out the door, while Carlie didn't even sniffle. People came and went in her life; that's what they did. It would be a miracle if these two came through and contacted her occasionally, maybe a monthly phone call and annual Christmas cards at best.

Again, the staff swooped in to check on her. Somehow, they didn't seem real, though. In fact, Carlie felt like a spectator looking at a curious play with unfamiliar actors playing disjointed parts in a badly written script. The events unfolding in front of her didn't really seem to pertain to her at all. Only the voice in her head that kept guiding her kept her on the track of seeming normalcy.

Time to eat. Brush your teeth. Pack your clothes. Go see Dr. White.

Even Dr. White looked suspiciously like a fictitious character acting stiffly in his performance of a mediocre psychiatrist. He went through the motions of asking how she'd slept, how she was coping with news about her father, and if she felt ready to go to Terrell.

So, Patty must have told him. And since when does anyone feel ready to go to Terrell? No one gets there by choice; it always involves court commitment, so what kind of stupid question is that? She numbly muttered, "fine", "fine", and "yes" at the appropriate times. *This play-acting is boring and a waste of time and energy. I'm only ready to move on in order to get Terrell out of the way, so I can get my freedom back.*

"Not so quickly," Jesus warned. "You still need to get real with me about the storm within."

What storm? I don't feel a storm. In fact, I don't feel anything.

"That's only temporarily. Just because you don't feel it doesn't mean it isn't happening. Hold onto Me as tightly as you can; the turbulence is about to hit."

Dr. White jotted something down and stared at his oblivious patient. "Where are you right now? Carlie? What are you thinking?"

Carlie looked straight at him but showed no recognition that he talked to her. *Why does this man want to know what I'm thinking? How on earth would it benefit me to let him inside my mind? Trust is not an option, not with him of all people. He's plainly as fake as they come.*

Her eyes locked in on his perfectly aligned and oh-so-white chompers. *Braces, I bet. Braces for a crooked man to have straight teeth.*

"I'll make a straight path for you. Follow me."

Okay, Jesus. Forge ahead. I'm with you. Me and all my baggage.

"Give it to Me."

What?

"The baggage. The fear, the dread, the anger and resentment. Give it all to Me."   *I thought I did that already.*

"Do it again. Do it every day, every hour, every minute."

Every second?

"Absolutely."

Dr. White stood and opened the door. Carlie didn't hear a word he said, but Patty came and gave her a shot in each arm while Carlie sat as still as stone.

206

The only person she saw after that was Jeffrey. He looked so far away, but he tried to tell her something. His voice got lost somewhere in the cacophony of unreal conversations with random medical words being flung about solemnly. Jeffrey made a gesture of talking on a phone. Carlie nodded, and the doors of the psychiatric unit opened.

Carlie must have slept soundly, because she didn't even remember the trip to Terrell. She simply awakened to echoes bouncing off the institution's barren walls. The staff ushered her into a warm shower, where she scrubbed and dressed in fresh clothes before being escorted to the cafeteria. The food tasted about as savory as cardboard, and the sea of expressionless faces around her told her that they had become mere puppets, medicated and mindless souls bound to sallow flesh. Then the endless interrogations began.

Name? Carlie Sweetwater. Where was she? At Terrell State Hospital. Date? No, thanks, she wanted to wait for the right man to come along. That answer retrieved a slight smile from the staff ever so briefly before they continued to probe. Did she hear or see anything that no one else seemed to hear or see? She truthfully couldn't tell what anyone else heard or saw. Did she entertain any thoughts of suicide? Absolutely not. Had she come up with any suicide plans or have any intentions to do so? No, not now; not the slightest. Was she still receiving messages from Jesus or Dr. Emmanuel?

She grimaced and held her aching head. "Dr. Manuel, the surgeon at Parkland, operated on me, didn't he? I mean he doesn't practice here, too, does he? I haven't seen him since I left Parkland."

"And what about Jesus?" asked her new psychiatrist who introduced himself as Dr. Paul Patel.

Carlie looked up as the voice within told her very plainly that He was still with her. She opened her mouth and amazed herself at what came out. "If you mean the Son of God, yeah. I'm a Christian, so I believe He is always with me. You know, I am entitled to my religious beliefs even in the nut hut."

The new psychiatrist with a foreign accent and dark skin smiled. "Yes, yes, you may continue to believe; this is true, but do you see Him or hear His voice. Does He have special messages just for you?"

"Let Me take this," Jesus intervened.

Again, the words just flowed seamlessly from Carlie. "I don't hear an actual voice or see His being, but by faith I experience Him. I am prompted by His Spirit, which is why I am no longer suicidal. I belong to Him. I have a purpose now. How about you?"

The psychiatrist's smile grew broader. "I also am Christian, and yes, I also have purpose." He tapped his desk thoughtfully. "How is your mood?"

"What mood? I'm too medicated to feel anything."

"Good point. I will take you off the antipsychotics, and we will monitor you for any difficulties. If you have problems, you will tell the nurse, right?"

"Sure."

The next few days Carlie spent coming out of the mental haze, but that didn't make adjusting to the state hospital easy. For one thing, the same psychiatrist acted like a completely different doctor the following day.

He waved her into his office and cracked a clever grin. "Now the antipsychotic medication has been discontinued, and you are thinking clearer, right?"

Carlie nodded and settled into the chair facing him. She didn't know what to expect, but an ominous feeling came over her.

"Be careful," Jesus warned. "Keep quiet and listen to me."

Dr. Peter Patel leaned forward with his elbows resting on his desk. "So now we find out what is really happening in your head. What does Jesus tell you now?"

"Now?" Carlie paused as if listening. "Nothing."

"You don't hear him?" His voice contained the distinct tinge of disbelief that Carlie had encountered many times in her journey through various hospitals. He picked up his pen and looked expectantly at her like she might start levitating at any given moment.

Again, she hesitated. "No."

"Do you see him, maybe wearing a scrub suit and posing as a doctor?"

She couldn't help but snicker. "No."

His bushy eyebrows arched. "Is this funny to you? After all, you told the staff at Parkland that you saw Jesus dressed as a doctor and had many conversations with him."

Carlie felt like prey being stalked by a stealthy cougar. She could sense in his eyes that he readied himself to pounce. "No, it's not funny."

"Then you think this is a plausible sighting?" His eyes bored into her without blinking.

She shifted into the chair. What had she done to deserve this? She had followed the rules. There hadn't been any melt downs, no trips to seclusion, no angry sparring with the staff. She had been lying low, trying to fly under the radar, get out as quickly as possible to get on with her own life...to face whatever legal crap awaited her. In her mind, she found Terrell just a pit stop, only an inconvenience on her way out of the system, and she merely had to play it cool and not draw too much attention to herself.

"It sounds downright crazy to me," she blurted, remembering how she'd reacted when she first saw Jesus.

"Does it? So, were you crazy when you were in Parkland, but now you aren't? Is this what you're trying to tell me?" He scribbled something down.

Carlie rubbed her forehead. *Where are you, Jesus? You told me to listen, to trust You. Every minute, every second, give it to You. I feel like this guy is trying his best to get me to look mentally cuckoo, so this would be a good time for You to jump right in with some of Your special insight.*

Still nothing from Jesus. Just this insidious doctor in this dull, little office.

"Well, I am waiting for an answer if you aren't too busy with internal dialog," he quipped.

"Internal…"

"You know, the conversation you are having in your head. Do you need me to repeat my question?"

Carlie nodded warily. *So much for I'm a Christian, too.*

"You're basically telling me that you became mentally insane, psychotic, crazy while at Parkland, but you've regained your sanity here." It sounded much more like a statement than a question.

Carlie crossed her arms defensively and leaned back in her chair. "Surely, they told you that they resuscitated me when I came into the ER, and they kept me on a ventilator in ICU while being in a coma. Then I almost died again when I became septic. And I'm sure they told you I had delirium because of the sepsis, and so I guess that's why I haven't seen Jesus since I woke up in ICU." There. How much plainer could it be?

"You didn't see him in the psychiatric unit?"

"No." She shifted in her chair.

"Or hear him speak to you?"

She sighed. "I'm not hearing any voices. I thought I explained this a few days ago. It's more like a spiritual insight or message, not something I hear with my ears."

Dr. Patel scribbled briefly. "You let me know if you do hear a voice."

"Sure," Carlie promised with her voice, but her mind screamed that she should never volunteer any information to this man. What was his deal? Did he have multiple personalities or something? She couldn't exactly put her finger on what went wrong between her first session and today, with him acting as fickle as they came. It struck her that most psychiatrists probably entered the field because they themselves were not quite right, but this guy seemed so sinister and two-faced that he almost made Dr. White look like a compassionate, well-meaning doctor.

The Storm

Pressure built in Carlie's head as her stomach churned furiously. She glared at the carbon pork chop, bland macaroni and cheese and limp green beans that passed for lunch. It looked like tasteless crap and tasted even worse than it looked. She shoved the offensive tray out of her way. Maybe the table was slippery, or she put a little too much anger into her shove, but—for whatever reason—the tray slid over the edge and met the floor with a clatter.

The drug-laden patients around her turned zombie-like in unison to look. An odd, skinny woman missing most of her teeth started chanting, "It's the fall, not the summer, not the summer of love, and I'll ride my love bug into the winter as wars wage and boys age and lads become men. Do it again and again." She rambled on with the sort of psychotic nonsense that belonged at a state mental facility, yet it only seemed to agitate the rest of the population.

A huge mammoth of a man covered in tattoos of skulls pounded his tray with his fist, sending macaroni and green beans flying. Another patient, a young man with jet black hair cut down to his scalp on one side and hanging in his eyes on the other let, out a loud whoop and threw the entire contents of his plate against the wall. Some guy who looked to be in his thirties put a spin on his plate and sent it flying like a Frisbee across the room, hitting a middle-aged woman whose irritable expression conveyed that she wouldn't tolerate being messed with. She picked up her plate and charged the offender.

From Carlie's one simple action, a riot broke out in the dining room. Food flew everywhere, and someone cried out that she'd been cut by broken glass. The staff came running over to contain the trouble makers and get the other patients into the day room next door. Carlie decided to slip out with the more docile patients to avoid what would surely come next, so she pulled some macaroni out of her hair and beat a quick retreat.

"Murderer!" shrieked the nearly toothless woman, pointing a bony finger at Carlie. "Don't let her near the baby. Help! HEELLLP!" she wailed, her hand trembling as she continued pointing at Carlie.

That just did it. Carlie already had her hands full dealing with a sneaky snake of a psychiatrist and an upcoming trial, not to mention being separated from her first good friend in like forever. Plus, she would have to testify about the fact that she—not Daddy—accidentally killed her baby brother. She had a hard-enough time thinking about it, much less having to tell her story in a courtroom where lawyers would analyze and question everything she said. With everything she dealt with, she didn't need some looney old hag yelling that she was a murderer.

"Shut up," she snapped. "You're crazy, and no one likes crazy."
I ought to know; that's why I find myself here, alone...again.

"Have you forgotten that I'm with you?" The voice seemed far away.

"Then why am I stuck here? What did I do to deserve this? I was just a kid trying to survive a messed-up childhood. This sucks. My whole life pretty much sucks. So, there you have it. One step forward, two steps back. Is that what you had in mind for me? What do you want from me? I've tried. I've really tried. They all just want to sabotage me, make me think I'm crazy. Well, I'm not! I'M. NOT. CRAZY. Period. Any questions?" Carlie hadn't realized she literally screamed these words until she saw everyone staring at her. Then a nurse came at her with a couple of syringes.

"Heaven forbid I should have any thoughts or feelings! Medicate the snot right out of me. Here." She pulled up her sleeve and offered her arm. "Harmonious living through Haldol; achieve more through Ativan and better yourself with Benadryl. That's the magic cocktail, right? That's the psych answer for everything."

A muscular male tech held her hands while the nurse gave the two shots. Carlie's verbal floodgates had already opened wide, and she showed no intention of slowing her torrential outpouring of anger, medicated or not. She let the tech lead her to a quiet room while she ranted and railed at the entire hospital staff.

"Yeah, just play mind games with me. Lock me up, shoot me full of drugs, treat me like I'm nothing. That's all I am to you, an inconvenient piece of trash. This place is a joke; there's no help, no hope of getting better in a place like this. Now let go of me." She shoved the tech aside and plopped down on the bed.

"Go on and gloat," she growled. "Aren't you the big man? I bet you get off on this sort of thing, don't you?"

He glared but said nothing as he backed up to the doorway and let the nurse in. Both looked so ridiculously somber that Carlie burst into laughter, leaving them speechless.

Carlie sneered, "Oh, aren't you two the power couple! You can bully a psych patient and somehow manage to chart everything so it will look like I'm crazy instead of you. And Dr. Patel is crazier than any of us, and you can tell him I said that. Oh, and be sure he knows that I'm eventually getting out of here and telling the world what he's putting me through. Tell him…"

"Which Dr. Patel?" asked the nurse.

Carlie lifted her head from the pillow. "What are you talking about? Of course, the Dr. Patel who is treating me." Then she mumbled under her breath, "Are you really that stupid?" and rolled over.

But the nurse didn't go away. "Before you go to sleep, I need to explain why we had to medicate you."

"Oh, goody, like I haven't heard this speech before." Sarcasm dripped from her voice.

"Well, you may at least be interested in knowing that there are two Dr. Patels, twin brothers named Peter and Paul. You have talked with both. Didn't you notice their first names were different? They always introduce themselves as Peter or Paul Patel."

Carlie turned and propped herself up on her elbows. Her head already felt woozy. "Twin brothers?"

The nurse nodded. "You aren't the first to confuse them, so I thought it might be helpful to explain who they are. Even though they use their full names, many patients just see what they think is the same person and overlook the difference."

Even through the descending Haldol fog Carlie could hear the quiet voice inside her spirit. "She is doing you a favor, you know."

Carlie grimaced at the nurse. "Thanks a lot for not pointing out this little fact until I totally freaking lost it. This place is crazier than I'll ever be."

The nurse's jaw tightened. "Well since you started a food fight and frightened all the other patients by screaming and acting in a hostile manner, we had to intervene with an emergent med."

"To shut up the looney tune. Besides, I didn't start the food fight." Carlie clenched her fist. *So, you think that was me being hostile? Just come over here and I'll show you hostile.*

"Don't do it," warned the inner voice.

The nurse looked only mildly annoyed as she continued her monologue. "We can unlock the door when you show calm, cooperative and nonthreatening behavior; then…"

"Just shut the hell up and get out of my hair. I'm a professional psych patient, so I've heard this canned speech before. Besides, I let you give me the shots, and I walked down here and didn't even fight back."

"You pushed me," Big Man grumbled.

"And you were in my personal space, so get over it," she snapped.

The tech's eyes grew narrow and his muscles tensed. "You don't get to shove people in here." He stepped closer.

"Oh, come on over here, Mr. Big Man. You think you can intimidate me? Huh?" she screamed.

The nurse held up her hand authoritatively. "Stop," she commanded sternly, and the tech froze. "We won't feed into this sort of behavior. Good night." She disappeared behind the thick wooden door with the tiny snoop-hole plexiglass window, through the toilet room and into the hall, and the tech followed suit except that he stopped outside the first door and stood guard.

"I see your dog is well trained," Carlie yelled. Deep inside she knew that she wasn't helping her cause, but she felt way too angry to care. She'd deal with the aftermath tomorrow.

It must have been midnight when Carlie woke up with a full bladder, but at least she awakened in time to keep her bed dry. She wearily sat up on the bed and tried to focus on her surroundings. In the dark, barren room a little light from the hallway lingered around the small window as if it was afraid to come in and illuminate the entire room. She could discern the shadow of someone lurking behind the door, watching her every move. These psychiatric facilities always treated her like this when she got locked up in seclusion. Someone would be posted at the door, probably just to mess with her head since someone else monitored her by camera. Anyway, whatever the rationale, these methods appeared to be standard with every psychiatric hospital that she had "visited". None of them showed much originality in their methodology. She sat up.

"Oh, great, another seclusion room," she muttered to herself. She began waving to the unseen staff member who would be watching the camera monitor. Nothing happened, so she stumbled over to the door and gave a test. Still locked. She began knocking. "I gotta go pee," she yelled.

A scrawny woman dressed in green scrubs and a sweater motioned to someone down the hall before answering Carlie. "Just a moment; I'll get someone." She sounded nervous, so Carlie guessed that she might be new.

"Hurry, or there's gonna be a mess on the floor." She couldn't help but grin to herself. She knew how to make the staff about as miserable as she felt.

The wooden door creaked open, and Carlie managed to navigate her way to the toilet in the seclusion anteroom with minimal stumbling. The two techs who guarded her stepped back, blocking the exit door after she landed on the commode with a thud. Just as she reached to flush, she heard the footsteps of yet another person approaching, probably a nurse. They always showed up to assess how explosive their patient was once she awakened from the good-night juice.

She bolted back to the bed, ignoring the groaning of the door and the approaching footsteps, and pulled the blanket over her head.

"We need to talk," a masculine voice said.

Carlie peered out from her blanket. "So, talk."

He turned the light on, blinding her. She closed her eyes.

"Sit up and look at me," he commanded.

"The light's too bright and I'm too tired. Just say what you gotta say."

"No, I want to make sure there is no misunderstanding. I want eye contact in the light where I can see you, so the question is if you're going to cooperate." His tone conveyed the expectation that she should comply.

Carlie instantly knew he meant business, but she felt much too sedated and not in the mood to look into the light and maybe still a tad miffed at the stupid twin doctors for tricking her. She sat upright in bed, popped her eyes open and blasted, "Just what the hell do you want? I'm fine if you stop screwing with me. What the..."

"Enough. Apparently, you aren't ready for the door to be unlocked." He turned and closed the thick door behind him.

Carlie heard the lock thud into place and some not-so-hushed tones talking about how much hostility she possessed. Carlie grinned and rolled over. In less time than it took for her to come up with a snarky comment, she fell back to sleep.

Going Nowhere Fast

Morning brought the day shift faces—nurses, techs, and Dr. Peter from the Patel clan of human vermin. Carlie found that her mood hadn't become any more charitable than during yesterday's explosion, so she let loose on anyone and everyone who came into the seclusion room. She even lunged at the not-so-good doctor in a furious attempt to get her hands around his neck. She immediately got subdued and shot up with the good stuff.

The medication only gave the staff temporary breaks from her outbursts. Jesus' prediction about the upcoming storm found fulfillment each time Carlie regained consciousness. Since her drug-induced slumber only lasted six to eight hours before her bladder awakened her, she would open her eyes briefly to assess her environment before wailing and screaming at the tops of her lungs. In fact, the force of her rage hit her so hard that she feared her head would explode.

Why am I still here? I had the perfect plan, and I did everything right even after Emily screwed everything up for me. I can't take it anymore...not one more day, not one more insincere doctor or nurse or horrible hospital. Let me out of here. Please, God, let me go. There's no point to my life, no point at all. Surely, you see what a mess I am. Put an end to me. PLEASE!

Then the next person would venture in to assess her, and she would lash out again. Night, day, night; time marched past in the same endless cycle. Torture, every second bringing searing pain to her entire soul. Sorrow, anguish, regret, loneliness, anger and, yes, not-so-quiet despair. Tears and cursing gushed like a river at flood stage, roaring and spilling over the natural boundaries of human emotion.

She tried banging her head on the wall and got restrained for her efforts. Now she felt even more trapped than ever before. She gasped and sputtered, spitting at the staff whenever they inched closer and cursed the day she was born. The staff gathered outside her door and conferred in hushed tones. When would she wear herself out?

Dr. Paul Patel pulled up a chair beside her bed. "You are clearly deeply distressed. The level of your suffering tells me that you can't handle it any more, at least not on your own. What can I do to help you?"

Hoarse from weeping and wailing for the past hour, Carlie only whispered, "Let me go."

Dr. Patel rubbed his chin thoughtfully. "Judging from your behavior, I fear for your safety. I can't just let you go, not until you can show me that you aren't a danger to yourself or anyone else. What are you willing to do to show me that you won't hurt anyone?"

Carlie had no answer. She just let out a soft moan. Her head throbbed, and her throat felt raw from shrieking and bellowing like someone possessed. Her stomach churned, and she felt utterly weary.

Dr. Patel didn't back off. "You told me once about your faith, but all I see now is fear. Even if you don't trust me or my brother or any of the nurses or therapists here, tap into what helped you at Parkland. I read their report. You showed real progress. Let's go back to what worked for you there."

Unfortunately, Carlie didn't hear Jesus speak any words of calm assurance. She only felt turmoil and a deep sense of shame. She failed once again. She did have something good, but she simply couldn't hang on to it. Then, again, if she couldn't hang onto it, was it even real? Dr. White thought she hallucinated. Dr. Manuel, the surgeon, blamed her delirious state for confusing him for the Son of God. Only Patty believed her—Patty and Taylor.

How she missed Taylor! She'd even settle for talking with Patty right now! *Wait. How did I know about Patty's scar and Dad's appeal? Those were realities, not hallucinations or delusions. But how could things go this wrong? I mean, I said I trusted Jesus. I thought I trusted him. How could he let things get so out-of-control?* She groaned again.

"I'm still here. Remember that you have to look for Me."

"Please just let me die. Don't keep me trapped..."—sob— "in this"—sniffle—"vicious cycle." More sobs made her attempts to talk coherently an exercise in futility, and the river of tears saturated her pillow case.

Dr. Patel shook his head solemnly. "We can't just let you die, even though your pain is great. We have to help you heal."

Dr. Emmanuel's voice sounded like it came from somewhere far away, though it whispered inside her spirit. "Yes, there really is healing, and you were on the right path before this setback.

Remember how it felt? Remember being loved and being able to give your burden to me?"

Snot mingled with tears on Carlie's face, but with her restrained hands plastered at her sides, she strained to wipe her face on her shoulder. As he turned to leave, Dr. Patel motioned to Big Man, who didn't appear impressed with Carlie's display of distress at all. He came at her with a cold, wet washcloth and firmly rubbed her face down, holding it over her mouth and nose just long enough to let her know he held power over her, and he wasn't to be messed with. Dr. Patel had already slipped out, promising that they would talk later when she behaved more calmly, so he didn't witness Big Man using excessive force.

In a flash, Carlie visualized this brute suffocating her. She sensed his anger and resentment and instantly knew how to use it. Big Man's hand covered her nose and mouth, so she bit him. Retribution came immediately as he squeezed her throat until she blacked out.

She couldn't see the other staff rushing in to pull Big Man off her. Carlie only knew that when she woke up, someone had taken her out of restraints, and her fierce foe had disappeared from her doorway. A young Filipino nurse hastily told her to return to her regular room and admonished her not to attack anyone else.

However, Carlie had no intention of budging so quickly. "Hey, you're supposed to process this whole incident with me. You know that I'm aware of how things happen on a psych unit. I want to know why I'm being released."

The petite nurse leaned against the wall. "You bit Bret, and he restrain you. You get injured as you fight him."

Carlie laughed and sat straight up. "Let's get this right: I bit him while in restraints, so he held me down even though restraints already seriously restricted any movement on my part, yet somehow I accidentally injured myself by fighting back? No way. I'll tell you what really happened. Dr. Patel told him to wipe my face, but he pressed down trying to suffocate me, so I bit him in self-defense. Then he strangled me. That's what really happened no matter what he told you." Carlie massaged her neck.

"This is very serious accusation you make." That concerned nurse face showed up again—that same hideous expression of insincerity.

"Yes, and it's my right to report it to Advocacy and Texas Department of Health and hospital administration. I need to use the phone now."

It wasn't an idle bluff; Carlie finally held some leverage, and she determined to play her hand right up until she walked out those doors. While making her phone calls, she noticed that none of the other patients were around, not that it mattered since they probably had to be in therapy of some sort. The scrawny female tech who looked and sounded like a product of rural inbreeding shadowed her in the background trying to act nonchalant.

Carlie growled, "I get to talk in privacy, so get lost."

The tech beat a quick retreat, but hushed voices in the hall suggested that other staff members hovered close by. *They're rattled. Finally, someone is turning the tables on them. Now what was Big Man's real name?*

As soon as she finished her three phone calls, Carlie discovered that her belongings had been packed for her in brown paper sacks so the staff could push her off to a different unit. The nurses and techs offered no explanation other than saying she required "decreased stimulation in a more secure environment". She figured that the real reason must be that they couldn't handle her, especially now that there would be an investigation.

"Well, what environment is more secure than a seclusion room?" she demanded.

They stared at her grimly. "Will you cooperate or not?"

"Okay, I know the real reason. You don't want me here when the investigator comes. I get that. You're in trouble, and you know it, so you want to ship me off, hide the evidence."

Her four escort techs said nothing, so she looked up and down the vacant hallway outside her room. She still didn't see Big Man. She rubbed her neck again for show. "Where's the guy who did this to me?" she demanded.

Her nurse mumbled that she didn't have to worry about him; besides, the time had come for her to go and gave the nod to her accomplices. "Again, I must ask, 'Will you walk with us willingly, or must we restrain you?'"

Carlie didn't want to get tied down again, so she trudged obediently to the next unit, surrounded by her escorts, still plotting what she would say and how she would say it when the investigator questioned her. After all, presentation was key. She needed to earn credibility.

Think, think. The camera! Surely, they recorded Big Man's assault. If a picture's worth a thousand words... But what if they destroy evidence? I've got to get a court-appointed attorney. I can fight this commitment here and get justice.

Thick doors opened to swallow her, and two nurses, one male and one female, along with two similarly diverse techs, ushered her in. They gave brief, to-the-point introductions, not that Carlie would remember their names anyhow. Then they issued a host of instructions that sounded more like commands. First, she must remain in her room at all times until staff deemed her safe to return to a community environment. If she so much as set one foot outside her room, enforcement would be immediate. Meals and therapy would come to her, and if she needed anything she could wave at the camera. There would be no excuses. Did she understand?

The male nurse, Randy, accomplished all the necessary assessments in record time. Carlie knew this, having been well versed in psychiatric admissions. After giving her solemn promise not to hurt herself or anyone else and to let the staff know if she felt violent tendencies rising, the staff left her in quiet solitude.

Now, she took to solitude like a fish takes to water—just her and Jesus and whoever watched the camera. She sighed.

Here we go. You were right. After all, you always are, with you being God and all. It's just that I don't get it. All shades of lunacy came erupting out of me just after I started turning to you and feeling better in the process. I finally had a couple of friends— between you and Taylor. Then I came here and felt utterly abandoned, so I guess my conviction wavered erratically. Your voice became harder for me to hear, and when I did hear you, I didn't like what you told me.

Why couldn't we just be done with it? That would be the humane thing to do. You promised me a spectacular suicide. When do I get what you promised?

"When you surrender everything—all your anger and pain and confusion—and die to yourself completely by living only through me and for me."

I tried. It didn't work.

"It didn't? Or you didn't stay with it? I never break a promise. I have the wisdom and the power to bring true healing and genuine peace to your troubled heart, but you must relinquish your own agenda and preconceived notions and let me take you beyond your imagination according to my plan—not just once or twice but every day. Are you willing to start again with Me today?"

I want to—I really do.

"But you're back to not trusting."

I don't know how.

"Faith—another word for trust—comes from hearing My word. Where's the Bible Patty gave you?"

I don't know, probably in my stuff in one of these paper bags.

"Well, look for it, and look for Me...unless you want to remain miserable—your choice."

Carlie picked through her few articles of clothing and found her Bible. Holding it close to her heart, she closed her eyes to block out the outside world. This time had to be different.

God, I know that I'm sorry. You've been patient with me, trying to guide me, and I've been impatient and obstinate with you. I want to be different, but I don't know how to change, so I need you to work inside me. Otherwise, I don't stand a chance.

They say that this Bible here is your word, and that it's powerful. I'm afraid that I won't be able to understand it, so I'll really need to rely on you there, too.

I don't know why you want me, or what you want to do with me. Please just do what you have to do.

Carlie's First Christmas in August

Lifting the Bible out of the paper sack proved to be the easy part. *Where do you start reading this thing? It's got like sixty-six different books within the book—I remember that from Sunday School—and who can figure out what it means?*

lie opened the brown leather book to somewhere close to the middle and began to read, "Woe to that wreath, the pride of Ephraim's drunkards, to the fading flower, his glorious beauty, set on the head of a fertile valley—to that city, the pride of those laid low by wine!" She scratched her head.

Isaiah 28, verse 1. Oh, yeah, Isaiah belonged to a group of Old Testament prophets. They habitually issued stern warnings and prophecies of doom, didn't they? She shuddered. *Can't see this being helpful.*

Out of curiosity and a smidgen of determination to prove her point about the old prophet's lack of relevance, she flipped some pages and settled on another couple of verses at the end of chapter fifty-seven: "But the wicked are like the tossing sea, which cannot rest, whose waves cast up mire and mud. 'There is no peace,' says my God, 'for the wicked.'"

Carlie tossed it on the bed and leaped to her feet. *Oh, yeah? So, you're calling me wicked 'cause I obviously don't have any peace. Thanks a lot.*

She began to pace around her bed, thoughts swirling rapidly. *I can't go on this way. It seemed better with Jesus before, but I also had Taylor around. Having a friend—it felt good. Even Patty helped—can't believe I'd even think that—but she did help in her own psych nurse way. And, yeah, for once in my life things got better instead of worse... until I came here.*

Here I'm so lonely, but not quite alone. Occasionally I still hear his voice; I hear Dr. Emmanuel—not the surgeon named Manuel, but the one who promised he'd always be with me. I don't get him, though. Why did he let me get lost in all this madness here?

"You're not lost in this place; it is not the issue. The doubt, the rage, the pain—it's all inside you. You're too busy being tuned into your thoughts and feelings, and they're screaming at you so loudly inside your head that you don't hear my voice much anymore." Carlie instantly recognized that this authoritative voice as truth, this message of reason and sanity.

"So how do I get back to listening to your voice? Help me, please. I'm desperate!" She clutched her head with both hands and let the tears flow.

Jesus said, "Look for me, and you will find me."

Is this sort of like hide-and-seek? I don't know. Where do I find Jesus?

 struck. *The New Testament. That's where Jesus showed up in the Bible. That's where I'll find answers. Let me flip over to the back part.* She turned the pages. *Not Hosea, Jonah or Micah. Where does the New Testament start?*

She turned to the end of Malachi, and—lo and behold—a whole page that said nothing other than "The New Testament" greeted her. This must be where the magic words came from, the clues, the formulas that would help her find Jesus and end her suffering by somehow causing her to die to herself. Yes, she'd heard that phrase somewhere before. It must have been in that white, wooden church in that little town, Wills Point, where her first foster parents took her every Sunday. The preacher had grasped the pulpit firmly and admonished his congregation with a quivering voice. She shuddered. Bits and pieces came back to her quite unexpectedly.

Still not feeling it, Jesus. Her eyes rested on the last chapter of Malachi, across from the page announcing the New Testament. "'Surely the day is coming; it will burn like a furnace. All the arrogant and every evildoer will be stubble, and the day that is coming will set them on fire,' says the Lord Almighty. 'Not a root or a branch will be left to them. But for you who revere my name, the sun of righteousness will rise with healing in its rays. And you will go out and frolic like well-fed calves. Then you will trample on the wicked; they will be ashes under the soles of your feet on the day when I act,' says the Lord Almighty."

This is some crazy crap for sure—oh, excuse me, God. I don't mean to say...well, I do have to admit—just being honest—this is more confusing than helpful.

"Keep searching, and you'll keep finding," prompted the inner voice again.

But it all sounds like a bunch of religious jabber, and it's scary with people getting burned up and other people frolicking like calves on their ashes. And I can't get that preacher out of my mind with his pale white skin, shiny bald head and bony fingers that always seemed to point right at me. He looked like the Grim

Reaper in a suit, and I always felt like he accused me of not quite living up to whatever standard of conduct is required of me.

"I'm not condemning you; I'm the One who justifies you. I'm here to make you whole."

Well, why doesn't this Bible just say so? Instead of all this creepy stuff?

Carlie groaned, but—seeing as how she had nothing else to do in her room—she dutifully plunged ahead in reading from the beginning of Matthew. It started out with a list of Jesus' family tree. She only recognized a few names and then got bored. *I don't even want to know my family tree,* she fumed, but then she got to the Christmas story—except it was missing the singing angels and the shepherds. *Wait, what's wrong with this Bible?* She decided on a sneak peek over in Mark, the next book, but since it started off by jumping ahead to John the Baptist preaching, she flipped over to whatever came next.

There it is. Luke. She settled back on her bed, leaning against the wall and plunged into the Christmas story that she remembered, only more. *Didn't recall that part with Zechariah and Elizabeth.* It seemed kind of weird with Zechariah being struck mute and Baby John jumping in Elizabeth's womb at the sound of Mary's voice, but when Joseph and Mary made their journey to Bethlehem and the Baby Jesus lay in a manger with angels singing and shepherds visiting, all felt right with the world.

An inexplicable calm and a sudden interest in reading more took her by surprise. She sensed a different kind of conflict—satisfy her urge for more or sit a spell and soak up the—what was that feeling? It felt like home, a home she'd never had.

"You see that I love you now, don't you?" Jesus asked softly.

The shepherds and the Baby in the manger invited her, and she wanted to crawl into that manger herself to lay down beside the

Baby to touch his little fingers and tell him she loved him and watch his tiny face smiling up at hers. Then she remembered what she read in Matthew about King Herod trying to kill the newborn king.

Whoa, I thought I had it rough. At least no one tried to kill me as an infant. The abuse I suffered started a few years later, I think.

Honestly, she couldn't remember NOT being abused. She shook her head. *I don't want to go there again.*

"But you need to go there to get healing." The answer came in a gentle tone, but it still caused her to grimace.

You sound like Patty. She's always pestering me about dealing with stuff from years ago.

"Maybe Patty sounds like me. Besides, if you can't handle the past, how can you face the future?"

You mean the appeal? I don't even want to think about it. How is that fair? I get abused when I'm a too little to take up for myself, and now I've got to relive all those horrible recollections— all for my abuser's benefit! Where's the justice in that?

Her heart began to race, and her muscles tightened. Carlie dug her fingernails into her baggy jeans and closed her eyes. Instead of visualizing the dark closet, she saw the Christ Child wrapped in swaddling clothes, the way she'd always pictured him, smiling at her, and her heart gratefully slowed.

*Today I'm celebrating Christmas. Today I'm just enjoying your gift, that you came for me. I don't understand it. I just want to...*she inhaled deeply...*breathe it, live it, rejoice in it.* She couldn't believe she'd used the word "rejoice" for the first time ever. It sounded like the correct churchy term, but she'd never experienced any rejoicing, really couldn't be sure what it looked or felt like to rejoice. *Is that okay for me to use that word?*

"Yes, you may rejoice forevermore. This is exactly what I want for you."

Let me just stay in this moment.

There she sat—content, rejoicing even. These emotions she'd heard other people talking about had never belonged to her. She sensed a strangely pleasant emotion caressing her soul. How could this be?

"Stay with me, and I will take care of your past, present and future. Do you believe?"

Right then and there she did believe. She could trust the Baby. Perhaps the Bible held an important key that would enable her to succeed for once in her life. Maybe this could work for her after all. A small flicker of hope, a glimpse of light at the end of the tunnel—however far away—proved to be enough for now. She would make it through this day. She would not succumb to the madness that threatened to consume her.

Preschool Carlie pulled the covers over her and snuggled deeper into her bed for just a few more minutes. She could faintly hear her first foster mom singing, "O, come all ye faithful, joyful and triumphant." A hint of baking chocolate chip cookies tantalized her nostrils. Her senses told her that she had escaped the trauma and terrifying violence, and her foster parents kept her safe for the first time in her short life. Amos, the gentle German Shepherd, burrowed under the quilt and licked her face as a not-too-subtle wake up call. Time to let the goats out of their pen for the day. She giggled and pulled on her cowgirl clothes and a jacket.

Living on a farm contained so much fun. Carlie absolutely adored the momma kitty in the barn with her wandering litter of seven curious fur balls. They explored the back yard fearlessly and pounced upon each other with great glee. As Carlie and

Amos walked over to the goat pen the kittens followed, mewing loudly and holding their flagpole tails up high. The goats greeted Carlie and Amos eagerly, bleating their readiness to satisfy their voracious appetites. They headed out to pasture without much prompting from Amos, who kept a watchful eye on them anyway.

Carlie sat beside the kittens and teased them with a twig, laughing at their antics with great amusement. She'd always wanted a kitten. They possessed a unique blend of cuteness combined with fierce predatory instincts that made them the most amusing animals ever. She picked one up, rubbed his ears, and listened as he purred.

It would be Christmas soon. Foster Mommy promised to make it special for her, baking her favorite cookies, holding her closely while she read the story of the Savior's birth, decorating the entire house with colored lights and holly. The tree towered over any that Carlie had ever seen in her parents' little double wide trailer house, and it was real. It even smelled like the outdoors.

This memory of the best time in her life revived adult Carlie's spirits as it popped into her consciousness. Even back at Ms. Momma and Mr. Papa's house, she suffered from terrifying nightmares, but at least she hadn't been forced to tell and retell her story a million times yet. Sure, she had to tell the police and some lady who was called a social worker her story a couple of times, but they found her this wonderful place to stay. Little Carlie thought that she would be able to forget all the yucky stuff, to enjoy this good feeling forever...this Christmas on a farm feeling. Maybe she'd even live happily every after.

That horrible closet may have been part of a nightmare and nothing more. Everything tended to be spookier in the deep darkness of night. She celebrated daytime, bright and sunny, and maybe—just maybe—the farm would become her only home, meaning that nothing else mattered.

Unfortunately, for some unknown reason, official-looking adults summoned her to their offices and insisted on asking her questions over and over. "Where did your daddy touch you?" "How did he hit your mommy?" "Did you see him hurt your brother?" "How many gunshots did you hear?"

Little Carlie wanted to have nothing to do with those discussions. "No! That is my scary dream. I don't want to play with you; I want to play with the kittens. They don't ask bad questions."

These same adults knowingly told her she could paint and draw and have a good time with them, but she didn't enjoy any of her times with them at all. Not like Christmas at the farm. Oh, they acted very impressed when she painted what they told her— pictures of her bad dream, but she hated those pictures. In fact, those pictures made her feel anxious and angry, and she tried to destroy them several times. Temper tantrums with screaming, crying and throwing crayons followed many of these sessions. Once she even hit the lady who asked her to draw.

She so desperately wanted to get back to the farm, back to kittens and chocolate chip cookies and safety. Her good memories. Her pleasant place.

Adult Carlie opened her eyes. *I did have something good in my life. I usually only remember the crud; that's what haunts me, and that's what all the therapists want to talk to death, but I really did have something...something good. Truly good."*

Brownie Points

It was hot as a Carolina Reaper pepper outside. Even though Carlie had been locked up since her Fourth of July suicide attempt, she could tell the early September sun sizzled everything under its rule. The lawn barely had any green to speak of despite the sprinklers going off in the wee hours of the morning. Carlie shook her head at their futile attempt to keep what landscaping that remained from completely withering up.

Might as well just put in a bunch of cacti and be done with it. Carlie pressed her hand against the very warm glass. It reminded her of how scorched her own life felt. *Ah, air conditioning! How did the settlers ever make it through these 100 plus degree summers? At least I can be glad that I wasn't born back then.*

Since discovering her one happy memory and discussing it with Jesus, Carlie made a point to look for whatever good she could find in her miserable life. So far, she had a very short list, but air conditioning surely made it. *And Taylor. God, I need to thank you for Taylor. I guess I should call her, but that means I'd have to call what's-his-name. Uh, what WAS his name?*

"Jeffrey. You never know; he might become a good friend, too." Jesus tended to be much more optimistic than Carlie.

She just wrinkled up her nose. *Yeah. Well, I'm not seeing it.*

"And you foresaw that you would become good friends with Taylor?"

Okay, I didn't know we'd become as close as we did, but I did feel drawn to her, mostly because she reminded me of my mom. Carlie sighed and became silent even in her head. Her poor battered mom, sweet little doormat who never stood up for herself. Carlie loved her but didn't want to end up like her, so she kept ever vigilant, never trusting.

The sound of a mower outside the window caught her attention. A bronze man wearing a wide straw hat rode the lawnmower slowly back and forth, back and forth. She felt mesmerized. The man and the humming of his mower, the heat waves shimmering upward from the cars in the parking lot, the quiet of the unit that morning.

Carlie sat at her desk and opened the Bible Patty had given her. *What would Patty think if she could see me now? Would she act all smug and tell me it was about time I got real about everything?*

"You know her better than that. She'd be proud. And happy."

Carlie's eyes widened in surprise. *Would she really? I mean, no one's been proud of me before.*

"I am. I'm proud to call you my daughter," came the voice inside her head. "After all, I made you."

Yeah, but you've done better work than this. Carlie pointed to her chubby frame incredulously.

"Beautiful, my daughter. And I'm making you even more beautiful."

Carlie bunched up her baggy clothes. Her jeans barely stayed up, proving that being in a coma for about a month and then being served cardboard at the state hospital had its benefits. *Okay, I'm not as chunky as I used to be, but I still wouldn't call this beautiful.*

"Do you really think I'm talking about anything as fleeting as your figure?" Jesus didn't sound amused—just sad. "That might be what society defines as beauty, but I go a tad deeper."

I've noticed that about you. You're...intense. You're making me more...don't know—just something I've never been before and don't know how to be, and I'm not even sure what you're making me."

Carlie thought about it. She'd been reading the Bible with Jesus every day. She'd reached the conclusion that she needed his insights to sort it all out and come up with something meaningful. And, boy, had he come up with a lot!

Satan tempted Jesus to turn rocks into bread after not having anything to eat for forty days, and she thought that he tempted her to scratch the eyes out of the psychiatric staff holding her prisoner. Yep, she'd been through a rough patch, but at least she'd eaten during the past forty days. Jesus pointed out that He lived on the word that comes from God, so that had to be the Bible, right? If she could just get her head wrapped around it, maybe her homicidal fantasy and even her suicidal dreams would simply vanish along with the devil who brought them.

Hmm. The devil—my father. So much alike. Maybe the same. When I feel my worst—it's my father's voice telling me that I'm trash.

"But now you have a new Father."

Father is a loaded word. She felt like a wild mustang had just kicked her in the stomach, but she didn't have long to brood about it, because she heard brisk clacking of high heels on tile coming closer and closer. Then they paused, and she heard a knock on her open door, jolting her back to the here and now.

A nurse and a smartly dressed woman with a clipboard stood in her doorway. "Carlie, this is Margaret Wilson from Texas Department of Health. She has some questions for you." The nurse set another chair in Carlie's room for Margaret, who promptly shook Carlie's hand before sitting down.

This could get interesting. Carlie angled her chair to face the investigator. "I'm glad you're here." *There, that sounded like a good start. Polite and sincere. Not rushing into making accusations. I almost sound like I have self-control or something. Now just hold it together. Act like a sane person.*

Margaret smiled, but it looked forced. Not a good sign. Carlie wondered what the staff had already told them. The middle-aged woman in front of her dressed professionally in a black skirt and white blouse. She had pulled her auburn hair up in a conservative style away from her freckled face, and her green eyes studied Carlie intently.

"Tell me what happened here, starting with when you went to seclusion."

Okay, I can do this. I can do this. God, help me do this.

Carlie returned her forced smile and took a deep breath. Her story went quite well, hitting all the important points about the two Dr. Patels playing mind games with her, and her being angry about getting shipped off to the state hospital after being on the psych unit at Parkland, her unintentional act of starting a riot in the dining room, and—yes—being angry enough to push that big, gruff tech out of her personal space once she already walked into the seclusion room. After all, maybe a little truth in self-disclosing might go a long way.

238

Whatever the case, Margaret's facial expression didn't give any clues about whether she believed a word, but at least she dutifully took notes on her clipboard. Occasionally she paused to ask a question and jotted down Carlie's reply, so Carlie figured that she would have to be satisfied knowing that everything in her side of the story got documented.

Carlie admitted to being very angry and uncooperative—though who could blame her under the circumstances? All her life the experts had taken her history of abuse and used it to torture her. Yes, she actually said that, because it was her truth—maybe not what they wanted to hear—but it was her reality, nonetheless.

Margaret paused at that point to ask if anyone in the mental health profession had ever helped her. Oh, how she hated that question!

"This one nurse a Parkland. I couldn't stand her because she always preached to me about dealing with my issues and finding new coping skills, and she'd make me work on all sorts of stuff. She'd give me assignments and then she'd check up on my progress. It got to be the most annoying thing ever, and I'd just make up stuff to get her off my back." She paused.

"So how did she help you?"

"Well, she never gave up. And I guess sometimes I'd think about the stuff she'd talk with me about. And she believed me. I, uh, I don't feel like most people believe me. I feel like most nurses and doctors just groan and think 'great, we got stuck with HER again, and she's just a drama queen, and we're sick of her and her drama.' And the never-ending line-up of therapists are like 'tell us what happened to you' and it makes me sick rehashing the horror stories. And what good does it do?"

Margaret shifted in her wooden chair, scribbling furiously. "I'm getting the picture that you felt suspicious of the staff here." Carlie nodded. "And with all your experience with psychiatric facilities and staff, how does this facility measure up?"

Not expecting that one. Carlie shifted uncomfortably. "What do you mean?"

"Is this facility better, worse, or about the same as the other hospitals?"

"Oh, I guess pretty much the same except the food is crap, and the building is ancient. And that reminds me that I did like one of the techs at Parkland, because she'd save extra brownies for me." Even as the words came out of her mouth, she thought they might be a mistake. *Oh, no. This lady's gonna take one look at me and think I don't need any extra brownies.*

Instead, Margaret smiled—not the fake smile—but a genuine eyes-dancing and mouth wide open smile. "I really like brownies, too, so I can totally understand why you'd like that tech." Her smile faded. "So now tell me about the tech here, uh, Brody Camfield. Just what happened between the two of you?"

"Well, like I said, I did push him away from me once they put me in seclusion, and after that he'd just glare at me, and I could see the hate in his eyes. Of course, they shot me up with drugs, and I went to sleep, but then I woke up feeling like a trapped animal. The nurses and techs treated me like 'whoa, there's the crazy girl; don't get too close' and I'd yell at them for being stupid. I felt like a captive to this vicious cycle of anger, drugs, waking up to them treating me like a criminal, and me getting angry all over again. I got so bent out of shape that I banged my head on the wall, so they restrained me supposedly to protect me from myself, but if they'd just left me alone, I wouldn't have been so out-of-control angry."

Margaret went back to taking notes though her eyes showed more interest than before the brownie comment. *Go figure.*

"Anyway, one of the Patel twins—I still can't tell them apart—came into the seclusion room talking with me and I cried up a storm and made a mess of myself with all the tears and snot, and I couldn't wipe my face seeing as how I had been—you know—restrained. Dr. Patel told Big...I mean Brody...the tech who'd been glaring at me, uh, he told him to wash my face. So, he gets this washcloth practically dripping with cold water and pushes down on my face, like holding his hand over my mouth and nose..."

"He held his hand over your mouth and nose?"

"Yes, well, he held the wet cloth against me and pushed down with his hand, and I couldn't breathe."

"How long did he hold your face down like this, so you couldn't breathe?"

"Uh, I don't know. I mean I had no way to time it; nor did I think of anything other than biting him, so I did just that and he let go. Of course, then he tried to choke me to death, but the other staff came to my rescue."

"And then?"

"My face and neck looked kind of purplish for a while. I think they took pictures of it. And I called to file a complaint. Then they moved me to this floor and told me to stay in this room, 'cause they didn't want me out with other people."

"So how are you doing here in this room by yourself?"

"Much better," Carlie admitted. "I mean, I can think—you know—I can sort things out. It's like I can finally breathe a little without all their idiocy up in my business, and it feels better—more peaceful."

Margaret glanced out the window thoughtfully before refocusing on Carlie. "Okay, let me check my understanding. You feel very uncomfortable with people who are mental health professionals. Instead of feeling cared for, you feel trapped, maybe a bit scared by being trapped, and very angry, to the point that you called it 'out-of-control anger'. Is that correct?"

"Yeah, but that doesn't give him the right to try to kill me!" Carlie's voice rose just a tad more defensively than she wished.

"No, it doesn't," Margaret said softly.

"And how do I know he won't try again?"

"You won't be seeing him here again. In fact, you should only see him when you testify against him. Can you do that—testify?"

Carlie hung her head and moaned. "Relive it again?"

"You have described a criminal act. Can you hold it together to testify in court?"

What's one more courtroom, one more trial, one more witness stand? Carlie nodded grimly. "I suppose so."

What's New?

As soon as the investigator left, a tall African American nurse with a stunning figure came in. Shift change always brought new faces, and Carlie hadn't met this one before. She didn't exactly look bland like most of the psych nurses; for one thing she wore stylish, form-fitting scrubs and accessorized with appropriate bling, and secondly, she spoke directly and called things like she saw them without any sugar-coating, putting it out there plainly and emphatically. Even her facial expressions hadn't become muted like engraved images of feigned concern. In fact, Carlie didn't think she looked at all like a nurse. She must not have practiced the clinical look very well.

"I'm Clarice, your night nurse, and, girl, you need some new clothes. What are these? Hand-me downs from your fat granny? Oh, no, you are way too young to be sporting that look. No wonder you got the glum face."

While Carlie tried to decide whether to tell her off or agree with her, Clarice plunged ahead. "Okay, first we do a proper assessment, and of course I have to assess my other patients and get meds set up, but after I get everyone medicated and settled down, how 'bout you and me doing some on-line shopping?"

Now she had Carlie's attention. "For real?"

"Why not? I've got a tablet, and you've got a credit card or a bank card, don't you? And I know you've been hospitalized for a couple of months, which means you haven't been out spending your check. You don't want to leave here looking all saggy baggy, do you?"

"Leave here? No one's talked with me about leaving. Am I about to be discharged?"

Clarice held up her hand. "Now don't get too excited. I'm not saying you're ready to go yet, but you're making progress and will be rejoining community group therapy sessions Monday, from what I hear. And if you keep making progress... Well, we're a hospital and we don't keep people forever."

That sounded like music to Carlie's ears. She quickly answered all the assessment questions and even threw in some extra information such as how she'd have to testify in two court cases and especially dreaded her dad's appeal what with her newly recovered memory of accidentally killing her little brother. Clarice took notes and commented on Carlie having some life. Her tone of voice clearly meant some dreadful life, not what-an-exciting-life. Maybe this nurse really got her.

Then Clarice asked the question she'd gotten so often in her life: "Carlie Sweetwater, say, you aren't related to Charlie Sweetwater, are you? The hall of fame Cowboy?"

Carlie shook her head. "My pawpaw's name is Charlie, and he's a crusty rancher who happens to own cattle, but I don't think he's famous for anything good. Besides, his ranch isn't any better than anyone else's. That dirty old man—ugh! I don't like thinking about him."

Besides, Carlie had a lot more to think about: her conversation with the investigator, the possibility of a shopping trip inside a psych hospital—a first time ever event for her—and how soon she might get released. Her mind raced from one topic to the next.

What a day! I made it through the investigation with Margaret today. That means Big Man Brody is out of the way. What a relief! He could be scary. But, yuck, another trial.

I really do need some more clothes. She bunched up the excessive waistline of her jeans. *I wonder what size I wear now. Oh, God, help me figure that one out. It's been so long since I've shopped for clothes. How much money do I have in my checking account anyway? Should be enough for a halfway decent wardrobe. How much longer will I be here? Will I need summer clothes or fall? It will probably still be hot when I leave.*

Yikes! Where will I live? Can't go back to the old boarding house. I burned that bridge. Wish I could burn this bridge, too. Never heard of a state mental hospital putting you on a blacklist. Wonder if it's possible. Hmm.

Oh, I need to call Taylor, but I'll have to talk to Jeffrey to find her. Where did I put his number? What do I do next, Jesus?

Not hearing any divine instructions, Carlie picked up her Bible and opened it to a verse about a seven-headed red dragon that posed himself to eat a pregnant woman's baby as soon as she gave birth. Interesting, but not helpful, even if she did find it in the New Testament book of—she glanced at the top of the page—Revelation. Well, that explained a lot. She took a stab at it again and landed in the book of Luke. She read the parable of the persistent widow who kept hounding a judge who didn't exactly care about people or God but gave in and ordered justice for the woman simply because she wouldn't go away until he heard her case.

So, what does that mean? I need to start petitioning the judge who will be hearing my father's appeal? Would that get me out of testifying and having to spill the beans about Bubba? Her heart skipped a beat or two. *Wait, maybe this has some possibilities. Let's try this again and see if there's something else I should do.*

This time she flipped too far back and found herself in the Old Testament. It was Hosea, chapter 9, and it talked about being unfaithful to God and loving the wages of a prostitute. Her eyes widened briefly before a skeptical scowl clouded her face.

Jesus, my Bible must be broken. I thought I could find what I'm supposed to do by reading it, but it's more confusing than anything.

"Want a snack or something to drink?" the tech asked while knocking on her door and poking his head in all at the same time. He whisked her water pitcher from her bedside table and waited for an answer.

"Naw, nothing sounds good right now." Carlie barely glanced at him.

"Whatcha reading? Doing your Bible study again? You read the Bible more than any other patient I've known. You must be an expert at it."

Carlie laughed. "Me—an expert? No way. I'm very new to reading it, and it's quite confusing. I'm looking for answers and not having much luck."

"What kind of answers?" He peered at Hosea's passage. "Thinking about prostitution?"

They both had a good laugh at that. Neither of them had even heard of Hosea before, and both had grown up going to church and felt pretty sure that God didn't want people getting into prostitution. Laughing brought Carlie's defenses down a bit, so she told the tech she wanted to figure out what she needed to do next but opening the Bible to random passages hadn't given her the answers she expected.

"Well, I'm no preacher or Sunday School teacher, but I'm pretty sure it doesn't work like that," he said. "I think you're supposed to just read it and get to know God better, and you ask him to kind of guide you in life. If you just open the Bible and point, expecting that will give you answers—well, that's kind of like magical thinking. I'll be back with some fresh ice water."

With that he left, but Carlie thought he'd made a good point. *Maybe she'd been guilty of expecting magic from the Bible instead of being realistic. But what about my life seems like reality? Maybe a reality show, but not like most people's version of reality. Whatever, no more open and point when in a pinch.*

"That was actually a good lesson to learn," came the familiar voice.

Jesus, you're still there?

"Always."

I'm glad. I really need a friend. I miss Taylor, but... Maybe I should just get it over with and go call Jeffrey. Carlie search the desk drawer for the folded scrap of paper that had his number.

Jeffrey's phone rang a about six or seven times, and Carlie thought about hanging up when she heard a deep voice greeting her. "Hello?"

"Hey, Jeffrey. It's me, uh, Carlie, you know from the psych unit at Parkland. Are you out yet?"

Oh, hi, Carlie. Glad you called. I'm out and I've been keeping in touch with Tay...I mean Jillian. I always forget her new name."

"So, she went with Jillian Taylor?" Carlie vaguely remembered suggesting the name but still felt honestly surprised that someone would take her advice about anything.

"Yeah, and she's doing great getting her career back on track, but she's pretty lonely. She can use all the friends she can get right now. How about you? How are you doing? Did you just get out of Terrell?"

"No, I'm still here. It's been horrible, and I've been in seclusion most of the time until recently."

"Oh." The uncomfortable pause that followed surely meant "so what's new?" since his tone of voice didn't register any surprise.

Carlie bit her lower lip. What on earth did she think, blabbing to Jeffrey of all people? "Hey, how are you doing? You're talking now, so that's got to be a good sign." Again, she bit her lip. Had she offended him?

"I'm back at work and maintaining pretty well, but I'm still going to therapy." Another awkward pause gave Carlie time to sort through possible responses. Before she came up with something halfway decent to say, Jeffrey offered Jillian's new phone number and urged her to call. Then came the real shocker: "You know she's living on the other side of Fort Worth. Call me when you're ready for discharge, and I'll come pick you up and take you over to see her."

"Oh, uh, sure, thanks. That's really kind of you."

Another gap in the conversation. Carlie fidgeted. Did she have anything else to say? "Um, I'll let you go. Thanks for her number."

"Sure. Bye for now."

Having extricated herself from the clumsiest conversation ever, Carlie quickly dialed her one good friend.

Jillian answered promptly and exclaimed enthusiastically when she heard Carlie's voice. "Carlie! You're okay? It's so good to hear your voice! How are you? It seems like it's been so long— what about three or four weeks? I was afraid things weren't going very well for you. Are you finally home, wherever that may be? Tell me everything." Her words gushed out without allowing her to take a breath.

Carlie smiled. This conversation flowed much better than the one she'd just had with Jeffrey.

Words and laughter continued to flow unhampered between the two as they got caught up. Carlie told the whole story of being in seclusion and Big Man Brody's assault—"that's terrible!!!"—and the investigator's interview. "Well, he should land in jail!" Then the new nurse who promised to let her shop for new clothes tonight. "Good. You deserve some new clothes; get something cute."

As for Jillian, she managed to get divorced rather quickly, because the extent of her abuse expedited the process. Now she taught first grade clear over on the west side of Fort Worth and was DYING to see Carlie as soon as she got discharged. In fact, she wondered if they might make good roommates since she had a modest two-bedroom apartment close to her school.

Carlie had barely begun to obsess over where she could live when they cut her loose, but she'd be delighted to share an apartment with Jillian, assuming she could afford the rent.

On and on they chattered until Clarice brought her evening medication. She interrupted just long enough for the ritual of scanning Carlie's bracelet and meds, a quick swallow and mouth check before heading down the hall.

Then Jillian made a comment that hit Carlie like a cannonball in the gut. "Isn't Jeffrey such a sweet guy? He's just been so helpful. I'd be pulling my hair out if not for him. Who would have thought that such a quiet guy could have such depth and sensitivity?"

Carlie closed her eyes tightly. "Are you like in a relationship with him? I mean, I'm just concerned that you just got out of a bad marriage, and you probably need some time to heal before jumping into another relationship." There. It had to be said, and she said it with conviction.

Jillian groaned. "Relationship? No, nothing more than friends. He turned out to be a neat guy; that's all."

"You're sure there's nothing more, 'cause I don't want you to get hurt and it just seems too fast..."

"No. Definitely not anything else. He's just made a tough situation a lot more bearable, and he's offered to move you out here if you're okay with that."

"Yeah, that's nice of him. I guess I'm not big on trusting men."

A Good Day

Shopping online turned out to be more productive than what Carlie could have imagined, and with Clarice measuring her and helping her pick out the appropriate sizes, she felt comfortable with her purchases. She learned how to search by brands, colors and styles. Electronic shopping proved much more effective than driving around from store to store trying on clothes, hoping they had something decent in her size—which they rarely did.

Of course, she discovered that she'd shrunk three to four sizes depending on the brand, and that opened more fashion options within the constraints of her limited budget. Being on disability usually meant shopping at the big box discount stores and wearing what XXL petite selections they had made her look rather frumpy and bland. But here she'd become a downsized version of her previous self, considering choices she'd never enjoyed before. On top of that, Clarice had a flair for putting together a fun and sassy wardrobe that didn't break the bank. Carlie felt pleased when she sat back and viewed her online shopping cart.

She couldn't get to sleep that night. Carlie kept imagining the new more stylish version of her former self walking out of the state hospital. She still wouldn't be mistaken for some anorexic model, but she at least would look more like what she considered normal, and with some fashion sense for a change and a new apartment where people didn't know the old Carlie—well, it seemed like starting over.

Every fifteen minutes one of the techs stuck his head in the door for about a second, and upon being satisfied that she remained precisely where she was supposed to be and presumably breathing, he took off to the next room. Carlie heard the door across the hall squeak and rolled over. Tick tock. She looked at her watch. One o'clock in the morning. Nurses took turns making rounds on the hour, so she sat up expectantly. Maybe she could talk with Clarice about her insomnia.

Unfortunately, it was an ole sourpuss nurse who demanded to know why she sat up at this hour and crisply informed her that sleeping was the recommended therapy at night. "So, what do you need—something for sleep or anxiety? What's keeping you awake?"

Carlie felt annoyed. *Because, of course, it's got to be something twisted and bad to keep one of inmates awake. I ought to tell her I'm struggling with my homicidal tendencies.*

"You don't want to go there," Jesus warned. For having such a quiet voice in her inner spirit, He sure spoke with force.

She froze. His warning hit home; she certainly didn't want to go backwards when the end of this hospital stay might be in sight.

"Well?" The nurse maintained a tight schedule that didn't include time for small talk.

"I just have a lot on my mind. Can I have a sleeping pill?"

"A much more civilized response," came the divine affirmation.

"I'll check with your nurse." The woman in the doorway made a note on her clipboard and disappeared.

Wait, something really must be wrong! Why do I feel so, so weird? Carlie sprang to her feet and checked her face in the mirror above the sink. She touched her face. Something seemed to be missing. Carlie leaned forward and inspected several angles. She looked different than the old Carlie. Some difference besides the weight loss, something in her eyes caught her attention. They widened and then squinted, turning her head from side to side without breaking eye contact with herself in the mirror. *What is it?*

Her eyes looked...softer. Yes. Much softer. Her heart felt lighter. This marked uncharted territory. She didn't miss the old, seething-with-anger glare or the accompanying emotions of churning with anxiety or floundering in the depths of despair and depression. Not to say that she'd become normal. She couldn't even say for sure what normal was, but she knew for sure it didn't look like her, no matter how much healing had occurred. She pulled up a chair and sat in front of her pensive reflection.

That face staring back at her belonged to an injured soul, to be sure, so why the strange serenity?

"Peace, be still."

She smiled. That's what Jesus said to calm a storm when he and his disciples crossed a lake in a boat, and the disciples awakened him yelling that they were all going to die. Then he spoke those famous words, and the storm instantly disappeared. She remembered the story from Sunday School and from recently reading it in the Bible for herself. It seemed like a fairy tale back in childhood, but she had plenty of first-hand experience with storms. Not weather-related turbulence but the emotional tornadoes that wrecked everything in her life repeatedly.

Carlie propped her chin on her hand. *Did you just silence my storm? Not that I had one of my major Carlie-gone-ballistic episodes, but there's always—and I mean every single minute— this underlying intense pressure. And the pressure always seems to blow me into a whirlwind that I can't stop. But you, did you just make it go away...like forever?*

"Bringing peace is what I do. But not just a one-size-fits-all and one-time-lasts always kind of peace; it's a personal, moment by moment kind of peace. It comes from knowing me, staying in me."

The clickety clack of the computer on wheels announced Clarice's presence before she even entered the room. "Can't sleep?"

"No. I guess this day just seemed too good. I'm not used to having good days. It feels, uh, unnatural—at least for me. I'd like to grow accustomed to this feeling."

Clarice grinned. "Something tells me you're on the right track." She reached for Carlie's arm and scanned the hospital wrist band. "I've got your sleeping pill."

Carlie settled back in her bed with her Bible. *Might as well read while waiting for the sleeping pill to take effect. Wish they'd work as quickly in real life as they do on TV. Someone swallows a pill and he's out in an instant.*

She opened her Bible to where she'd placed a slip of paper to serve as a bookmark. John—as in the gospel of—chapter 14. Oh, yes, she'd read it this morning and was strangely affected by its promise of peace. And peace was something she felt right now. Could it be a coincidence or truly a God thing?

As much as she intended to read chapter 15, she found herself immersed in 14 again. Of course, that spawned a lengthy chat with Jesus as she laid out all the junk about her life that stirred her up so.   Instead of getting her dander up again when she rehearsed her grievances, she felt so mellow and peaceful that she fell into a deep slumber with the light still on.

In the morning Carlie awakened refreshed and eager to read chapter 15. It worked better than caffeine. She felt energized with purpose. God had chosen her. He loved her. She resolved to keep abiding in Him like a branch that stays connected to the grapevine, and he promised to make her "fruitful". She perceived that meant productive, as in good things coming from her once hot-mess of a life. So, what exactly did he have in mind for her? And why her—of all people? This had to be some outrageous fairy tale, especially the part about it being true. She could feel his power, and with it, she readied herself for the day.

When she entered the therapy room, Carlie saw one patient leaning back in her chair with her arms crossed and sporting a sullen countenance. *Oh. Been there; not fun.* Another woman kept her eyes averted to the floor with her cheek planted in the palm of her hand and her supporting elbow resting on the arm of her chair. *Sorry for your pain.* A third misfit with clenched jaw literally vibrated with jittery legs, and another slumped in near lifeless fashion.

They look so miserable. I wish I could just package up what I've found and give it to them, Jesus.

The short thirty-something female therapist glanced at her list. "Welcome to group therapy. I'm Kate for those of you who are new. Let's briefly introduce ourselves before we begin. Brenda, will you start?"

Miss Surly snarled, "I'm Brenda, and I don't feel like playing. That's all you need to know."

A couple of middle-aged looking women announced their names in more of a matter-of-fact manner. The young jitter-legged gal rapidly spewed a string of adjectives describing herself—none of which would pass for normal in the real world— and added her name, Summer, almost as an afterthought. A wrinkled patient with long gray hair and an eerie, blank stare periodically smacked her lips and stuck her tongue out in the process while her fingers constantly made a pill-rolling motion. She didn't say anything but her name, and that came after a considerable delay.

Carlie saw each fellow hostage of the mental health system— really saw them for the first time. These hurting, confused people looked a lot like her...at least the old her. Her oh-so-happy-that-it-could-turn-cartwheels heart spilled out her mouth when her turn came.

"I'm Carlie, and my whole life has been seriously screwed up until now. I've never felt good about anything. I've never been happy or content or any of those so-called normal things, and I've never believed it was possible because of me being such damaged goods. I never had hope or purpose or felt loved. Until now."

Seeing several well-medicated heads turn her way, she continued, "My last suicide attempt succeeded until they did CPR on me and stuck me on a ventilator in ICU where I lingered in a coma for a month. And that's the beginning of something good happening in my life." She paused.

Kate nodded encouragingly, "Please go on. What happened?"

"It might sound strange, but I met Jesus."

Brenda rolled her eyes, and Kate's expression changed from curious to incredulous.

"Hey, I didn't believe it at first either. I saw him dressed in scrubs and a lab coat in the ED, and he brought me back from death's door—and, yes, death has a literal door and bright light if it's leading to eternal bliss with God. If not, it's like a long, oppressively dark and excruciatingly hot elevator shaft, plunging further and further into torment and despair beyond anything that words can describe."

Brenda snickered. "So which direction did you go?"

"I actually died twice, and they resuscitated me both times, so I experienced both. But that's not the point." Carlie didn't want to get bogged down in the details and felt impatient to move on to telling them about talking with Jesus.

The youngest member of the group, nineteen-year-old Summer, ejected herself from her seat as if she was on fire. "I knew it. I knew that's where I headed on my own personal highway to hell." She paced feverishly. "The demon known as Saber Hound always dogs my every step. See!" She held up her right arm for everyone to see her jagged scar. "This is where he bit me when I was just four-years-old. And here," she pulled her hair back and pointed out another uneven scar, "is where he smashed me in the head with a rock when I was ten." She started making bizarre gestures with her hands and mumbling what must have either been a foreign language or irrational gobbledygook.

Kate motioned for a tech to take Summer to her nurse while talking in an even voice. "Summer, I see this topic is disturbing you. Maybe our friend, Charlene, can help you find your nurse and get some medication to help you feel better. You're going to be okay here, Summer. We're here to protect you and keep you safe."

Summer froze and looked dubious about whether anyone could be safe anywhere, but when Charlene offered to walk with her, she grabbed the tech's hand and bolted out the door.

As soon as the commotion died down, Carlie tried explaining about her talks with Jesus and what he'd taught her so far in the gospel of John. She received a rather cold reception from her peers topped off by a command from Kate to let Betsy talk now and to meet her in her office to "discuss these matters" after group.

Trying out "Normal"

Carlie quickly found herself back in her room with her Bible confiscated. The staff pronounced her guilty of "religious pre-occupation" with "grandiose delusions" and told her that she needed to deal with the real world. Okay, maybe her wording could stand some improvement. After all, announcing that she'd met Jesus in a psych unit did have drawbacks.

They thought I was talking crazy like Joylyn back at Parkland. Even after I explained about the near-death experience and what I got out of reading the Bible and discussing things with You. I thought what I said made sense. Of course, Summer's stretch of the imagination reaction didn't help, but then she can't help being psychotic, I suppose.

"You do remember what you read in the fifteenth chapter of John, don't you?" Jesus nudged her. "If they treated Me the way they did, and you belong to Me, how are they going to treat you? It comes with the territory once you are no longer a part of this world."

Well, I'm in good company then. I guess I didn't expect the backlash, but it still doesn't take away the purpose and the peace I feel. It's just confusing. I mean that chapter also talked about testifying about You, and isn't that what I did?

"You did testify. You told them about what you experienced with Me, but they can't understand at this point. Pray for them and leave the rest to Me."

Later that afternoon one of the Patel brothers questioned her thoroughly and made copious notes before declaring that he wouldn't put her back on Zyprexa at this time. He mentioned that he was concerned about her sudden elevation in mood and wanted to keep an eye on her to make sure she didn't go into mania.

Carlie tried to keep a straight face. If she indicated she felt upset, they'd assume she was defensive about her "delusions" and irritable, and they'd keep her longer. If she acted happy, they would assume she'd become manic. If she hung out with the real psychotic people on the unit, they'd see that as somehow affirming their belief that she must be bending the edges of sanity herself. If she stayed in her room, she would be isolating. How on earth could she possibly win in this hell hole?

"But you're not here alone, remember?"

Carlie shuffled into the day room and plopped in front of the TV and pretended to watch some meaningless show. *Act normal; act normal. Yeah, right, I'm an expert on normal.*

"No, but you know how to act," assured Jesus.

I do?

"Look at the staff. What are they doing?"

A nurse talked with a patient over in the corner. She leaned in, giving the patient her undivided attention. A tech made her fifteen-minute rounds and checked patients off her list. Another tech pushed the supper trays down the hall.

They're acting busy. So, what do I do to stay busy in here? They took my Bible, so I don't have anything to read or do.

"You can help set out the food trays."

Well, it's better than being bored to death and worrying about how to get out of here. She headed to the dining room to lend a hand to the process.

The tech gladly accepted her assistance, and soon the rest of the patient population sought out their trays and commenced eating. Carlie found herself sitting next to the elderly lady who kept smacking her lips. At least she didn't chatter on and on. Carlie could avoid looking at the whole protruding tongue thing and simply focus on her food. *Act normal.*

Other patients steered clear. *Okay, eat. That's all I have to do right now.* She took a bite. *Cardboard. Masquerading as mystery meat smothering in some kind of salty gravy. Yuck. Mashed potatoes and green beans, just a bite or two will do.* She managed to dispatch about half of the so-called food quickly, so she didn't have to taste it very long and washed it down with iced tea. *Salad and a roll. Might as well. It tasted almost good, so* she didn't have to rush through this part. *Peach cobbler. How could they screw that up?* Thankfully she enjoyed the taste enough that she could eat it slowly. She didn't want to bolt back to her room too quickly.

As other patients exited, Carlie offered to help the tech put all the trays back in the food service cart. The tech smiled and said she appreciated the offer, but she had to record how much each person ate first.

Carlie found that interesting. "You keep a record of how much we eat? Why?"

"The doctors want to know."

"Really? They want to know how much we eat? Why? And what else do you record?"

The tech shrugged. "They want to know how much you eat, how many hours you sleep, how your hygiene is, how you interact. It gives them a picture of how you're doing."

And it gives me an idea of how to act.

The tech started collecting the plastic silverware. "Why are you so curious? You know we check on everyone all the time and make notes."

"Yeah, I just never thought about what the doctors wanted to know about us."

A plan started to formulate. Carlie noted the location of the trash cans related to the tables. She could work with this new information. Maybe helping the staff out would help her out, as in out of this hospital.

The next morning's group therapy went better for Carlie. She explained that she meant that she'd had a spiritual awakening, a come-to-Jesus encounter that changed her perspective slowly but surely, and not some psychotic delusion.

Kate politely thanked her for sharing but remained unconvinced from what Carlie could tell. Most of the patients didn't even blink an eye. At least no allegations of religious preoccupation came from any of the staff.

"Ask for your Bible back," Jesus said.

Really? Now? Don't you think it's too soon?

"Trust Me."

As soon as group therapy was over, Carlie made her way over to Kate. "Can I have my Bible back? It brings me comfort, and there's not much else to do around here."

Kate motioned for her to sit down. "I know you just recently got out of room restriction, and from what I see you are adjusting fairly well to being in the general population on our women's unit. While you were isolated, you read most of the day. It seemed to help you cope since you had no other outbursts. Even yesterday, you handled my concerns about your religious preoccupation calmly. I'm still concerned about having you isolating in your room with your Bible, but I'm willing to let you have it an hour a day if you continue to show good progress."

Carlie nodded solemnly. *Don't look too happy now; I don't want to be labeled as bipolar on top of everything else that they've called me.* "Believe me, I want to make progress. What can I do? Do you have any assignments I can work on?" She almost bit her tongue saying that. *Nurse Patty would have a heart attack if she heard me now.*

Kate lifted her eyebrows, and a faint smile tugged at the corners of her lips. "I believe I have just the thing for you. Now, you will have to check out a pencil from the nurses' station and work on this where they can observe you."

Carlie nodded again. *What else is new?*

With her newly formed plan, Carlie worked her tail off writing assignments for Kate, slipping ill-tasting food into the trash cans unobserved, checking out her Bible for the allotted hour a day of reading, and making sure she got her nightly sleeping pill in time to get her full eight hours of sleep. She mingled with her peers, carefully finding the ones who didn't look like they watched a different movie from the rest of the world or about to jump down the throats of anyone who got in their way.

One day her new clothes came in. She bubbled with excitement, but careful to show only what she thought would be an acceptable level of elation lest she should show up on someone's mania radar. She rushed to her room to try on her purchases.

The light pink blouse really complimented her complexion. The first pair of jeans fit like a glove, maybe a bit snug, but since she didn't eat much here she'd probably be just right for them in no time at all. On to the next outfit. She could hardly wait to see Clarice again. She'd be duly impressed.

Finding herself delighted with each purchase, she pondered which one to wear first. The pink blouse really caught her eye, but she favored a folksy, almost hipster outfit because it appeared so far removed from anything she'd ever owned before. Then the very sleek and flattering black tee shirt with a tiger's face smugly staring at anyone who dared to look at her made her feel proud of the weight she'd lost. Maybe she should go with the casual but flattering tee shirt since it was late in the afternoon and save the more fashionable apparel for tomorrow's group therapy.

She studied her reflection in the mirror approvingly and ran her fingers through her once shoulder-length bob. Three months of growth brought new possibilities. Stay longer? Maybe pull it back? Maybe she should thumb through some of the magazines she'd noticed in the day room to get an idea about hairstyles. That seemed like a normal thing to do, right?

She walked to the day room, carrying herself as tall as her five-foot-five-inch frame could stand. For the first time since she'd come to Terrell, her jeans didn't require being cinched up with a short Velcro strip to keep them from falling off. It felt good to look more decent, more normal. *There's that word again.*

Settling on the couch with an armload of periodicals, she started thumbing through pages looking for inspiration. *Too curly and way too much maintenance. Don't want to go that short. Yikes, who would really wear a style that outlandish?*

One of the night techs saw her searching through magazines and asked what she was looking for. Carlie glanced up. The tech had a cute hairstyle, kind of an asymmetrical pixie cut. Carlie didn't know if she could see herself handling that look; in fact, the more she considered it, the more she became convinced that it wouldn't be a good match for her wavy hair.

More important than picking out a new do, she wanted this interaction to be meaningful. She decided to play her new starring role as the well-put-together, normal Carlie and observe the staff's reaction.

"I'm looking for a new hairstyle, but I haven't found anything yet." She studied the tech more closely. "Hey, yours is the best I've seen so far. Would you mind sending me a selfie that I can take with me when I go for my next haircut?"

Lana thanked her for her compliment but regretfully explained that she wasn't allowed to text or e-mail patients. She did pull out her cell phone and show Carlie a website that had a picture of her exact style. "This is where I found it in the first place," she said. "And look at these." She scrolled through rows and columns of the latest styles. They had a good laugh at some of the more bizarre ones.

"Oh, this one definitely," Carlie exclaimed. "I always wanted to look like a porcupine on steroids"

"Or how about being a goth clown?" Lana asked. "That would get everyone's attention."

"Probably wouldn't help me land a job."

Lana lifted her eyebrows inquisitively. "What kind of job are you hoping to find?"

"I'm   not   sure   yet."

Freedom

Kate beckoned Carlie into her office after group therapy one morning. Carlie had been cranking out the assignments on using effective coping skills for managing her anger and depression and writing up plans for where she would go, what she would do and how she would follow up with outpatient psychiatric care once she got discharged. Kate held up Carlie's latest submission.

"Impressive," she gleamed like a proud mother raising a prodigy. "I'm truly amazed at how far you've come in such a short time."

Carlie shifted in her chair. "It doesn't feel like a short time. It feels like I've been here an eternity."

"Well, you spent almost an entire week in seclusion and another week spent on room restriction, so you've only been coming to group and individual therapy for a couple of weeks."

"Two and a half to be precise, but who's counting? And that's on top of however long I was here before everything unraveled and I went to seclusion." Carlie tucked her hair behind her ear.

Kate smiled. "Apparently you are keeping track of your time here. I understand this isn't where you'd want to be."

Carlie grimaced. "It's that obvious? I mean, I do understand why I've been forced to come here. After a very serious suicide attempt, I unmistakably needed some help. Then wigging out like I did when I first transferred from Parkland didn't exactly scream of mental health." She tried to sound earnest though her insides bristled.

After all, I'm supposed to be a docile pushover in order to be a good psych patient, right? Be careful about what emotions you show; guard your true thoughts.

"Stay cool," the inner voice warned.

"Yes," Kate studied her face intently. "But it's unusual to find someone who accepts our help this quickly after initially reacting so violently. So—tell me the truth—what happened? You went from having hostile outbursts to behaving like a star patient almost overnight. I'm even getting good reports from the nursing staff. You're eating more, sleeping all night and helping with the food trays. It's like someone flipped a switch in your head, so tell me about it."

Oh, God, help! This could be dangerous. If I tell the truth, she'll go back to saying I'm religiously preoccupied.

"Trust Me," came the familiar reply.

Carlie took a deep breath. *I don't really have any better option, so here goes.* "You know that I started making progress in Parkland, right?"

Kate nodded. "I read the report."

"Well, for the first time in my life I had a really good friend plus a sense that God was doing something in me. It all seemed so strange, even scary. I found myself in uncharted territory—at least for me. Then I came here and felt so alone, and I doubted that I could go on here. I felt like somehow I left the good changes behind at Parkland, along with my friend and maybe even God. I know it probably doesn't make sense to anyone else, but that's how I felt." She paused for a moment before continuing to gauge how Kate appeared to be receiving her words. So far, it looked good, so she summoned the courage to continue.

"Anyway, I became so confused by the Patel twins and thought they tried to play with my mind. And I really didn't mean to start a food fight in the dining room. It happened accidentally; I felt angry and didn't realize how hard I shoved my tray. Once I went into the anger mode, I just couldn't seem to get out of it. It really did me good to simply be left alone for the next week. That gave me time to read my Bible and get my head back together without having to deal with other people."

Kate tapped her index finger thoughtfully. "Okay, I appreciate you sharing that. What I want to know now is what you suppose will happen the next time you get angry. After all, there will always be something in life to cause distress, and you won't always be able to hole up somewhere for a week while you sort things out. For example, I understand you're going to be placed on the witness stand to testify about your dad. That can't be easy. How will you cope?"

"I wrote about that in my last assignment." *Didn't you read it?*

"Yes, and what you wrote is outstanding, but I want to hear it from your lips."

"She wants to know if it comes from your heart," Jesus whispered.

"I'll be honest; I'm scared to death when I think about it. It's not just facing my dad again; it's telling what I recently remembered—that I killed my little brother—accidentally that is, but still..." *Yikes! Why does everything have to be so hard? Why do I have to keep rehearsing this over and over?*

"Remember that I've got this," came the reassurance.

She took a deep breath and continued. "I believe that if God showed me what I'd forgotten, He will give me the strength to face the trial and whatever else may come. You may call it religious preoccupation, but where else can I turn? Everything I've ever done in life has resulted in me losing control, attempting suicide, getting thrown into a psych unit. But that's because I had no hope. Now I have a very solid hope in God, that he has a plan for me even if I don't understand what his plan might bring."

"But what if God doesn't live up to your expectations?" Kate asked softly.

Carlie thought about all the surprises Jesus had sprung on her already and laughed. "God has never been what I expected, but He's exactly what I need."

Kate smiled. "Okay, so now you have hope, but what happens if the lawyers are demanding, you get overwhelmed and you don't receive any clear messages from God. Tell me more about your plan to cope with the trial if that happens."

Without batting an eye or the least hesitation, Carlie dove right in. "Before any other preparation, I must find a sense of peace by reading the fourteenth and fifteenth chapters of John and meditating on those words. As I meditate, I will pray for God's peace, and I will listen with my spirit for any direction He gives. Then I will meet with the prosecuting attorney to answer his questions. If I feel the tension rising—like my stomach getting twisted in knots and my muscles tensing and my heart racing—I will take several deep breaths and close my eyes and pray for just a moment to calm myself. Then I will answer whatever question he asks. I will simply tell the truth and let God handle the outcome. After all, it's not exactly in my hands, is it?"

Kate squinted and nodded thoughtfully. "And what about the actual trial?"

"I'm hoping my friend, Jillian, will be there. She already knows what really happened, so I can just look at her the whole time and tune out everyone else and their reactions. I will try to keep my replies brief, and if either attorney tries to push my buttons, I will close my eyes, deep breathe and count to ten before answering. If the judges ask what I'm doing, I will say that I'm a psych patient, and this is my plan for not losing control in the courtroom."

Kate chuckled. "And that's what impresses me about your plan. You're so brutally honest while protecting yourself."

"Uh, thanks. I also have a plan for handling myself if I feel I'm absolutely going to lose it."

"Yes, I loved that part. Go on and tell me about it."

"I will ask the judges for a break, so I don't end up back in the psych unit. If I'm not mentally sound, then they might as well know it on the front end instead of me going psycho on them. After all, I'm emotionally unstable because of what happened during my childhood—the very thing that I'm testifying about—so surely they will understand, especially since I've just been hospitalized for almost three months. All I need is time to pop a Xanax and let it kick in—maybe an hour tops."

"Good point. Be upfront about that with the court and perhaps the judges will be compassionate and not let either lawyer bully you. The only change that I would suggest is that you might want to take the Xanax before you testify to help diminish the chance of you getting overwhelmed. Since you've obviously put a lot of thought into your plan, I have one last assignment for you." She handed a paper to Carlie. "These are your discharge plans. Take this copy with you when you leave, so you don't get flustered and forget the good work you've done here. Dr. Paul Patel is ready to cut you loose, and he's already written the discharge order, so you'll need to call your friend to come pick you up."

"Today?" Carlie lifted her eyebrows.

"Unless you'd like to stay longer." Kate grinned.

Carlie sprang out of the chair. "For real?"

"Absolutely."

"I'll go call him now!"

"I thought your friend was a girl named Jillian." Kate picked up her pen as if to make a note.

"Yeah, but this guy who is a mutual friend will take me to her apartment because she moved, and he knows how to get to her new place."

"Okay, go make your arrangements." As Carlie bolted to the door, Kate added, "Oh, Carlie, just for the record, I'm pretty sure you thought I came down on you for religious reasons, but please understand that we often get patients who become delusional about God such as thinking they are God or Satan, or maybe a prophet. Others become overly preoccupied with receiving messages from God and develop unrealistic expectations and beliefs that set them up to act out in bizarre ways. All these extremes are very detrimental, so we discourage them. As we worked together, I could see that your visions during your near-death experience and what you read in your Bible served to encourage you and give you a focal point for hanging onto hope and peace of mind. I would never want to take away your faith. I only wanted to make sure you didn't base it on a delusion, a psychotic belief that would set you up for failure in the long run. You understand?"

Sure, lady. Whatever you say. Carlie nodded and trotted off to make her phone call, careful to mask her true feelings.

A few hours later Jeffrey showed up and carried all her worldly possessions in a couple of plastic bags to his car while Carlie marveled at the blinding bright and fiercely scorching September sun. In a few days it would be October, and the totally baked earth awaited autumn showers to rejuvenate north Texas. Carlie didn't care about the soaring temperature or the cracks in the soil from the long summer drought. She stopped to relish being outside. Freedom! How long she waited for this moment! Now she could come and go as she pleased, and she determined right then and there to never relinquish her freedom again.

They pulled out of the parking lot from the state hospital, past shady oak-lined lanes and historical two-story houses with white stately columns. Old fashioned southern charm mixed with twenty-first century small town traffic. Carlie hadn't really taken the time to consider the sights and sounds of the outside world that she missed while being preoccupied with fighting for sanity. She hungrily stared at the passing scenery.

Terrell would never become a large city like Dallas, but it was big for Kaufman County, and it carried a profoundly rural East Texas atmosphere. Carlie thought about her first foster home, farther east from Terrell, over in Van Zandt County near a town called Wills Point. Her good-memory place.

Jeffrey turned onto Highway 80 with its string of businesses.

"Oh, a Whataburger!" The familiar orange and white sign beckoned, signaling her mouth to start watering.

"Would you like to stop and get something to eat? It's going take about an hour and a half to two hours to get to Jillian's apartment, going through traffic this time of day, so we might as well travel with food in our stomachs. My treat." Jeffrey pulled his silver Toyota Camry into the parking lot as he talked. "I love their shakes."

"How about their onion rings? Would you want to split an order?"

"Sure, you're talking my language now. The Whataburger with cheese and jalapenos and the Avocado Bacon Burger are my favorites; how about you?"

"I'm more of a Whatachick'n or a Whataburger minus the pickles kind of gal."

And just like that, a conversation sparked a bond between two unlikely people. In fact, supper proved downright void of any awkward pauses. Jeffrey turned out to be an interesting guy with a weird family situation of his own.

As one thing led to another, Jeffrey ended up telling his story. Not only did his father found an esteemed law firm in Dallas, but his super-smart brother, Elliot, a former high school star quarterback back in the day, became a highly successful attorney in his own right and a partner in his dad's firm. His older sister, Samantha, had creamed all her tennis opponents in the state of Texas back in high school and sailed through med school at Harvard before becoming a respected cardiologist at UT Southwestern. Sister number two, Kimberly, excelled at basketball in high school and college and at stunning the masses with her radiant beauty. She now worked as a model who traveled the world. His mother truly loved him, the too clumsy to play sports, selectively mute, odd child, but she died of metastatic breast cancer during his early teenage years, leaving him to feel like a misplaced loser in a family of high achievers.

Carlie couldn't believe it. "You came from a wealthy family and ended up at Parkland like all us poor folks? No wonder your dad never came to visit; some of our underclass cooties might have worn off on him."

Jeffrey grinned. "Oh, the tragedy!"

"Probably his worst nightmare," Carlie added.

"A real horror freak show! What would he ever tell his golfing buddies at the club? 'Hey, I've got to run and see my idiot son at the county hospital?' He would never allow that type of scandal happen." He swallowed his last bit of burger and washed it down with his chocolate shake. "Want the last onion ring?"

Carlie shook her head, "No thanks, I'm stuffed. You eat it while I visit the ladies' room."

Her stomach began cramping before she got there. She hadn't eaten that much in about three months, so she'd definitely overdone a good thing. She grimaced. The first thing she did in the outside world—and she blew it. A simple thing like eating a meal. How on earth did she stand of chance of making it through all the other stuff? Insecurity hit like a tidal wave, and she found herself hyperventilating.

I've never been free before—never. It's always been this foster home or that looney bin or some boarding house for losers and nut cases. This is my first taste of freedom. My first time out of an institution of any sort. So, what do I really want to do?

Inside the restroom, Carlie gave herself a good talking to. *Come on, girl. You pulled it together long enough to get out of Psychville with some help from above. Thank you, Jesus, for getting me this far, but now comes the real challenge. Don't freak out. Don't go off on anyone. Keep it together. Keep listening to Jesus. Just don't go back. Oh, God, please keep me from going back in.*

It may have been a good speech as far as self-talk speeches go, but Carlie looked into her own soul and saw just how clueless she was. Her heart raced as she panted for air. *What comes next? Wait, I have a plan. I'll get a job. I'll become normal by acting the part.*

"Remember me? Trust me. I'm still in control."

She splashed some cold water in her face and worked at slowing down her breathing. Now that she left the hospital, she should be celebrating, not acting like a little, lost puppy. She'd be just fine by God's grace.

After all, this formerly mute, barely functioning guy seemed like a genuine, normal person now and acted like driving her clear across the metroplex during evening rush hour traffic was no big deal. If Jeffrey could do this, she could, too.

"But you're destined to kill yourself. You know you are." A sinister voice spoke from deep inside her heart.

She glared in the bathroom mirror. *What?*

"Don't listen. I've come to bring you life."

"REALLY? You're still the same hurting, scared little girl, daddy's girl with bats in her belfry. Who else could you be? There's no hope; it's all been an illusion.

"Liar...the truth is not in him."

I'm confused.

"Listen to me and live."

"Listen to me and die."

Carlie fumbled through her purse with trembling hands and fished out a Xanax. She swallowed and splashed some more cold water in her face. *Just get in that car. Get in that car. Go to Jillian's apartment. Stick with the plan. Oh, Jesus, give me strength! Between you and Jillian helping me I can become a normal gal.*

She wiped her face with a paper towel, set her jaw in fierce determination and rejoined Jeffrey. "I'm ready to go."

www.ingramcontent.com/pod-product-compliance
Lightning Source LLC
Chambersburg PA
CBHW072203170626
46813CB00003B/772